THE GRAFTERS

"DO YOU BEGIN TO SUSPECT THINGS?" SHE ASKED

THE
GRAFTERS

BY
FRANCIS LYNDE

ILLUSTRATED BY
ARTHUR I. KELLER

THE GREGG PRESS / RIDGEWOOD, N. J.

First published in 1904 by The Bobbs-Merrill Company
Republished in 1968 by
The Gregg Press Incorporated
171 East Ridgewood Avenue
Ridgewood, New Jersey, U.S.A.

Copyright© 1968 by
The Gregg Press, Inc.

Library of Congress Catalog Card Number: 68-20017

Printed in United States of America

AMERICANS IN FICTION

In the domain of literature the play may once have been the chief abstract and chronicle of the times, but during the nineteenth and twentieth centuries the novel has usurped the chief place in holding the mirror up to the homely face of society. On this account, if for no other, the Gregg Press series of reprints of American fiction merits the attention of all students of Americana and of librarians interested in building up adequate collections dealing with the social and literary history of the United States. Most of the three score and ten novels or volumes of short stories included in the series enjoyed considerable fame in their day but have been so long out of print as to be virtually unobtainable in the original editions.

Included in the list are works by writers not presently fashionable in critical circles—but nevertheless well known to literary historians—among them Joel Chandler Harris, Harriet Beecher Stowe, Thomas Bailey Aldrich, and William Gilmore Simms. A substantial element in the list consists of authors who are known especially for their graphic portrayal of a particular American setting, such as Gertrude Atherton (California), Arlo Bates (Boston), Alice Brown (New England), Edward Eggleston (Indiana), Mary Wilkins Freeman (New England), Henry B. Fuller (Chicago), Richard M. Johnston (Georgia), James Lane Allen (Kentucky), Mary N. Murfree (Tennessee), and Thomas Nelson Page (Virginia). There is even a novel by Frederic Remington, one of the most popular painters of the Western cowboy and Indian—and another, and impressive minor classic on the early mining region of Colorado, from the pen of Mary Hallock Foote. The professional student of American literature will rejoice in the opportunity afforded by the collection to extend his reading of fiction belonging to what is called the "local-color movement"—a major current in the development of the national belles-lettres.

Among the titles in the series are also a number of famous historical novels. Silas Weir Mitchell's *Hugh Wynne* is one of the very best fictional treatments of the American Revolution. John Esten Cooke is the foremost Southern writer of his day who dealt with the Civil War. The two books by Thomas Dixon are among the most famous novels on the Reconstruction Era, with sensational disclosures of the original Ku Klux Klan in action. They supplied the grist for the first great movie "spectacular"—*The Birth of a Nation* (1915).

Paul Leicester Ford's *The Honorable Peter Stirling* is justly ranked among the top American novels which portray American politics in action—a subject illuminated by other novelists in the Gregg list—A. H. Lewis, Frances H. Burnett, and Alice Brown, for example. Economic problems are forcefully put before the reader in works by Aldrich, Mrs. Freeman, and John Hay, whose novels illustrate the ominous concern over the early battles between labor and capital. From the sweatshops of Eastern cities in which newly arrived immigrants toiled for pittances, to the Western mining camps where the laborers packed revolvers, the working class of the times enters into various other stories in the Gregg list. The capitalist class, also, comes in for attention, with an account of a struggle for the ownership of a railroad in Samuel Merwin's *The Short-Line War* and with the devastating documentation of the foibles of the newly rich and their wives in the narratives of David Graham Phillips. It was Phillips whose annoying talent for the exposure of abuses led Theodore Roosevelt to put the term "muck-raker" into currency.

While it is apparent that local-color stories, the historical novel, and the economic novel have all been borne in mind in choosing the titles for this important series of reprints, it is evident that careful consideration has also been given to treatments of various minority elements in the American population. The Negro, especially, but also the Indian, the half-breed, Creoles, Cajuns—and even the West Coast Japanese—appear as characters in various of these novels or volumes of short stories and sketches. Joel Chandler Harris's *Free Joe* will open the eyes of readers who know that author solely as the creator of humorous old Uncle Remus. And there is a revelatory volume of dialect tales, written by a Negro author, *The Conjure Woman* by Charles W. Chesnutt.

In literary conventions and the dominating attitudes toward life, the works in the Gregg series range from the adventurous romance illustrated so well by Mayne Reid or the polite urbanity of Owen Wister to the mordant irony of Kate Chopin and the grimmer realism of Joseph Kirkland's own experiences on bloody Civil War battlefields or the depressing display of New York farm life by Harold Frederic. In short, the series admirably illustrates the general qualities of the fiction produced in the United States during the era covered, just as it generously mirrors the geographical regions, the people, and the problems of the times.

PROFESSOR CLARENCE GOHDES
Duke University
Durham, North Carolina

December, 1967

CONTENTS

TO MY GOOD FRIEND
MR. EDWARD YOUNG CHAPIN

THE GRAFTERS

I

In point of age, Gaston the strenuous was still no more than a lusty infant among the cities of the brown plain when the boom broke and the junto was born, though its beginnings as a halt camp ran back to the days of the later Mormon migrations across the thirsty plain; to that day when the advanced guard of Zophar Smith's ox-train dug wells in the damp sands of Dry Creek and called them the Waters of Merom.

Later, one Jethro Simsby, a Mormon deserter, set up his rod and staff on the banks of the creek, homesteaded a quarter-section of the sage-brush plain, and in due time came to be known as the Dry Creek cattle king. And the cow-camp was still Simsby's when the locating engineers of the Western Pacific, searching for tank stations in a land where water was scarce and hard to come by, drove their stakes along the north line of the quarter-section; and having named their last station Alphonse, christened this one Gaston.

From the stake-driving of the engineers to the spike-driving of the track-layers was a full decade. For hard times overtook the Western Pacific at Midland City, eighty miles to the eastward; while the State capital, two days' bronco-jolting west of Dry Creek, had railroad outlets in plenty and no inducements to offer a new-comer.

But, with the breaking of the cloud of financial depression, the Western Pacific succeeded in placing its extension bonds, and a little later the earth began to fly on the grade of the new line to the west. Within a Sundayless month the electric lights of the night shift could be seen, and, when the wind was right, the shriek of the locomotive whistle could be heard at Dry Creek; and in this interval between dawn and daylight Jethro Simsby sold his quarter-section for the nominal sum of two thousand dollars, spot cash, to two men who buck-boarded in ahead of the track-layers.

This purchase of the "J-lazy-S" ranch by Hawk and Guilford marked the modest beginning of Gaston the marvelous. By the time the temporary sidings were down and the tank well was dug in the damp sands, it was heralded far and wide that the Western Pacific would make the city on the banks of Dry Creek—a city consisting as yet only of the Simsby ranch shacks—its western terminus. Thereupon followed one of the senseless rushes that populate the waste places of the earth and give the professional city-builder his reason for being. In a fortnight after the driving of the silver spike the dusty plain was dotted with the black-roofed shelters of the Argonauts; and by the following spring the plow was furrowing the cattle ranges in ever-widening circles, and Gaston had voted a bond loan of three hundred thousand dollars to pave its streets.

Then under the forced draft of skilful exploitation, three years of high pressure passed quickly; years named by the promoters the period of development. In the Year One the very heavens smiled and the rainfall broke the record of the oldest inhabitant. Thus the region round about lost the word "arid" as a qualifying adjective, and the picturesque fictions of the prospectus makers were miraculously justified. In Year Two there was less rain, but still an abundant crop; and Jethro Simsby, drifting in from some unnamed frontier of a newer cow-country, saw what he had missed, took to drink, and shot himself in the lobby of the Mid-Continent Hotel, an ornate, five-storied, brick-and-terra-cotta structure standing precisely upon the site of the "J-lazy-S" branding corral.

It was in this same Year Two, the fame of the latest of western Meccas for young men having penetrated to the provincial backgrounds of New Hampshire, that David Kent came.

By virtue of his diploma, and three years of country practice in the New Hampshire county town where his father before him had read Blackstone and Chitty, he had his window on the fourth floor of the Farquhar Building lettered "Attorney and Counselor at Law"; but up to the day in the latter part of the fateful Year Three, when the overdue crash came, he was best known as a reckless plunger in real estate—this, mind you, at a moment when every third man counted his gains in "front feet", and was shouting himself hoarse at the daily brass-band lot sales.

When the bottom fell out in the autumn of Year Three, Kent fell with it, though not altogether as far or as hard as many another. One of his professional hold-fasts—it was the one that afterward became the bread-tackle in the famine time—was his position as local attorney for the railway company. By reason of this he was among the first to have a hint of the impending cataclysm. The Western Pacific, after so long a pause on the banks of Dry Creek, had floated its second mortgage bonds and would presently build on to the capital, leaving Gaston to way-station quietude. Therefore and wherefore—

Kent was not lacking in native shrewdness or energy. He foresaw, not the pitiable bubble-burst which ensued, indeed, but the certain and inevitable end of the speculative era. Like every one else, he had bought chiefly with promises to pay, and his paper in the three banks aggregated a sum equal to a frugal New Hampshire competence.

"How long have I got?" was the laconic wire which he sent to Loring, the secretary of the Western Pacific Advisory Board in Boston, from whom his hint had come. And when Loring replied that the grading and track-laying contracts were already awarded, there was at least one "long" on the Gaston real estate exchange who wrought desperately night and day to "unload".

As it turned out, the race against time was both a victory and a defeat. On the morning when the *Daily Clarion* sounded the first note of public alarm, David Kent took up the last of his bank promises-to-pay, and transferred his final mortgaged holding in Gaston realty. When it was done he locked himself in his office in the Farquhar Building and balanced the account. On leaving the New Hampshire country town to try the new cast for fortune in the golden West, he had turned his small patrimony into cash—some ten thousand dollars of it. To set over against the bill of exchange for this amount, which he had brought to Gaston a year earlier, there were a clean name, a few hundred dollars in bank, six lots, bought and paid for, in one of the Gaston suburbs, and a vast deal of experience.

Kent ran his hands through his hair, opened the check-book and hastily filled out a check payable to himself for the remaining few hundreds. When he reached the Apache National on the corner of Colorado and Texas Streets, he was the one hundred and twenty-seventh man in the queue, which extended around the corner and doubled back and forth in the cross-street to the stoppage of all traffic. The announcement in the *Clarion* had done its work, and the baleful flower of panic, which is a juggler's rose for quick-growing possibilities, was filling the very air of the street with its acrid perfume—the scent of all others that soonest drives men mad.

Major James Guilford, the president of the Apache National, was in the cage with the sweating paying tellers, and it was to him that Kent presented his check when his turn came.

"What! You, too, Kent?" said the president, re-proachfully. "I thought you had more backbone."

Kent shook his head.

"Gaston has absorbed nine-tenths of the money I brought here; I'll absorb the remaining tenth myself, if it's just the same to you, Major. Thank you." And the hundred and twenty-seventh man pocketed his sal-vage from the wreck and fought his way out through the jam at the doors. Two hours farther along in the forenoon the Apache National suspended payment, and the bank examiner was wired for.

For suddenness and thoroughgoing completeness the Gaston bubble-bursting was a record-breaker. For a week and a day there was a frantic struggle for enlargement, and by the expiration of a fortnight the life was pretty well trampled out of the civic corpse and the stench began to arise.

Flight upon any terms then became the order of the day, and if the place had been suddenly plague-smitten the panicky exodus could scarcely have been more headlong. None the less, in any such disorderly up-anchoring there are stragglers perforce: some left like stranded hulks by the ebbing tide; others riding by mooring chains which may be neither slipped nor capstaned. When all was over there were deserted streets and empty suburbs in ruthless profusion; but there was also a hungry minority of the crews of the stranded and anchored hulks left behind to live or die as they might, and presently to fall into cannibalism, preying one upon another between whiles, or waiting like their prototypes of the Spanish Main for the stray spoils of any luckless argosy that might drift within grappling distance.

Kent stayed partly because a local attorney for the railroad was as necessary in Gaston the bereaved as in Gaston the strenuous; partly, also, because he was a student of his kind, and the broken city gave him laboratory opportunities for the study of human nature at its worst.

He marked the raising of the black flag as the Gaston castaways, getting sorrily afloat one by one, cleared their decks for action. Some Bluebeard admiral there will always be for such stressful occasions, and David Kent, standing aside and growing cynical day by day, laid even chances on Hawk, the ex-district attorney, on Major Guilford, and on one Jasper G. Bucks, sometime mayor of Gaston the iridescent.

Afterward he was to learn that he had underrated the gifts of the former mayor. For when the famine time was fully come, and there were no more argosies drifting Gastonward for the bucaneers to sack and scuttle, it was Jasper G. Bucks who called a conference of his fellow werwolves, set forth his new cast for fortune, and brought the junto, the child of sheer desperation fiercely at bay, into being.

It was in the autumn of that first cataclysmic year that Secretary Loring, traveling from Boston to the State capital on a mission for the Western Pacific, stopped over a train with Kent. After a rather dispiriting dinner in the deserted Mid-Continent café, and some plowing of the field of recollection in Kent's rooms in the Farquhar Building, they took the deserted street in the golden twilight to walk to the railway station.

"It was a decent thing for you to do—stopping over a train with me, Grantham," said the host, when the five squares intervening had been half measured. "I have had all kinds of a time out here in this God-forsaken desert, but never until to-day anything approaching a chummy hour with a man I know and care for."

Kent had not spoken since they had felt their way out of the dark lower hall of the Farquhar Building. Up to this point the talk had been pointedly reminiscent; of the men of their university year, of mutual friends in the far-away "God's country" to the eastward, of the Gastonian epic, of all things save only two—the exile's cast for fortune in the untamed West, and one other.

"That brings us a little nearer to the things that be—and to your prospects, David," said the guest. "How are you fixed here?"

Kent shrugged.

"Gaston is dead, as you see; too dead to bury."

"Why don't you get out of it, then?"

"I shall some day, perhaps. Up to date there has been no place to go to, and no good way to arrive. Like some thousands of others, I've made an ass of myself here, Loring."

"By coming, you mean? Oh, I don't know about
that. You have had some hard knocks, I take it, but if
you are the same David Kent I used to know, they have
made a bigger man of you."

"Think so?"

"I'd bet on it. We have had the Gaston epic done
out for us in the newspapers. No man could live
through such an experience as you must have had without growing a few inches. Hello! What's this?"

A turned corner had brought them in front of a
lighted building in Texas Street with a straggling
crowd gathered about the porticoed entrance. As Loring spoke, there was a rattle of snare drums followed
by the *dum-dum* of the bass, and a brass band ramped
out the opening measures of a campaign march.

"It is a rally," said Kent, when they had passed far
enough beyond the zone of brass-throated clamorings
to make the reply audible. "I told you that the Gaston
wolf-pack had gone into politics. We are in the throes
of a State election, and there is to be a political speech-
making at the Opera House to-night, with Bucks in
the title rôle. And there is a fair measure of the dead-
ness of the town! When you see people flock together
like that to hear a brass band play, it means one of two
things: that the town hasn't outgrown the country
village stage, or else it has passed that and all other
stages and is well on its way to the cemetery."

"That is one way of putting it," Loring rejoined. "If things are as bad as that, it's time you were moving on, don't you think?"

"I guess so," was the lack-luster response. "Only I don't know where to go, or what to do when I get there."

They were crossing the open square in front of the wide-eaved passenger station. A thunderous tremolo, dominating the distant band music, thrilled on the still air, and the extended arm of the station semaphore with its two dangling lanterns wagged twice.

"My train," said Loring, quickening his step.

"No," Kent corrected. "It is a special from the west, bringing a Bucks crowd to the political rally. Number Three isn't due for fifteen minutes yet, and she is always late."

They mounted the steps to the station platform in good time to meet the three-car special as it came clattering in over the switches, and presently found themselves in the thick of the crowd of debarking ralliers.

It was a mixed masculine multitude, fairly typical of time, place and occasion; stalwart men of the soil for the greater part, bearded and bronzed and rough-clothed, with here and there a range-rider in picturesque leathern shaps, sagging pistols and wide-flapped sombrero.

Loring stood aside and put up his eye-glasses. It was his first sight near at hand of the untrammeled West *in puris naturalibus,* and he was finding the spectacle both instructive and diverting. Looking to Kent for fellowship he saw that his companion was holding himself stiffly aloof; also, he remarked that none of the boisterous partizans flung a word of recognition in Kent's direction.

"Don't you know any of them?" he asked.

Kent's reply was lost in the deep-chested bull-bellow of a cattleman from the Rio Blanco.

"Hold on a minute, boys, before you scatter! Line up here, and let's give three cheers and a tail-twister for next-Governor Bucks! Now, then—*everybody!* Hip, hip—"

The ripping crash of the cheer jarred Loring's eyeglasses from their hold, and he replaced them with a smile. Four times the ear-splitting shout went up, and as the echoes of the "tiger" trailed off into silence the stentorian voice was lifted again.

"Good enough! Now, then; three groans for the land syndicates, alien mortgagees, and the Western Pacific Railroad, by grabs! and to hell with 'em!"

The responsive clamor was a thing to be acutely remembered—sustained, long-drawn, vindictive; a nerve-wrenching pandemonium of groans, yelpings and catcalls, in the midst of which the partizans shuffled into loose marching order and tramped away townward.

"That answers your question, doesn't it?" said Kent, smiling sourly. "If not, I can set it out for you in words. The Western Pacific is the best-hated corporation this side of the Mississippi, and I am its local attorney."

"I don't envy you," said Loring. "I had no idea the opposition crystallized itself in any such concrete ill will. You must have the whole weight of public sentiment against you in any railroad litigation."

"I do," said Kent, simply. "If every complainant against us had the right to pack his own jury, we couldn't fare worse."

"What is at the bottom of it? Is it our pricking of the Gaston bubble by building on to the capital?"

"Oh, no; it's much more personal to these shouters. As you may, or may not, know, our line—like every other western railroad with no competition—has for its motto, 'All the tariff the traffic will stand,' and it bleeds the country accordingly. But we are forgetting your train. Shall we go and see how late it is?"

II

A MAN OF THE PEOPLE

Train Number Three, the Western Flyer, was late, as Kent had predicted—just how late the operator could not tell; and pending the chalking-up of its arriving time on the bulletin board, the two men sat on an empty baggage truck and smoked in companionable silence.

While they waited, Loring's thoughts were busy with many things, friendly solicitude for the exile serving as the point of departure. He knew what a handfast friend might know: how Kent had finished his postgraduate course in the law and had succeeded to his father's small practice in the New Hampshire county town where he was born and bred. Also, he knew how Kent's friends, college friends who knew his gifts and ability, had deprecated the burial; and he himself had been curious enough to pay Kent a visit to spy out the reason why. On their first evening together in the stuffy little law office which had been his father's, Kent

(14)

had made a clean breast of it: there was a young woman in the case, and a promise passed before Kent had gone to college. She was a farmer's daughter, with no notion for a change of environment; wherefore she had determined Kent's career and the scene of it, laying its lines in the narrow field of her own choosing.

Later, as Loring knew, the sentimental anchor had dragged until it was hopelessly off holding-ground. The young woman had laid the blame at the door of the university, had given Kent a bad half-year of fault-finding and recrimination, and had finally made an end of the matter by bestowing her dowry of hillside acres on the son of a neighboring farmer.

Thereafter Kent had stagnated quietly, living with simple rigor the life he had marked out for himself; thankful at heart, Loring had suspected, for the timely intervention of the farmer's son, but holding himself well in hand against a repetition of the sentimental offense. All this until the opening of the summer hotel at the foot of Old Croydon, and the coming of Elinor Brentwood.

No one knew just how much Miss Brentwood had to do with the long-delayed awakening of David Kent; but in Loring's forecastings she enjoyed the full benefit of the doubt. From tramping the hills alone, or whipping the streams for brook trout, David had taken to spending his afternoons with lover-like regularity at

the Croydon Inn; and at the end of the season had
electrified the sleepy home town by declaring his intention to go West and grow up with the country.

In Loring's setting-forth of the awakening, the motive was not far to seek. Miss Brentwood was ambitious, and if her interest in Kent had been only casual
she would not have been likely to point him to the
wider battle-field. Again, apart from his modest patrimony, Kent had only his profession. The Brentwoods
were not rich, as riches are measured in millions; but
they lived in their own house in the Back Bay wilder-
ness, moved in Boston's older substantial circle, and, in
a world where success, economic or other, is in some
sort the touchstone, were many social planes above a
country lawyer.

Loring knew Kent's fierce poverty-pride—none better. Hence, he was at no loss to account for the exile's
flight afield, or for his unhopeful present attitude.
Meaning to win trophies to lay at Miss Brentwood's
feet, the present stage of the rough joust with Fortune
found him unhorsed, unweaponed and rolling in the
dust of the lists.

Loring chewed his cigar reflectively, wishing his companion would open the way to free speech on the subject presumably nearest his heart. He had a word of
comfort, negative comfort, to offer, but it might not
be said until Kent should give him leave by taking the

initiative. Kent broke silence at last, but the prompting was nothing more pertinent than the chalking-up of the delayed train's time.

"An hour and twenty minutes: that means any time after nine o'clock. I'm honestly sorry for you, Grantham—sorry for any one that has to stay in this charnel-house of a town ten minutes after he's through. What will you do with yourself?"

Loring got up, looked at his watch, and made a suggestion, hoping that Kent would fall in with it.

"I don't know. Shall we go back to your rooms and sit a while?"

The exile's eyes gloomed suddenly.

"Not unless you insist on it. We should get back among the relics and I should bore you. I'm not the man you used to know, Grantham."

"No?" said Loring. "I sha'n't be hypocritical enough to contradict you. Nevertheless, you are my host. It is for you to say what you will do with me until train time."

"We can kill an hour at the rally, if you like. You have seen the street parade and heard the band play: it is only fair that you should see the menagerie on exhibition."

Loring found his match-box and made a fresh light for his cigar.

"It's pretty evident that you and 'next-Governor'

Bucks are on opposite sides of the political fence," he observed.

"We are. I should think a good bit less of myself than I do—and that's needless—if I trained in his company."

"Yet you will give him a chance to make a partizan of me? Well, come along. Politics are not down on my western programme, but I'm here to see all the new things."

The Gaston Opera House was a survival of the flush times, and barring a certain tawdriness from disuse and neglect, and a rather garish effect which marched evenly with the brick-and-terra-cotta fronts in Texas Street and the American-Tudor cottages of the suburbs, it was a creditable relic. The auditorium was well filled in pit, dress-circle and gallery when Kent and his guest edged their way through the standing committee in the foyer; but by dint of careful searching they succeeded in finding two seats well around to the left, with a balcony pillar to separate them from their nearest neighbors.

Since the public side of American politics varies little with the variation of latitude or longitude, the man from the East found himself at once in homely and remindful surroundings. There was the customary draping of flags under the proscenium arch and across the set-piece villa of the background. In the semicircle of chairs arched from wing to wing sat the local and visiting

political lights; men of all trades, these, some of them
a little shamefaced and ill at ease by reason of their
unwonted conspicuity; all of them listening with a
carefully assumed air of strained attention to the
speaker of the moment.

Also, there was the characteristic ante-election audience, typical of all America—the thing most truly typical in a land where national types are sought for mi-
croscopically: wheel-horses who came at the party call;
men who came in the temporary upblaze of enthusiastic
patriotism, which is lighted with the opening of the campaign, and which goes out like a candle in a gust of
wind the day after the election; men who came to ap-
plaud blindly, and a few who came to cavil and deride.
Loring oriented himself in a leisurely eye-sweep, and
so came by easy gradations to the speaker.

Measured by the standard of fitness for his office of
prolocutor the man standing beside the stage-properties
speaker's desk was worthy a second glance. He was
dark, undersized, trimly built; with a Vandyke beard
clipped closely enough to show the lines of a bull-dog
jaw, and eyes that had the gift, priceless to the public
speaker, of seeming to hold every onlooking eye in the
audience. Unlike his backers in the awkward semicircle, he wore a professional long coat; and the hands
that marked his smoothly flowing sentences were slim
and shapely.

"Who is he?" asked Loring, in an aside to Kent.

"Stephen Hawk, the ex-district attorney: boomer, pettifogger, promoter—a charter member of the Gaston wolf-pack. A man who would persuade you into believing in the impeccability of Satan in one breath, and knife you in the back for a ten-dollar bill in the next," was the rejoinder.

Loring nodded, and again became a listener. Hawk's speech was merely introductory, and it was nearing its peroration.

"Fellow citizens, this occasion is as auspicious as it is significant. When the people rise in their might to say to tyranny in whatsoever form it oppresses them, 'Thus far and no farther shalt thou go,' the night is far spent and the light is breaking in the east.

"Since the day when we first began to wrest with compelling hands the natural riches from the soil of this our adoptive State, political trickery in high places, backed by the puissant might of alien corporations, has ground us into the dust.

"But now the time of our deliverance is at hand. Great movements give birth to great leaders; and in this, our holy crusade against oppression and tyranny, the crisis has bred the man. Ladies and gentlemen, I have the pleasure of presenting to you the speaker of the evening: our friend and fellow citizen the Honorable Jasper G. Bucks, by the grace of

God, and your suffrages, the next governor of the State."

In the storm of applause that burst upon the dramatic peroration of the ex-district attorney, a man rose from the center of the stage semicircle and lumbered heavily forward to the footlights. Loring's first emotion was of surprise, tempered with pity. The crisis-born leader, heralded by such a flourish of rhetorical trumpets, was a giant in size; but with his huge figure, unshapely and ill-clad, all promise of greatness seemed to pause.

His face, broad-featured, colorless, and beardless as a boy's, was either a blank or an impenetrable mask. There was no convincement in the lack-luster gaze of the small, porcine eyes; no eloquence in the harsh, nasal tones of the untrained voice, or in the ponderous and awkward wavings of the beam-like arms. None the less, before he had uttered a dozen halting sentences he was carrying the audience with him step by step; moving the great concourse of listeners with his commonplace periods as a mellifluous Hawk could never hope to move it.

Loring saw the miracle in the throes of its outworking; saw and felt it in his own proper person, and sought in vain to account for it. Was there some subtile magnetism in this great hulk of a man that made itself felt in spite of its hamperings? Or was it merely that the people, weary of empty rhetoric and unkept promises, were ripe to welcome and to follow any man whose apparent earnestness and sincerity atoned for all his lacks?

Explain it as he might, Loring soon assured himself that the Honorable Jasper G. Bucks was laying hold of the sentiment of the audience as though it were a thing tangible to be grasped by the huge hands. Unlike Hawk, whose speech flamed easily into denunciation when it touched on the alien corporations, he counseled moderation and lawful reprisals. Land syndicates, railroads, foreign capital in whatever employment, were prime necessities in any new and growing commonwealth. The province of the people was not to wreck the ship, but to guide it. And the remedy for all ills lay in controlling legislation, faithfully and rigidly enforced.

"My friends: I'm only a plain, hard-handed farmer, as those of you who are my fellow townsmen can testify. But I've seen what you've seen, and I've suffered what you've suffered. Year after year we send our representatives to the legislature, and what comes of it? Why, these corporations, looking only to their own interests, as they're in duty bound to do, buys 'em if they can. You can't blame 'em for that; it's business—their business. But it is our business, as citizens of this great commonwealth, to prevent it. We have good laws on our statute books, but we need more of 'em; laws for control, with plain, honest men at the capital, in the judiciary, in every root and branch of the executive, to enforce 'em. With such laws, and such men to see that they are executed, there wouldn't be any more extortion, any more raising of the rates of transportation on the produce of our ranches and farms merely because the eastern market for that particular product happened to jump a few cents on the dollar.

"No, my friends; plain, hard-handed farmer though I be, I can see what will follow an honest election of the people, by the people, and for the people. The State can be—it ought to be—sovereign within its own boundaries. If we rise up as one man next Tuesday and put a ticket into the ballot-box that says we are going to make it so, and keep it so, you'll see a new commodity tariff put into effect on the Western Pacific Railroad the day after."

The speaker paused, and into the little gap of silence barked a voice from the gallery.

"That's what you say. But supposin' they don't do it?"

Loring was gazing steadfastly at the blank, heavy face, so utterly devoid of the enthusiasm the man was evoking in others. For one flitting instant he thought he saw behind the mask. The immobile face, the awkward gestures, the slipshod English became suddenly transparent, revealing the real man; a man of titanic strength, of tremendous possibilities for good or evil. Loring put up his glasses and looked again; but the figure of the flash-light inner vision had vanished, and the speaker was answering his objector as calmly as though the house held only the single critic to be set right.

"I'm always glad to hear a man speak right out in meeting," he said, dropping still deeper into the colloquialisms. "Supposing the corporations don't see the handwriting on the wall—won't see it, you say? Then, my friend, it will become the manifest duty of the legislature and the executive to make 'em see it: always lawfully, you understand; always with a just and equitable respect for the rights of property in which our free and glorious institutions are founded, but with level-handed justice, and without fear or favor."

A thunderous uproar of applause clamored on the heels of the answer, and the Honorable Jasper mopped his face with a colored handkerchief and took a swallow of water from the glass on the desk.

"Mind you, my friends, I'm not saying we are not going to find plenty of stumps and roots and a tough sod in this furrow we are going to plow. It's only the fool or the ignoramus who underrates the strength of his opponent. It is going to be just plain, honest justice and the will of the people against the money of the

Harrimans and the Goulds and the Vanderbilts and all
the rest of 'em. But the law is mighty, and it will pre-
vail. Give us an honest legislature to make such laws,
and an executive strong ˜enough to enforce 'em, and
the sovereign State will stand out glorious and triumphant as a monument against oppression.

"When that time comes—and it's a-coming, my
friends—the corporations and the syndicates will read
the handwriting on the wall; don't you be afraid of
that. If they should be a little grain thick-headed and
sort o' blind at first, as old King Belshazzar was, it may
be that the sovereign State will have to give 'em an
object-lesson—lawfully, always lawfully, you understand. But when they see, through the medium of
such an object-lesson or otherwise, as the case may be,
that we mean business; when they see that we, the
people of this great and growing commonwealth, mean
to assert our rights to live and move and have our being, to have fair, even-handed justice meted out to
ourselves, our wives and our little children, they'll come
down and quit watering their stock with the sweat of
our brows; and that hold-up motto of theirs, 'All the
tariff the traffic will stand,' will be no more known in
Israel!"

Again the clamor of applause rose like fine dust on
the throng-heated air, and Kent looked at his watch.

"It is time we were going," he said; adding: "I guess you have had enough of it, haven't you?"

Loring was silent for the better part of the way back to the railway station. When he spoke it was in answer to a delayed question of Kent's.

"What do I think of him? I don't know, David; and that's the plain truth. He is not the man he appears to be as he stands there haranguing that crowd. That is a pose, and an exceedingly skilful one. He is not altogether apparent to me; but he strikes me as being a man of immense possibilities—whether for good or evil, I can't say."

"You needn't draw another breath of uncertainty on that score," was the curt rejoinder. "He is a demagogue, pure and unadulterated."

Loring did not attempt to refute the charge.

"Are he and his party likely to win?" he asked.

"God knows," said Kent. "We have had so many lightning transformations in politics in the State that nothing is impossible."

"I'd like to know," was Loring's comment. "It might make some difference to me, personally."

"To you?" said Kent, inquiringly. "That reminds me: I haven't given you a chance to say ten words about yourself."

"The chance hasn't been lacking. But my business out here is—well, it isn't exactly a Star Chamber mat-

ter, but I'm under promise in a way not to talk about
it until I have had a conference with our people at the
capital. I'll write you about it in a few days."

They were ascending the steps at the end of the
passenger platform again, and Loring broke away from
the political and personal entanglement to give Kent
one more opportunity to hear his word of negative comfort.

"We dug up the field of recollection pretty thoroughly
in our after-dinner séance in your rooms, David, but I
noticed there was one corner of it you left undisturbed.
Was there any good reason?"

Kent made no show of misunderstanding.

"There was the excellent reason which must have
been apparent to you before you had been an hour in
Gaston. I've made my shot, and missed."

Loring entered the breach with his shield held well
to the fore. He was the last man in the world to assault a friend's confidence recklessly.

"I thought a good while ago, and I still think, that
you are making a mountain out of a mole-hill, David.
Elinor Brentwood is a true woman in every inch of
her. She is as much above caring for false notions of
caste as you ought to be."

"I know her nobility: which is all the more reason
why I shouldn't take advantage of it. We may scoff at
the social inequalities as much as we please, but we can't

laugh them out of court. As between a young woman who is an heiress in her own right, and a briefless lawyer, there are differences which a decent man is bound to efface. And I haven't been able."

"Does Miss Brentwood know?"

"She knows nothing at all. I was unwilling to entangle her, even with a confidence."

"The more fool you," said Loring, bluntly. "You call yourself a lawyer, and you have not yet learned one of the first principles of common justice, which is that a woman has some rights which even a besotted lover is bound to respect. You made love to her that summer at Croydon; you needn't deny it. And at the end of things you walk off to make your fortune without committing yourself; without knowing, or apparently caring, what your stiff-necked poverty-pride may cost her in years of uncertainty. You deserve to lose her."

Kent's smile was a fair measure of his unhopeful mood.

"You can't well lose what you have never had. I'm not such an ass as to believe that she cared greatly."

"How do you know? Not by anything you ever gave her a chance to say, I'll dare swear. I've a bit of qualified good news for you, but the spirit is moving me mightily to hold my tongue."

"Tell me," said Kent, his indifference vanishing in the turning of a leaf.

"Well, to begin with, Miss Brentwood is still unmarried, though the gossips say she doesn't lack plenty of eligible offers."

"Half of that I knew; the other half I took for granted. Go on."

"Her mother, under the advice of the chief of the clan Brentwood, has been making a lot of bad investments for herself and her two daughters: in other words, she has been making ducks and drakes of the Brentwood fortune."

Kent was as deeply moved as if the loss had been his own, and said as much, craving more of the particulars.

"I can't give them. But I may say that the blame lies at your door, David."

"At my door? How do you arrive at that?"

"By the shortest possible route. If you had done your duty by Elinor in the Croydon summer, Mrs. Brentwood would have had a bright young attorney for a son-in-law and adviser, and the bad investments would not have been made."

Kent's laugh was entirely devoid of mirth.

"Don't trample on a man when he's down. I was neither a prophet nor the son of a prophet. But how bad is the smash? Surely you know that?"

"No, I don't. Bradford was telling me about it the day I left Boston. He gave me to understand that the principal family holding at present is in the stock of a certain western railway."

"Did he happen to know the name of the stock?" asked Kent, moistening his lips.

"He did. Fate flirts with you two in the usual fashion. Mrs. Brentwood's little fortune—and by consequence, Elinor's and Penelope's—is tied up in the stock of the company whose platform we are occupying at the present moment—the Western Pacific."

Kent let slip a hard word directed at ill-advisers in general, and Loring took his cue from the malediction.

"You swear pretty feelingly, David. Isn't our property as good a thing as we of the Boston end have been cracking it up to be?"

"You know better about the financial part of it than I do. But—well, you are fresh from this anarchistic conclave at the Opera House. You can imagine what the stock of the Western Pacific, or of any other foreign corporation doing business in this State, will be worth in six months after Bucks and his crowd get into the saddle."

"You speak as if the result of the election were a foregone conclusion. I hope it isn't. But we were talking more particularly of Miss Brentwood, and your personal responsibilities." The belated train was whistling for the lower yard, and Loring was determined to say all that was in his mind.

"Yes; go on. I'm anxious to hear—more anxious than I seem to be, perhaps."

"Well, she is coming West, after a bit. She, and her sister and the mother. Mrs. Brentwood's asthma is worse, and the wise men have ordered her to the interior. I thought you'd like to know."

"Is she—are they coming this way?" asked Kent.

The train was in, and the porter had fetched Loring's hand-bag from the check-stand. The guest paused with one foot on the step of the sleeping-car.

"If I were you, David, I'd write and ask; I should, by Jove. It would be a tremendously cheeky thing to do, of course, having such a slight acquaintance with her as you have; but I'll be hanged if I shouldn't chance it. And in the mean time, if I don't go back East next week, you'll hear from me. When you do, or if you do, take a day off and run up to the capital. I shall need you. Good-by."

Kent watched the train pull out; stood looking after it until the two red eyes of the rear signals had disappeared in the dusty darkness of the illimitable plain. Then he went to his rooms, to the one which was called by courtesy his office, and without allowing himself time for a nice balancing of the pros and cons, squared himself at the desk to write a letter.

III

THE BOSTONIANS

It was precisely on the day set for the Brentwoods' westward flitting that the postman, making his morning round, delivered David Kent's asking at the house in the Back Bay sub-district. Elinor was busy packing for the migration, but she left Penelope and the maid to cope with the problem of compressing two trunkfuls into one while she read the letter, and she was reading it a second time when Mr. Brookes Ormsby's card came up.

"You go, Penelope," she begged. "There is so much to do."

"Not I," said the younger sister, cavalierly; "he didn't come to see me." Whereupon Elinor smoothed the two small wrinkles of impatience out of her brow, tucked her letter into her bosom, and went down to meet the early morning caller.

Mr. Brookes Ormsby, club-man, gentleman of athletic leisure, and inheritor of the Ormsby millions, was

(32)

pacing back and forth before the handful of fire in the drawing-room grate when she entered.

"You don't deserve to have a collie sheep-dog friend," he protested reproachfully. "How was I to know that you were going away?"

Another time Elinor might have felt that she owed him an explanation, but just now she was careful, and troubled about the packing.

"How was I to know you didn't know?" she retorted. "It was in the *Transcript.*"

"Well!" said Ormsby. "Things have come to a pretty pass when I have to keep track of you through the society column. I didn't see the paper. Dyckman brought me word last night at Vineyard Haven, and we broke a propeller blade on the *Amphitrite* trying to get here in time."

"I am so sorry—for the *Amphitrite*," she said. "But you are here, and in good season. Shall I call mother and Nell?"

"No. I ran out to see if I'm in time to do your errands for you—take your tickets, and so on."

"Oh, we shouldn't think of troubling you. James can do all those things. And failing James, there is a very dependable young woman at the head of this household. Haven't I 'personally conducted' the family all over Europe?"

"James is a base hireling," said the caller, blandly.

"And as for the capable young woman: do I or do I not recollect a dark night on the German frontier when she was glad enough to call on a sleepy fellow pilgrim to help her wrestle with a particularly thick-headed customs officer?"

"If you do, it is not especially kind of you to remind her of it."

He looked up quickly, and the masterful soul of the man, for which the clean-cut, square-set jaw and the athletic figure were the outward presentments, put on a mask of deference and humility.

"You are hard with me, Elinor—always flinty and adamantine, and that sort. Have you no soft side at all?"

She laughed.

"The sentimental young woman went out some time ago, didn't she? One can't be an anachronism."

"I suppose not. Yet I'm always trying to make myself believe other things about you. Don't you like to be cared for like other women?"

"I don't know; sometimes I think I should. But I have had to be the man of the house since father died."

"I know," he said. "And it is the petty anxieties that have made you put the woman to the wall. I'm here this morning to save you some of them; to take the man's part in your outsetting, or as much of it as I can.

When are you going to give me the right to come between you and all the little worries, Elinor?"

She turned from him with a faint gesture of cold impatience.

"You are forgetting your promise," she said quite dispassionately. "We were to be friends; as good friends as we were before that evening at Bar Harbor. I told you it would be impossible, and you said you were strong enough to make it possible."

He looked at her with narrowing eyes.

"It is possible, in a way. But I'd like to know what door of your heart it is that I haven't been able to open."

She ignored the pleading and took refuge in a woman's expedient.

"If you insist on going back to the beginnings, I shall go back, also—to Abigail and the trunk-packing."

He planted himself squarely before her, the mask lifted and the masterful soul asserting itself boldly.

"It wouldn't do any good, you know. I am going with you."

"To Abigail and the trunk-room?"

"Oh, no; to the jumping-off place out West—wherever it is you are going to hibernate."

"No," she said decisively; "you must not."

"Why?"

"My saying so ought to be sufficient reason."

"It isn't," he contended, frowning down on her good-naturedly. "Shall I tell you why you don't want me to go? It is because you are afraid."

"I am not," she denied.

"Yes, you are. You know in your own heart there is no reason why you should continue to make me unhappy, and you are afraid I might over-persuade you."

Her eyes—they were the serene eyes of cool gray that take on slate-blue tints in stressful moments—met his defiantly.

"If you think that, I withdraw my objection," she said coldly. "Mother and Penelope will be delighted, I am sure."

"And you will be bored, world without end," he laughed. "Never mind; I'll be decent about it and keep out of your way as much as you like."

Again she made the little gesture of petulant impatience.

"You are continually placing me in a false position. Can't you leave me out of it entirely?"

It is one of the prime requisites of successful mastership to know when to press the point home, and when to recede gracefully. Ormsby abruptly shut the door upon sentiment and came down to things practical.

"It is your every-day comfort that concerns me

chiefly. I am going to take all three of you in charge,
giving the dependable young person a well-earned holi-
day—a little journey in which she won't have to chaf-
fer with the transit people. Have you chosen your
route to the western somewhere?"

Miss Brentwood had the fair, transparent skin that
tells tales, and the blue-gray eyes were apt to confirm
them. David Kent's letter was hidden in the folds of
her loose-waisted morning gown, and she fancied it
stirred like a thing alive to remind her of its message.
Ormsby was looking past her to the old-fashioned or-
molu clock on the high mantel, comparing the time
with his watch, but he was not oblivious of the tell-
tale flush.

"There is nothing embarrassing about the choosing
of a route, is there?" he queried.

"Oh, no; being true Americans, we don't know one
route from another in our own country," she confessed. "But at the western end of it we want to go
over the Western Pacific."

Ormsby knew the West by rail routes as one who
travels much for time-killing purposes.

"It's a rather roundabout cow-path," he objected.
"The Overland Short Line is a good bit more direct;
not to mention the service, which is a lot better."

But Elinor had made her small concession to David
Kent's letter, and she would not withdraw it.

"Probably you don't own any Western Pacific stock," she suggested. "We do; and we mean to be loyal to our salt."

Ormsby laughed.

"I see Western Pacific has gone down a few points since the election of Governor Bucks. If I had any, I'd wire my broker to sell."

"We are not so easily frightened," she asserted; adding, with a touch of the austerity which was her Puritan birthright: "Nor quite so conscienceless as you men."

"Conscience," he repeated half absently; "is there any room for such an out-of-date thing in a nation of successfulists? But seriously; you ought to get rid of Western Pacific. There can be no possible question of conscience involved."

"I don't agree with you," she retorted with prompt decision. "If we were to sell now it would be because we were afraid it might prove to be a bad investment. Therefore, for the sake of a presumably ignorant buyer, we have no right to sell."

He smiled leniently.

"All of which goes to prove that you three lone women need a guardian. But I mustn't keep you any longer from Abigail and the trunks. What time shall I send the expediters after your luggage?"

She told him, and went with him to the door.

"Please don't think me ungrateful," she said, when she had thrown the night-latch for him. "I don't mean to be."

"I don't think anything of you that I ought not to think: in that I am as conscientious as even you could wish. Good-by, until this evening. I'll meet you all at the station."

As had come to be the regular order of things, Elinor found herself under fire when she went above stairs to rejoin her mother and sister.

Mrs. Brentwood was not indifferent to the Ormsby millions; neither had she forgotten a certain sentimental summer at the foot of Old Croydon. She was a thin-lipped little person, plain-spoken to the verge of unfriendliness; a woman in whom the rugged, self-reliant, Puritan strain had become panic-acidulous. And when the Puritan stock degenerates in that direction, it is apt to lack good judgment on the business side, and also the passivity which smooths the way for incompetence in less assertive folk.

Kent had stood something in awe, not especially of her personality, but of her tongue; and had been forced to acquiesce silently in Loring's summing-up of Elinor's mother as a woman who had taken culture and the humanizing amenities of the broader life much as the granite of her native hills takes polish—reluctantly, and without prejudice to its inner granular structure.

"Elinor, you ought to be ashamed to keep Brookes Ormsby dangling the way you do," was her comment when Elinor came back. "You are your father's daughters, both of you: there isn't a drop of the Grimkie blood in either of you, I do believe."

Elinor was sufficiently her father's daughter to hold her peace under her mother's reproaches: also, there was enough of the Grimkie blood in her veins to stiffen her in opposition when the need arose. So she said nothing.

"Since your Uncle Ichabod made such a desperate mess of that copper business in Montana, we have all been next door to poverty, and you know it," the mother went on, irritated by Elinor's silence. "I don't care so much for myself: your father and I began with nothing, and I can go back to nothing, if necessary. But you can't, and neither can Penelope; you'd both starve. I should like to know what Brookes Ormsby has done that you can't tolerate him."

"It isn't anything he has done, or failed to do," said Elinor, wearily. "Please let's not go over it all again, mother."

Mrs. Brentwood let that gun cool while she fired another.

"I suppose he came to say good-by: what is he going to do with himself this winter?"

The temptation to equivocate for pure perversity's sake was strong upon Elinor, and she yielded to it.

"How should I know? He has the *Amphitrite* and the Florida coast, hasn't he?"

Mrs. Brentwood groaned.

"To think of the way he squanders his money in sheer dissipation!" she exclaimed. "Of course, he will take an entire house-party with him, as usual, and the cost of that one cruise would set you up in housekeeping."

Penelope laughed with a younger daughter's license. She was a statuesque young woman with a pose, ripe lips, flashing white teeth, laughing eyes with an imp of mischief in them, and an exquisitely turned-up nose that was neither the Brentwood, which was severely classic, nor the Grimkie, which was pure Puritan renaissance.

"Which is to intimate that he won't have money enough left to do it when he comes back," she commented. "I wish there were some way of making him believe he had to give me what remains of his income after he has spent all he can on the Florida cruise. I'd wear Worth gowns and be lapped in luxury for the next ten years at the very least."

"He isn't going to Florida this winter," said Elinor, repenting her of the small quibble. "He is going West."

Mrs. Brentwood looked up sharply.

"With us?" she queried.

"Yes."

Penelope clasped her hands and tried to look soulful.

"Oh, Ellie!" she said; "have you—"

"No," Elinor retorted; "I have not."

IV

The westward journey began at the appointed hour in the evening with the resourceful Ormsby in command; and when the outsetting, in which she had to sustain only the part of an óbedient automaton, was a fact accomplished, Elinor settled back into the pillowed corner of her sleeping-car section to enjoy the unwonted sensation of being the one cared for instead of the caretaker.

She had traveled more or less with her mother and Penelope ever since her father's death, and was well used to taking the helm. Experience and the responsibilities had made her self-reliant, and her jesting boast that she was a dependable young woman was the simple truth. Yet to the most modern of girl bachelors there may come moments when the soul harks back to the eternal-womanly, and the desire to be petted and looked after and safe-conducted is stronger than the bachelor conventions.

Two sections away the inevitable newly married pair posed unconsciously to point the moral for Miss Brentwood. She marked the eagerly anticipative solicitude of the boyish groom, contrasting it now and then with Ormsby's less obtrusive attentions. It was all very absurd and sentimental, she thought; and yet she was not without a curious heart-stirring of envy provoked by the self-satisfied complacency of the bride.

What had that chit of a girl done to earn her immunity from self-defendings and the petty anxieties? Nothing, Elinor decided; at least, nothing more purposeful than the swimmer ·does when he lets himself drift with the current. None the less, the immunity was hers, undeniably, palpably. For the first time in her life Miss Brentwood found herself looking, with a little shudder of withdrawal and dismay, down the possible vista—possible to every unmarried woman of twenty-four—milestoned by unbroken years of spinsterhood and self-helpings.

Was she strong enough to walk this hedged-up path alone?—single-hearted enough to go on holding out against her mother's urgings, against Ormsby's masterful wooing, against her own unconquerable longing for a sure anchorage in some safe haven of manful care and supervision; all this that she might continue to preserve her independence and live the life which, despite its drawbacks, was yet her own?

There were times when she doubted her resolution; and this first night of the westward journey was one of them. She had thought at one time that she might be able to idealize David Kent, but he had gone his way to hew out his fortune, taking her upstirrings of his ambition in a purely literal and selfish sense, so far as she could determine. And now there was Brookes Ormsby. She could by no possibility idealize him. He was a fixed fact, stubbornly asserted. Yet he was a great-hearted gentleman, unspoiled by his millions, thoughtful always for her comfort, generous, self-effacing. Just now, for example, when he had done all, he had seemed to divine her wish to be alone and had betaken himself to the smoking-compartment.

"I promised not to bore you," he had said, "and I sha'n't. Send the porter after me if there is anything I have forgotten to do."

She took up the magazine he had left on the seat beside her and sought to put away the disquieting thoughts. But they refused to be dismissed; and now among them rose up another, dating back to that idealizing summer at the foot of Old Croydon, and having its genesis in a hard saying of her mother's.

She closed her eyes, recalling the words and the occasion of them. "You are merely wasting time and sentiment on this young upstart of a country lawyer, Elinor. So long as you were content to make it a sum-

mer day's amusement, I had nothing to say; you are
old enough and sensible enough to choose your own
recreations. But in justice to yourself, no less than
to him, you must let it end with our going home. You
haven't money enough for two."

Her eyes grew hot under the closed lids when she
remembered. At the time the hard saying was evoked
there was money enough for two, if David Kent would
have shared it. But he had held his peace and gone
away, and now there was not enough for two.

Elinor faced her major weakness unflinchingly. She
was not a slave to the luxuries—the luxuries of the very
rich. On the contrary, she had tried to make herself believe that hardness was a part of her creed. But latterly, she had been made to see that there was a for-
midable array of things which she had been calling
comforts: little luxuries which Brookes Ormsby's wife
might reckon among the simplest necessities of the
daily life, but which David Kent's wife might have
to forego; nay, things which Elinor Brentwood might
presently have to forego. For she compelled herself
to front the fact of the diminished patrimony squarely.
So long as the modest Western Pacific dividends were
forthcoming, they could live comfortably and without
pinching. But failing these—

"No, I'm not great enough," she confessed, with a little shiver. "I should be utterly miserable. If I could

afford to indulge in ideals it would be different; but I can't—not when one word of mine will build a barrier so high that all the soul-killing little skimpings can never climb over it. And besides, I owe something to mother and Nell."

It was the final straw. When any weakness of the human heart can find a seeming virtue to go hand in hand with it, the battle is as good as lost; and at that moment Brookes Ormsby, placidly refilling his short pipe in the smoking-room of the Pullman, was by no means in the hopeless case he was sometimes tempted to fancy himself.

As may be surmised, a diligent suitor, old enough to plan thoughtfully, and yet young enough to simulate the youthful ardor of a lover whose hair has not begun to thin at the temples, would lose no ground in a three days' journey and the opportunities it afforded.

In Penelope's phrase, Elinor "suffered him", enjoying her freedom from care like a sleepy kitten; shutting the door on the past and keeping it shut until the night when their through sleeper was coupled to the Western Pacific Flyer at A. & T. Junction. But late that evening, when she was rummaging in her handbag for a handkerchief, she came upon David Kent's letter and read it again.

"Loring tells me you are coming West," he wrote.

"I assume there is at least one chance in three that you will pass through Gaston. If you do, and if the hour is not altogether impossible, I should like to meet your train. One thing among the many the past two years have denied me—the only thing I have cared much about, I think—is the sight of your face. I shall be very happy if you will let me look at you— just for the minute or two the train may stop."

There was more of it; a good bit more: but it was all guarded commonplace, opening no window in the heart of the man David Kent. Yet even in the commonplace she found some faint interlinings of the change in him; not a mere metamorphosis of the outward man, as a new environment might make, but a radical change, deep and biting, like the action of a strong acid upon a fine-grained metal.

She returned the letter to its envelope, and after looking up Gaston on the time-table fell into a heart-stirring reverie, with unseeing eyes fixed on the restful blackness of the night rushing rearward past the car windows.

"He has forgotten," she said, with a little lip-curl of disappointment. "He thinks he ought to remember, and he is trying—trying because Grantham said something that made him think he ought to try. But it's no use. It was only a little summer idyl, and we have both outlived it."

She was still gazing steadfastly upon the wall of outer darkness when the porter began to make down the berths and Penelope came over to sit in the opposite seat. A moment later the younger sister made a discovery, or thought she did.

"Why, Elinor Brentwood!" she said. "I do believe you are crying!"

Elinor's smile was serenity undisturbed.

"What a vivid imagination you have, Nell, dear," she scoffed. Then she changed the subject arbitrarily: "Is mother quite comfortable? Did you have the porter put a screen in her window?—you know she always insists she can't breathe without it."

Penelope evaded the queries and took her turn at subject-wrenching—an art in which she excelled.

"We are on our own railroad now, aren't we?" she asked, with purposeful lack-interest. "And—let me see—isn't Mr. Kent at some little town we pass through?"

"It is a city," said Elinor. "And the name is Gaston."

"I remember now," Penelope rejoined. "I wonder if we shall see him?"

"It is most unlikely. He does not know we are coming, and he wouldn't be looking for us."

Penelope's fine eyes clouded. At times Elinor's

thought-processes were as plain as print to the younger sister; at other times they were not.

"I should think the least we could do would be to let him know," she ventured. "Does anybody know what time the train passes Gaston?"

"At seven-fifteen to-morrow evening," was the unguarded reply; and Penelope drew her own conclusions from the ready answer and the folded time-table in Elinor's lap.

"Well, why don't you send him a wire? I'm sure I should."

"Why should I?" said Elinor, warily.

"Oh, I don't know: any other young woman of his acquaintance would, I fancy. I have half a mind to do it myself. *I* like him, if you don't care for him any more."

Thus Penelope; and a little while afterward, finding herself in the library compartment with blanks and pen and ink convenient and nothing better to do, she impulsively made the threat good in a ten-word message to Kent.

"If he should happen to drop in unexpectedly it will give Ellie the shock of her life," she mused; and the telegram was smuggled into the hands of the porter to be sent as occasion offered.

Those who knew Mr. Brookes Ormsby best were wont

to say that the world of action, a world lusting avidly for resourceful men, had lost the chance of acquiring a promising leader when he was born heir to the Ormsby millions. Be that as it may, he made the most of such opportunities for the exercising of his gift as came to one for whom the long purse leveled most barriers; had been making the most of the present leaguer of a woman's heart—a citadel whose capitulation was not to be compassed by mere money-might, he would have said.

Up to the final day of the long westward flight all things had gone well with him. True, Elinor had not thawed visibly, but she had been tolerant; Penelope had amused herself at no one's expense save her own—a boon for which Ormsby did not fail to be duly thankful; and Mrs. Brentwood had contributed her mite by keeping hands off.

But at the dining-car luncheon on the last day's run, Penelope, languishing at a table for two with an unresponsive Ormsby for a vis-à-vis, made sly mention of the possible recrudescence of one David Kent at a place called Gaston: this merely to note the effect upon an unresponsive table-mate.

In Penelope's observings there was no effect perceptible. Ormsby said "Ah?" and asked if she would have more of the salad. But later, in a contemplative half-hour with his pipe in the smoking-compartment, he let the scrap of information sink in and take root.

Hitherto Kent had been little more than a name to him; a name he had never heard on Elinor's lips. But if love be blind in the teens and twenties, it is more than apt to have a keen gift of insight in the thirties and beyond. Hence, by the time Ormsby had come to the second filling of his pipe, he had pieced together bits of half-forgotten gossip about the Croydon summer, curious little reticences on Elinor's part, vague hints let fall by Mrs. Brentwood; enough to enable him to chart the rock on which his love-argosy was drifting, and to name it—David Kent.

Now to a well-knit man of the world—who happens to be a heaven-born diplomatist into the bargain—to be forewarned is to be doubly armed. At the end of the half-hour of studious solitude in the smoking-room, Ormsby had pricked out his course on the chart to a boat's-length; had trimmed his sails to the minutest starting of a sheet. A glance at his watch and another at the time-table gave him the length of his respite. Six hours there were; and a dining-car dinner intervened. Those six hours, and the dinner, he decided, must win or lose the race.

Picturing for ourselves, if we may, how nine men out of ten would have given place to panic-ardor, turning a possible victory into a hopeless rout, let us

hold aloof and mark the generalship of the tenth, who
chances to be the heaven-born.

For five of the six precious hours Ormsby merely
saw to it that Elinor was judiciously marooned. Then
the dining-car was reopened and the evening meal was
announced. Waiting until a sufficient number of passengers had gone forward to insure a crowded car,
Ormsby let his party fall in with the tail of the procession, and the inevitable happened. Single seats
only could be had, and Elinor was compelled to dine
in solemn silence at a table with three strangers.

Dinner over, there remained but twenty minutes
of the respite; but the diplomatist kept his head, going
back to the sleeping-car with his charges and dropping
into the seat beside Elinor with the light of calm assurance in his eye.

"You are quite comfortable?" he began. "Sha'n't
I have the Presence in the buffet make you a cup of
tea? That in the diner didn't deserve the name."

She was regarding him with curious anger in the
gray eyes, and her reply quite ignored the kindly
offer of refreshment.

"You are the pink of dragomans," she said. "Don't
you want to go and smoke?"

"To be entirely consistent, I suppose I ought to,"
he confessed, wondering if his throw had failed. "Do
you want me to go?"

"I have been alone all the afternoon: I can endure it a little while longer, I presume."

Ormsby permitted himself a single heart-throb of exultation. He had deliberately gone about to break down her poise, her only barrier of defense, and it began to look as if he had succeeded.

"I couldn't help it, you know," he said, catching his cue swiftly. "There are times when I'm obliged to keep away from you—times when every fiber of me rebels against the restraints of the false position you have thrust me into. When I'm taken that way I don't dare play with the fire."

"I wish I could know how much you mean by that," she said musingly. Deep down in her heart she knew she was as far as ever from loving this man; but his love, or the insistent urging of it, was like a strong current drifting her whither she would not go.

"I mean all that an honest man can mean," he rejoined. "I have fought like a soldier for standing-room in the place you have assigned me; I have tried sincerely—and stupidly, you will say—to be merely your friend, just the best friend you ever had. But it's no use. Coming or going, I shall always be your lover."

"Please don't," she said, neither coldly nor warmly. "You are getting over into the domain of the very young people when you say things like that."

It was an unpleasant thing to say, and he was not beyond wincing a little. None the less, he would not be turned aside.

"You'll overlook it in me if I've pressed the thing too hard on the side of sentiment, won't you? Apart from the fact that I feel that way, I've been going on the supposition that you'd like it, if you could only make up your mind to like me."

"I do like you," she admitted; "more than any one I have ever known, I think."

The drumming wheels and a long-drawn trumpet blast from the locomotive made a shield of sound to isolate them. The elderly banker in the opposite section was nodding over his newspaper; and the newly married ones were oblivious, each to all else but the other. Mrs. Brentwood was apparently sleeping peacefully three seats away; and Penelope was invisible.

"There was a time when I should have begged hard for something more, Elinor; but now I'm willing to take what I can get, and be thankful. Will you give me the right to make you as happy as I can on the unemotional basis?"

She felt herself slipping.

"If you could fully understand—"

"I understand that you don't love me, in the novel-ist's sense of the word, and I am not asking more than you can give. But if you can give me the little now, and more when I have won it—don't curl your lip at me, please: I'm trying to put it as mildly as I can."

She was looking at him level-eyed, and he could have sworn that she was never calmer or more self-possessed.

"I don't know why you should want my promise—or any woman's—on such conditions," she said evenly.

"But I do," he insisted.

The lights of a town suburb were flitting past the windows, and the monotonous song of the tires was drowned in the shrill crescendo of the brakes. She turned from him suddenly and laid her cheek against the grateful cool of the window-pane. But when he took her hand she did not withdraw it.

"Is it mine, Elinor?" he whispered. "You see, I'm not asking much."

"Is it worth taking—by itself?"

"You make me very happy," he said quietly; and just then the train stopped with a jerk, and a shuffling bustle of station-platform noises floated in through the open deck transoms of the car.

As if the solution of continuity had been a call to arouse her, Elinor freed her hand with a swift little wrench and sat bolt upright in her corner.

"This station—do you know the name of it?" she

asked, fighting hard for the self-control that usually came so easily.

Ormsby consulted his watch.

"I am not quite sure. It ought to be——"

He broke off when he saw that she was no longer listening to him. There was a stir in the forward vestibule, and the porter came in with a hand-bag. At his heels was a man in a rough-weather box-coat; a youngish man, clean-shaven and wind-tanned to a healthy bronze, with an eager face and alert eyes that made an instant inventory of the car and its complement of passengers. So much Ormsby saw. Then Penelope stood up in her place to greet the new-comer.

"Why, Mr. Kent!" she exclaimed. "Are you really going on with us? How nice of you!"

Elinor turned coolly upon her seat-mate, self-posses-sion once more firmly seated in the saddle.

"Did you know Mr. Kent was going to board the train here?" she asked abruptly.

"Do you mean the gentleman Penelope has waylaid? I haven't the pleasure of his acquaintance. Will you introduce us?"

V

JOURNEYS END—

It had been a day of upsettings for David Kent, beginning with the late breakfast at which Neltje, the night watchman at the railway station, had brought him Penelope's telegram.

At ten he had a case in court: Shotwell *vs.* Western Pacific Co., damages for stock-killing; for the plaintiff —Hawk; for the defendant—Kent. With the thought that he was presently going to see Elinor again, Kent went gaily to the battle legal, meaning to wring victory out of a jury drawn for the most part from the plaintiff's stock-raising neighbors. By dint of great perseverance he managed to prolong the fight until the middle of the afternoon, was worsted, as usual, and so far lost his temper as to get himself called down by the judge, MacFarlane.

Whereupon he went back to the Farquhar Building and to his office and sat down at the type-writer to pound out a letter to the general counsel, resigning

(58)

his sinecure. The Shotwell case was the third he had lost for the company in a single court term. Justice for the railroad company, under present agrarian conditions, was not to be had in the lower courts, and he was weary of fighting the losing battle. Therefore—

In the midst of the type-rattling the boy that served the few occupied offices in the Farquhar Building had brought the afternoon mail. It included a letter from Loring, and there was another reversive upheaval for the exile. Loring's business at the capital was no longer a secret. He had been tendered the resident management of the Western Pacific, with headquarters on the ground, and had accepted. His letter was a brief note, asking Kent to report at once for legal duty in the larger field.

"I am not fairly in the saddle yet, and shall not be for a week or so," wrote the newly appointed manager. "But I find I am going to need a level-headed lawyer at my elbow from the jump—one who knows the State political ropes and isn't afraid of a scrap. Come in on Number Three to-day, if you can; if not, send a wire and say when I may look for you. Or, better still, wire anyway."

David Kent struggled with his emotions until he had got his feet down to the solid earth again. Then he tore up the half-written resignation and began to smite things in order for the flight. Could he make

Number Three?   Since that was the train named in
Penelope's message, nothing short of a catastrophe
should prevent his making it.

He did make it, with an hour to spare; an hour
which he proceeded to turn into a time of sharp trial
for the patient telegraph operator at the station, with
his badgerings of the man for news of Number Three.
The train reported—he took it as a special miracle
wrought in his behalf that the Flyer was for this once
abreast of her schedule—he fell to tramping up and
down the long platform, deep in anticipative prefigur-
ings. The mills of the years grind many grists besides
the trickling stream of the hours: would he find Miss
Brentwood as he had left her? Could he be sure of
meeting her on the frank, friendly footing of the Croydon summer? He feared not; feared all things—lover-
like.

He hoped there would be no absence-reared barrier
to be painfully leveled. A man among men, a leader
in some sort, and in battle a soldier who could hew
his way painstakingly, if not dramatically, to his end,
David Kent was no carpet knight, and he knew his
lack. Would Elinor make things easy for him, as she
used to daily in the somewhat difficult social atmosphere of the exclusive summer hotel?

Measuring it out in all its despairing length and
breadth after the fact, he was deeply grateful to Pe-

nelope. Missing her ready help at the moment of cata-
clysms when he entered the sleeping-car, he might have
betrayed himself. His first glance lighted on Elinor
and Ormsby, and he needed no gloss on the love-text.
He had delayed too long; had asked too much of the
Fates, and Atropos, the scissors-bearing sister, had
snipped his thread of hope.

It is one of the consequences of civilization that we
are denied the privilege of unmasking at the behest of
the elemental emotions; that we are constrained to
bleed decorously. Making shift to lean heavily on
Penelope, Kent came through without doing or saying
anything unseemly. Mrs. Brentwood, who had been
sleeping with one eye open, and that eye upon Elinor
and Ormsby, made sure that she had now no special
reason to be ungracious to David Kent. For the
others, Ormsby was good-naturedly suave; Elinor was
by turns unwontedly kind and curiously silent; and
Penelope—but, as we say, it was to Penelope that Kent
owed most.

So it came about that the outcome of the cataclysm
was a thing which happens often enough in a conven-
tionalized world. David Kent, with his tragedy fresh
upon him, dropped informally into place as one of the
party of five; and of all the others, Penelope alone suspected how hard he was hit. And when all was said;
when the new *modus vivendi* had been fairly estab-

lished and the hour grew late, Kent went voluntarily
with Ormsby to the smoking-compartment, "to play the
string out decently," as he afterward confessed to
Loring.

"I see you know how to get the most comfort out of
your tobacco," said the club-man, when they were com-
panionably settled in the men's room and Kent produced his pipe and tobacco pouch. "I prefer the pipe
myself, for a steady thing; but at this time of night a
light Castilla fits me pretty well. Try one?" tendering
his cigar-case.

Fighting shrewdly against a natural prompting to
regard Ormsby as an hereditary enemy, Kent forced
himself to be neighborly.

"I don't mind," he said, returning the pipe to its
case. And when the Havanas were well alight, and
the talk had circled down upon the political situation in the State, he was able to bear his part with a
fair exterior, giving Ormsby an impressionistic outline
of the late campaign and the conditions that had made
the sweeping triumph of the People's Party possible.

"We have been coming to it steadily through the last
administration, and a part of the preceding one," he explained. "Last year the drought cut the cereals in
half, and the country was too new to stand it without
borrowing. There was little local capital, and the eastern article was hungry, taking all the interest the law

allows, and as much more as it could get. This year the crop broke all records for abundance, but the price is down and the railroads, trying to recoup for two bad years, have stiffened the freight rates. The net result is our political overturn."

"Then the railroads and the corporations are not primarily to blame?" said Ormsby.

"Oh, no. Corporations here, as elsewhere, are looking out for the present dollar, but if the country were generally prosperous, the people would pay the tax carelessly, as they do in the older sections. With us it has been a sort of Donnybrook Fair: the agricultural voter has shillalahed the head he could reach most easily."

The New Yorker nodded. His millions were solidly placed, and he took no more than a sportsman's interest in the fluctuations of the stock market.

"Of course, there have been all sorts of rumors East: 'bull' prophecies that the triumph of the new party means an era of unexampled prosperity for the State— and by consequence for western stocks; 'bear' growlings that things are sure to go to the bow-wows under the Bucks régime. What do you think of it?"

Kent blew a series of smoke rings and watched them rise to become a part of the stratified tobacco cloud overhead before replying.

"I may as well confess that I am not entirely an unprejudiced observer," he admitted. "For one thing, I am in the legal department of one of the best-hated of the railroads; and for another, Governor Bucks, Meigs, the attorney-general, and Hendricks, the new secretary of State, are men whom I know as, it is safe to say, the general public doesn't know them. If I could be sure that these three men are going to be able to control their own party majority in the Assembly, I should take the first train East and make my fortune selling tips in Wall Street."

"You put it graphically. Then the Bucks idea is likely to prove a disturbing element on 'Change?"

"It is; always providing it can dominate its own majority. But this is by no means certain. The political earthquake is essentially a popular protest against hard conditions brought about, as the voters seem to believe, by the oppressions of the alien corporations and extortionate railroad rates. Yet there are plenty of steady-going, conservative men in the movement; men who have no present idea of revolutionizing things. Marston, the lieutenant-governor, is one of that kind. It all depends on whether these men will allow themselves to be whipped into line by the leaders, who, as I am very well convinced, are a set of conscienceless demagogues, fighting solely for their own hand."

Ormsby nodded again.

"You are likely to have good hunting this winter, Mr. Kent. It hasn't begun yet, I take it?"

"Oh, no; the Assembly does not convene for a fortnight, and nobody short of an inspired prophet can foretell what legislation will be sprung. But one thing is safe to count on: the leaders are out for spoils. They mean to rob somebody, and, if my guess is worth anything, they are sharp enough to try first to get their schemes legalized by having enabling laws passed by the Assembly."

"Um," said the eastern man. Then he took the measure of his companion in a shrewd overlook. "You are the man on the ground, Mr. Kent, and I'll ask a straightforward question. If you had a friend owning stock in one of the involved railways, what would you advise?"

Kent smiled.

"We needn't make it a hypothetical case. If I had the right to advise Mrs. Brentwood and her daughters, I should counsel them to sit tight in the boat for the present."

"Would you? But Western Pacific has gone off several points already."

"I know it has; and unfortunately, Mrs. Brentwood bought in at the top of the market. That is why I counsel delay. If she sells now, she is sure to lose. If she holds on, there is an even chance for a spasmodic upward reaction before worse things happen."

"Perhaps: you know more about the probabilities than I pretend to. But on the other hand, she may lose more if she holds on."

Kent bit deep into his cigar.

"We must see to it that she doesn't lose, Mr. Ormsby."

The club-man laughed broadly.

"Isn't that a good bit like saying that the shallop must see to it that the wind doesn't blow too hard for it?"

"Possibly. But in the sorriest wreck there is usually some small chance for salvage. I understand Mrs. Brentwood's holding is not very large?"

"A block of some three thousand shares, held jointly by her and her two daughters, I believe."

"Exactly: not enough to excite anybody's cupidity; and yet enough to turn the scale if there should ever be a fight for a majority control."

"There is no such fight in prospect, is there?"

"No; not that I know of. But I was thinking of the possibilities. If a smash comes there will be a good deal of horse-swapping in the middle of the stream— buying up of depressed stocks by people who need the lines worse than the original owners do."

"I see," said Ormsby. "Then you would counsel delay?"

"I should; and I'll go a step farther. I am on the inside, in a way, and any hint I can give you for Miss —for Mrs. Brentwood's benefit shall be promptly forthcoming."

"By Jove! that's decent," said Ormsby, heartily. "You are a friend worth having, Mr. Kent. But which 'inside' do you mean—the railroad or the political?"

"Oh, the railroad, of course. And while I think of it, my office will be in the Quintard Building; and you—I suppose you will put up at the Wellington?"

"For the present, we all shall. It is Mrs. Brentwood's notion to take a furnished house later on for herself and daughters, if she can find one. I'll keep in touch with you."

"Do. It may come to a bit of quick wiring when our chance arrives. You know Loring—Grantham Loring?"

"Passably well. I came across him one summer in the mountains of Peru, where he was managing a railroad. He is a mighty good sort. I had mountain fever, and he took me in and did for me."

"He is with us now," said David Kent; "the newly appointed general manager of the Western Pacific."

"Good!" said the club-man "I think a lot of him;

he is an all-around dependable fellow, and plenty capable. I'm glad to know he has caught on higher up."

The locomotive whistle was droning again, and a dodging procession of red-eyed switch-lights flicked past the windows. Kent stood up and flung away the stump of his cigar.

"The capital," he announced. "I'll go back with you and help out with the shawl-strap things." And in the vestibule he added: "I spoke of Loring because he will be with us in anything we have to do in Mrs. Brentwood's behalf. Look him up when you have time—fourth floor of the Quintard."

VI

The session, the shortest in the history of the State, and thus far the least eventful, was nearing its close; and the alarmists who had prophesied evil and evil only of the "Populist" victory were fast losing credit with the men of their own camp and with the country at large.

After the orthodox strife over the speakership of the House, and the equally orthodox wrangle over contested seats, the State Assembly had settled down to routine business, despatching it with such unheard-of celerity as to win columns of approval from the State press as a whole; though there were not wanting a few radical editors to raise the ante-election cry of reform, and to ask pointedly when it was to begin.

Notwithstanding the lack of alarms, however, the six weeks had been a period of unceasing vigilance on the part of the interests which were supposed to be in jeopardy. Every alien corporation owning property and

(69)

doing business in the State had its quota of watchful defenders on the ground; men who came and went, in the lobbies of the capitol, in the visitors' galleries, at the receptions; men who said little, but who saw and heard all things down to the small talk of the corridors and the clubs, and the gossip of the hotel rotundas.

David Kent was of this silent army of observation, doing watch-dog duty for the Western Pacific; thankful enough, if the truth be told, to have a thing to do which kept him from dwelling overmuch upon the wreck of his hopes. But in the closing days of the session, when a despatchful Assembly, anxious to be quit of its task, had gone into night sittings, the anodyne drug of work began to lose its effect.

The Brentwoods had taken furnished apartments in Tejon Avenue, two squares from the capitol, and Kent had called no oftener than good breeding prescribed. Yet their accessibility, and his unconquerable desire to sear his wound in the flame that had caused it, were constant temptations, and he was battling with them for the hundredth time on the Friday night when he sat in the House gallery listening to a perfunctory debate which concerned itself with a bill touching State waterways.

"Heavens! This thing is getting to be little short of deadly!" fumed Crenshawe, his right-hand neighbor, who was also a member of the corps of observation.

"I'm going to the club for a game of pool. Won't you come along?"

Kent nodded and left his seat with the bored one. But in the great rotunda he changed his mind.

"You'll find plenty of better players than I am at the club," he said in extenuation. "I think I'll smoke a whiff or two here and go back. They can't hold on much longer for to-night."

Five minutes later, when he had lighted a cigar and was glancing over the evening paper, two other members of the corporation committee of safety came down from the Senate gallery and stopped opposite Kent's pillar to struggle into their overcoats.

"It's precisely as I wrote our people two weeks ago— a timidity scare, pure and simple," one of them was saying. "I've a mind to start home to-morrow. There is nothing doing here, or going to be done."

"No," said the other. "If it wasn't for House Bill Twenty-nine, I'd go to-night. They will adjourn to-morrow or Monday."

"House Bill Twenty-nine is much too dead to bury," was the reassuring rejoinder. "The committee is ours, and the bill will not be heard of again at this session. If that is all you are holding on for—"

They passed out of earshot, and Kent folded his newspaper absently. House Bill Twenty-nine had been the one measure touching the sensitive "vested interests";

the one measure for the suppression of which the corporations' lobby had felt called on to take steps. It
was an omnibus bill put forth as a substitute for the existing law defining the status of foreign corporations.
It had originated in the governor's office,—a fact which
Kent had ferreted out within twenty-four hours of its
first reading,—and for that reason he had procured a
printed copy, searching it diligently for the hidden
menace he was sure it embodied.

When the search proved fruitless, he had seen the bill
pass the House by a safe majority, had followed it to the
Senate, and in a cunningly worded amendment tacked
on in the upper house had found what he was seeking.
Under the existing law foreign corporations were subject to State supervision, and were dealt with as presumably unfriendly aliens. But the Senate amendment
to House Bill Twenty-nine fairly swept the interstate
corporations, as such, out of existence, by making it obligatory upon them to acquire the standing of local corporations. Charters were to be refiled with the secretary
of State; resident directories and operating headquarters
were to be established within the boundaries and jurisdiction of the State; in short, the State proposed, by the
terms of the new law, to deal only with creatures of its
own creation.

Kent saw, or thought he saw, the fine hand of the
junto in all this. It was a still hunt in which the long-

est way around was the shortest way home. Like all
new-country codes, the organic law of the State favored
local corporations, and it might be argued that a bill
placing the foreign companies on a purely local footing
was an unmixed blessing to the aliens. But on the
other hand, an unprincipled executive might easily make
the new law an engine of extortion. To go no further
into the matter than the required refiling of charters:
the State constitution gave the secretary of State quasi-
judicial powers. It was within his province to pass
upon the applications for chartered rights, and to deny
them if the question *pro bono publico* were involved.

Kent put two and two together, saw the wide door of
exactions which might be opened, and passed the word
of warning among his associates; after which he had
watched the course of the amended House Bill Twenty-
nine with interest sharp-set, planning meanwhile with
Hildreth, the editor of the *Daily Argus*, an exposé
which should make plain the immense possibilities for
corruption opened up by the proposed law; a journal-
istic salvo of publicity to be fired as a last resort.

The measure as amended had passed the Senate without debate, and had gone back to the House. Here, after
the second reading, and in the very hour when the
Argus editorial was getting itself cast in the linotypes,
there was a hitch. The member from the Rio Blanco,
favoring the measure in all its parts, and fearful only

lest corporation gold might find a technical flaw in it, moved that it be referred to the committee on judiciary for a report on its constitutionality; and, accordingly, to the committee on judiciary it had gone.

Kent recalled the passing of the crisis, remembering how he had hastened to telephone the *Argus* editor to kill the exposé at the last moment. The incident was now a month in the past, and the committee had not yet reported; would never report, Kent imagined. He knew the personnel of the committee on judiciary; knew that at least three members of it were down on the list, made up at the beginning of the session by his colleagues in the army of observation, as "approach-ables". Also, he knew by inference at least, that these three men had been approached, not without success, and that House Bill Twenty-nine, with its fee-gathering amendment, was safely shelved.

"It's an ill-smelling muck-heap!" he frowned, re-calling the incidents of the crisis at the suggestion let fall by the two outgoing lobbyists. "And so much of this dog-watch as isn't sickeningly demoralizing is deadly dull, as Crenshawe puts it. If I had anywhere to go, I'd cut the galleries for to-night."

He was returning the newspaper to his pocket when it occurred to him that his object in buying it had been to note the stock quotations; a daily duty which, for Elinor's sake, he had never omitted. Whereupon he reopened it and ran his eye down the lists. There was a decided upward tendency in westerns. Overland Short Line had gained two points; and Western Pacific—

He held the paper under the nearest electric globe to make sure: Western Pacific, preferred, was quoted at fifty-eight and a half, which was one point and a half above the Brentwood purchase price.

One minute later an excited life-saver was shut in the box of the public telephone, gritting his teeth at the inanity of the central operator who insisted on giving him "A-1224" instead of "A-1234," the Hotel Wellington.

"No, no! Can't you understand? I want twelve-thirty-four; one, two, *three,* four; the Hotel Wellington."

There was more skirling of bells, another nerve-trying wait, and at last the clerk of the hotel answered.

"What name did you say? Oh, it's you, is it, Mr. Kent? Ormsby? Mr. Brookes Ormsby? No, he isn't here; he went out about two minutes ago. What's that you say? *Damn?* Well, I'm sorry, too. No message that I can take? All right. Good-by."

This was the beginning. For the middle part Kent burst out of the telephone-box and took the nearest short-cut through the capitol grounds for the street-car corner. At a quarter of nine he was cross-questioning the clerk face to face in the lobby of the Wellington. There

was little more to be learned about Ormsby. The club-
man had left his key and gone out. He was in evening
dress, and had taken a cab at the hotel entrance.

Kent dashed across to his rooms and, in a feverish
race against time, made himself fit to chase a man in
evening dress. There was no car in sight when he came
down, and he, too, took a cab with an explosive order
to the driver: "124 Tejon Avenue, and be quick
about it!"

It was the housemaid that answered his ring at the
door of the Brentwood apartment. She was a Swede, a
recent importation; hence Kent learned nothing beyond the bare fact that the ladies had gone out. "With
Mr. Ormsby?" he asked.

"Yaas; Aye tank it vill pee dat yentlemans."

The pursuer took the road again, rather unhopefully.
There were a dozen places where Ormsby might have
taken his charges. Among them there was the legislative
reception at Portia Van Brock's. Kent flipped a figurative coin, and gave the order for Alameda Square. The
reception was perhaps the least unlikely place of the
dozen.

He was no more than fashionably late at the Van
Brock house, and fortunately he was able to reckon himself among the chosen few for whom Miss Portia's door
swung on hospitable hinges at all hours. Loring had
known her in Washington, and he had stood sponsor for

Kent in the first week of the exile's residence at the capital. Thereafter she had taken Kent up on his own account, and by now he was deep in her debt. For one thing, she had set the fashion in the matter of legislative receptions—her detractors, knowing nothing whatever about it, hinted that she had been an amateur social lobbyist in Washington, playing the game for the pure zest of it—and at these functions Kent had learned many things pertinent to his purpose as watch-dog for the railroad company and legal adviser to his chief— things not named openly on the floor of the House or of the Senate chamber.

There was a crush in the ample mansion in Alameda Square, as there always was at Miss Van Brock's "open evenings," and when Kent came down from the cloak-room he had to inch his way by littles through the crowded reception-parlors in the search for the Brent-wood party. It was unsuccessful at first; but later, catching a glimpse of Elinor at the piano, and another of Penelope inducting an up-country legislator into the mysteries of social small-talk, he breathed freer. His haphazard guess had hit the mark, and the finding of Ormsby was now only a question of moments.

It was Miss Van Brock herself who told him where to look for the club-man—though not at his first asking.

"You did come, then," she said, giving him her hand

with a frank little smile of welcome. "Some one said you were not going to be frivolous any more, and I wondered if you would take it out on me. Have you been at the night session?"

"Yes; at what you and your frivolities have left of it. A good third of the Solons seem to be sitting in permanence in Alameda Square."

"'Solons'," she repeated. "That recalls Editor Brownlo's little joke—only he didn't mean it. He wrote of them as 'Solons,' but the printer got it 'solans'. The member from Caliente read the article and the word stuck in his mind. In an unhappy hour he asked Colonel Mack's boy—Harry, the irrepressible, you know— to look it up for him. Harry did it, and of course took the most public occasion he could find to hand in his answer. 'It's geese, Mr. Hackett!' he announced triumphantly; and after we were all through laughing at him the member from the warm place turned it just as neatly as a veteran. 'Well, I'm Hackett,' he said."

David Kent laughed, as he was in duty bound, but he still had Ormsby on his mind.

"I see you have Mrs. Brentwood and her daughters here: can you tell me where I can find Mr. Brookes Ormsby?"

"I suppose I could if I should try. But you mustn't hurry me. There is a vacant corner in that davenport beyond the piano: please put me there and fetch me an ice. I'll wait for you."

He did as he was bidden, and when she was served he stood over her, wondering, as other men had wondered, what was the precise secret of her charm. Loring had told him Miss Van Brock's story. She was southern born, the only child of a somewhat ill-considered match between a young California lawyer, wire-pulling in the national capital in the interest of the Central Pacific Railroad, and a Virginia belle tasting the delights of her first winter in Washington.

Later, the young lawyer's state, or his employers, had sent him to Congress; and Portia, left motherless in her middle childhood, had grown up in an atmosphere of statecraft, or what passes for such, in an era of frank commercialism. Inheriting her mother's rare beauty of face and form, and uniting with it a sympathetic gift in grasp of detail, political and other, she soon became her father's confidante and loyal partizan, taking the place, as a daughter might, of the ambitious young wife and mother, who had set her heart on seeing the Van Brock name on the roll of the United States Senate.

Rensselaer Van Brock had died before the senatorial dream could be realized, but not before he had made a sufficient number of lucky investments to leave his daughter the arbitress of her own future. What that

future should be, not even Loring could guess. Since
her father's death Miss Van Brock had been a citizen
of the world. With a widowed aunt for the shadowiest
of chaperons, she had drifted with the tide of inclina-
tion, coming finally to rest in the western capital for
no better reason, perhaps, than that some portion of
her interest-bearing securities were emblazoned with the
great seal of this particular western State.

Kent was thinking of Loring's recountal as he stood
looking down on her. Other women were younger—
and with features more conventionally beautiful; Kent
could find a round dozen within easy eye-reach, to say
nothing of the calm-eyed, queenly *improvisatrice* at the
piano—his constant standard of all womanly charm and
grace. Unconsciously he fell to comparing the two, his
hostess and his love, and was brought back to things
present by a sharp reminder from Portia.

"Stop looking at Miss Brentwood that way, Mr. David. She is not for you; and you are keeping me waiting."

He smiled down on her.

"It is the law of compensation. I fancy you have
kept many a man waiting—and will keep many another."

There was a little tang of bitterness in her laugh.

"You remind me of the time when I went home from
school—oh, years and years ago. Old Chloe—she was

my black mammy, you know—had a grown daughter of her own, and her effort to dispose of her 'M'randy' was a standing joke in the family. In answer to my stereotyped question she stood back and folded her arms. 'Naw, honey; dat M'randy ain't ma'ied yit. She gwine be des lak you; look pretty, an' say, *Howdy! Misteh Jawnson,* an' go 'long by awn turrer side de road.'"

"A very pretty little fable," said Kent. "And the moral?"

"Is that I amuse myself with you—all of you; and in your turn you make use of me—or you think you do. Of what use can I be to Mr. David Kent this evening?"

"See how you misjudge me!" he protested. "My errand here to-night is purely charitable. Which brings me back to Ormsby: did you say you could tell me where to look for him?"

"He is in the smoking-room with five or six other tobacco misanthropes. What do you want of him?"

"I want to say two words in his ear; after which I shall vanish and make room for my betters."

Miss Van Brock was gazing steadfastly at the impassioned face lighted by the piano candles.

"Is it about Miss Brentwood?" she asked abruptly.

"In a way—yes," he confessed.

She rose and stood beside him—a bewitching figure of a woman who knew her part in the human comedy and played it well.

"Is it wise, David?" she asked softly. "I am not denying the possibilities: you might come between them
if you should try—I'm rather afraid you could. But
you mustn't, you know; it's too late. You've marred her,
between you; or rather that convention, which makes a
woman deaf, blind and dumb until a man has fairly
committed himself, has marred her. For your sake she
can never be quite all she ought to be to him: for his
sake she could never be quite the same to you."

He drew apart from her, frowning.

"If I should say that I don't fully understand what
you mean?" he rejoined.

"I should retort by saying something extremely un-
complimentary about your lack of perspicacity," she
cut in maliciously.

"I beg pardon," he said, a little stiffly. "You are laboring under an entirely wrong impression. What I
have to say to Mr. Brookes Ormsby does not remotely
concern the matter you touch upon. It's an affair of
the Stock Exchange."

"As if I didn't know!" she countered. "You merely
reminded me of the other thing. But if it is only a
business secret you may as well tell me all about it at
first hands. Some one is sure to tell me sooner or later."

Now David Kent was growing impatient. Down in
the inner depths of him he was persuaded that Ormsby

might have difficulty in inducing Mrs. Brentwood to sell her Western Pacific stock even at an advance; might require time, at least. And time, with a Bucks majority tinkering with corporate rights in the Assembly, might well be precious.

"Forgive me if I tell Ormsby first," he pleaded. "Afterward, if you care to know, you shall."

Miss Van Brock let him go at that, but now the way to the smoking-den on the floor above was hedged up. He did battle with the polite requirements, as a man must; shaking hands or exchanging a word with one and another of the obstructors only as he had to. None the less, when he had finally wrought his way to the smoking-room Ormsby had eluded him again.

He went back to the parlors, wondering how he had missed the club-man. In the middle room of the suite he found Portia chatting with Marston, the lieutenant-governor; and a young woman in the smartest of reception gowns had succeeded to Elinor's place at the piano.

"You found him?" queried the hostess, excusing herself to the tall, saturnine man who had shared the honors at the head of the People's Party ticket with Jasper G. Bucks.

"No," said Kent. "Have you seen him?"

"Why, yes; they all came to take leave just a few moments after you left me. I thought of telling Mr. Ormsby you were looking for him, but you shut me off so snippily—"

"Miss Van Brock! What have you done? I must go at once."

"Really? I am complimented. But if you must, you must, I suppose. I had something to tell you—something of importance; but I can't remember what it was now. I never can remember things in the hurry of leave-takings."

As we have intimated, Kent had hitherto found Miss Portia's confidences exceedingly helpful in a business way, and he hesitated. "Tell me," he begged.

"No, I can't remember it: I doubt if I shall ever remember it unless you can remind me by telling me why you are so desperately anxious to find Mr. Ormsby."

"I wonder if you hold everybody up like this," he laughed. "But I don't mind telling you. Western Pacific preferred has gone to fifty-eight and a half."

"And Mr. Ormsby has some to sell? I wish I had. Do you know what I'd do?" She drew closer and laid a hand on his arm. "I'd sell—by wire—to-night; at least, I'd make sure that my telegram would be the first thing my broker would lay his hands on in the morning."

"On general principles, I suppose: so should I, and

for the same reason. But have I succeeded in remind-
ing you of that thing you were going to tell me?"

"Not wholly; only partly. You said this matter of
Mr. Ormsby's concerned Miss Brentwood—in a way—
didn't you?"

"You will have your pound of flesh entire, won't you?
The stock is hers, and her mother's and sister's. I want
Ormsby to persuade them to sell. They'll listen to him.
That is all; all the all."

"Of course!" she said airily. "How simple of me not
to have been able to add it up without your help. I
saw the quotation in the evening paper; and I know,
better, perhaps, than you do, the need for haste. Must
you go now?" She had taken his arm and was edging
him through the press in the parlors toward the entrance hall.

"You haven't paid me yet," he objected.

"No; I'm trying to remember. Oh, yes; I have it
now. Wasn't some one telling me that you are interested in House Bill Twenty-nine?"

They had reached the dimly lighted front vestibule,
and her hand was still on his arm.

"I was interested in it," he admitted, correcting the
present to the past tense.

"But after it went to the House committee on judiciary you left it to more skilful, or perhaps we'd better
say, to less scrupulous hands?"

"I believe you are a witch. Is there anything you don't know?"

"Plenty of things. For example, I don't know exactly how much it cost our good friends of the 'vested interests' to have that bill mislaid in the committee room. But I do know they made a very foolish bargain."

"Beyond all doubt a most demoralizing bargain, which, to say the best of it, was only a choice between two evils. But why foolish?"

"Because—well, because mislaid things have a way of turning up unexpectedly, you know, and—"

He stopped her in a sudden gust of feverish excitement.

"Tell me what you mean in one word, Miss Van Brock. Don't those fellows intend to stay bought?"

She smiled pityingly.

"You are very young, Mr. David—or very honest. Supposing those 'fellows', as you dub the honorable members of the committee on judiciary, had a little plan of their own; a plan suggested by the readiness of certain of their opponents to rush into print with statements which might derange things?"

"I am supposing it with all my might."

"That is right; we are only supposing, you must remember. We may suppose their idea was to let the excitement about the amended bill die down; to let people

generally, and one fiercely honest young corporation attorney in particular, have time to forget that there was
such a thing as House Bill Twenty-nine. And in such
a suppositional case, how much they would be surprised,
and how they would laugh in their sleeves, if some one
came along and paid them handsomely for doing precisely what they meant to do."

David Kent's smile was almost ferocious.

"My argument is as good now as it was in the beginning: they have yet to reckon with the man who will
dare to expose them."

She turned from him and spoke to the footman at the
door.

"Thomas, fetch Mr. Kent's coat and hat from the
dressing-room." And then to Kent, in the tone she might
have used in telling him of the latest breeziness of the
member from the Rio Blanco: "I remember now what
it was that I wanted to tell you. While you have been
trying to find Mr. Ormsby, the committee on judiciary
has been reporting the long-lost House Bill Twenty-
nine. If you hurry you may be in time to see it passed
—it will doubtless go through without any tiresome debate. But you will hardly have time to obstruct it by
arousing public sentiment through the newspapers."

David Kent shook the light touch of her hand from
his arm and set his teeth hard upon a word hot from
the furnace of righteous indignation. For a moment he

fully believed she was in league with the junto; that she had been purposely holding him in talk while the very seconds were priceless.

She saw the scornful wrath in his eyes and turned it aside with a swift denial.

"No, David; I didn't do that," she said, speaking to his inmost thought. "If there had been anything you could do—the smallest shadow of a chance for you—I should have sent you flying at the first word. But there wasn't; it was all too well arranged—"

But he had snatched coat and hat from the waiting Thomas and was running like a madman for the nearest cab-stand.

VII

Kent's time from Alameda Square to the capitol was
the quickest a flogged cab-horse could make, but he
might have spared the horse and saved the double fee.
On the broad steps of the south portico he, uprushing
three at a bound, met the advance guard of the gallery
contingent, down-coming. The House had adjourned.

"One minute, Harnwicke!" he gasped, falling upon
the first member of the corporations' lobby he could
identify in the throng. "What's been done?"

"They've taken a fall out of us," was the brusk reply. "House Bill Twenty-nine was reported by the
committee on judiciary and rushed through after you
left. Somebody engineered it to the paring of a finger-
nail: bare quorum to act; members who might have
filibustered weeded out, on one pretext or another, to a
man; pages all excused, and nobody here with the privilege of the floor. It was as neat a piece of gag-work
as I ever hope to see if I live to be a hundred."

Kent faced about and joined the townward dispersal with his informant.

"Well, I suppose that settles it definitely; at least, until we can test its constitutionality in the courts," he said.

Harnwicke thought not, being of the opinion that the vested interests would never say die until they were quite dead. As assistant counsel for the Overland Short Line, he was in some sense the dean of the corps of observation, and could speak with authority.

"There is one chance left for us this side of the courts," he went on; "and now I think of it, you are the man to say how much of a chance it is. The bill still lacks the governor's signature."

Kent shook his head.

"It is his own measure. I have proof positive that he and Meigs and Hendricks drafted it. And all this fine-haired engineering to-night was his, or Meigs'."

"Of course; we all know that. But we don't know the particular object yet. Do they need the new law in their business as a source of revenue? Or do they want to be hired to kill it? In other words, does Bucks want a lump sum for a veto? You know the man better than any of us."

"By Jove!" said Kent. "Do you mean to say you would buy the governor of a state?"

Harnwicke turned a cold eye on his companion as

they strode along. He was of the square-set, plain-spoken, aggressive type—a finished product of the modern school of business lawyers.

"I don't understand that you are raising the question of ethics at this stage of the game, do I?" he remarked.

Kent fired up a little.

"And if I am?" he retorted.

"I should say you had missed your calling. It is baldly a question of business—or rather of self-preservation. We needn't mince matters among ourselves. If Bucks is for sale, we buy him."

Kent shrugged.

"There isn't any doubt about his purchasability. But I confess I don't quite see how you will go about it."

"Never mind that part of it; just leave the ways and means with those of us who have riper experience—and fewer hamperings, perhaps—than you have. Your share in it is to tell us how big a bid we must make. As I say, you know the man."

David Kent was silent for the striding of half a square. The New England conscience dies hard, and while it lives it is given to drawing sharp lines on all the boundaries of culpability. Kent ended by taking the matter in debate violently out of the domain of ethics and standing it upon the ground of expediency.

"It will cost too much. You would have to bid high—not to overcome his scruples, for he has none;

but to satisfy his greed—which is abnormal. And, besides, he has his pose to defend. If he can see his way
clear to a harvest of extortions under the law, he will
probably turn you down—and will make it hot for you
later on in the name of outraged virtue."

Harnwicke's laugh was cynical.

"He and his little clique don't own the earth in fee
simple. Perhaps we shall be able to make them grasp
that idea before we are through with them. We have
had this fight on in other states. Would ten thousand
be likely to satisfy him?"

"No," said Kent. "If you add another cipher, it
might."

"A hundred thousand is a pot of money. I take it
for granted the Western Pacific will stand its pro-
rate?"

The New England conscience bucked again, and Kent
made his first open protest against the methods of the
demoralizers.

"I am not in a position to say: I should advise against
it. Unofficially, I think I can speak for Loring and
the Boston people. We are not more saintly than other
folk, perhaps; and we are not in the railroad business
for health or pleasure. But I fancy the Advisory Board
would draw the line at bribing a governor—at any
rate, I hope it would."

"Rot!" said Harnwicke. And then: "You'll reap

the benefits with other interstate interests; you'll have
to come in."

Kent hesitated, but not now on the ground of the
principle to be defended.

"That brings in a question which I am not competent
to decide. Loring is your man. You will call a conference of the 'powers,' I take it?"

"It is already called. I sent Atherton out to notify
everybody as soon as the trap was sprung in the House.
We meet in the ordinary at the Camelot. You'll be
there?"

"A little later—if Loring wants me. I have some
telephoning to do before this thing gets on the wires."

They parted at the entrance to the Camelot Club,
and Kent went two squares farther on to the Wellington. Ormsby had not yet returned, and Kent went to
the telephone and called up the Brentwood apartments.
It was Penelope that answered.

"Well, I think you owe it," she began, as soon as he
had given his name. "What did I do at Miss Van
Brock's to make you cut me dead?"

"Why, nothing at all, I'm sure. I—I was looking
for Mr. Ormsby, and—"

"Not when I saw you," she broke in flippantly. "You
were handing Miss Portia an ice. Are you still looking
for Mr. Ormsby?"

"I am—just that. Is he with you?"

"No; he left here about twenty minutes ago. Is it anything serious?"

"Serious enough to make me want to find him as soon as I can. Did he say he was coming down to the Wellington?"

"Of course, he didn't," laughed Penelope. And then: "Whatever is the matter with you this evening, Mr. Kent?"

"I guess I'm a little excited," said Kent. "Something has happened—something I can't talk about over the wires. It concerns you and your mother and sister. You'll know all about it as soon as I can find Ormsby and send him out to you."

Penelope's "Oh!" was long-drawn and gasping.

"Is any one dead?" she faltered.

"No, no; it's nothing of that kind. I'll send Ormsby out, and he will tell you all about it."

"Can't you come yourself?"

"I may have to if I can't find Ormsby. Please don't let your mother go to bed until you have heard from one or the other of us. Did you get that?"

"Ye-es; but I should like to know more—a great deal more."

"I know; and I'd like to tell you. But I am using the public telephone here at the Wellington, and—Oh, damn!" Central had cut him out, and it was some minutes before the connection was switched in again.

"Is that you, Miss Penelope? All right; I wasn't quite through. When Ormsby comes, you must do as he tells you to, and you and Miss Elinor must help him convince your mother. Do you understand?"

"No, I don't understand anything. For goodness' sake, find Mr. Ormsby and make him run! This is perfectly dreadful!"

"Isn't it? And I'm awfully sorry. Good-by."

Kent hung up the receiver, and when he was asking a second time at the clerk's desk for the missing man, Ormsby came in to answer for himself. Whereupon the crisis was outlined to him in brief phrase, and he rose to the occasion, though not without a grimace.

"I'm not sure just how well you know Mrs. Hepzibah Brentwood," he demurred; "but it will be quite like her to balk. Don't you think you'd better go along? You are the company's attorney, and your opinion ought to carry some weight."

David Kent thought not; but a cautious diplomatist, having got the idea well into the back part of his head, was not to be denied.

"Of course, you'll come. You are just the man I'll need to back me up. I sha'n't shirk; I'll take the mother into the library and break the ice, while you are squaring things with the young women. Penelope won't care the snap of her finger either way; but Elinor has some notions that you are fitter to cope with than

I am. After, if you can give me a lift with Mrs. Hepzibah, I'll call you in. Come on; it's getting pretty
late to go visiting."

Kent yielded reluctantly, and they took a car for the
sake of speed. It was Penelope who opened the door
for them at 124 Tejon Avenue; and Ormsby made it
easy for his coadjutor, as he had promised.

"I want to see your mother in the library for a few
minutes," he began. "Will you arrange it, and take
care of Mr. Kent until I come for him?"

Penelope "arranged" it, not without another added
pang of curiosity, whereupon David Kent found himself the rather embarrassed third of a silent trio gathered about the embers of the sitting-room fire.

"Is it to be a Quaker meeting?" asked Penelope,
sweetly, when the silence had grown awe-inspiring.

Kent laughed for pure joy at the breaking of the
spell.

"One would think we had come to drag you all off to
jail, Ormsby and I," he said; and then he went on to
explain. "It's about your Western Pacific stock, you
know. To-day's quotations put it a point and a half
above your purchase price, and we've come to persuade
you to unload, *pronto,* as the member from the Rio
Blanco would say."

"Is that all?" said Penelope, stifling a yawn. "Then

I'm not in it: I'm an infant." And she rose and went to the piano.

"You haven't told us all of it: what has happened?" queried Elinor, speaking for the first time since her greeting of Kent.

He briefed the story of House Bill Twenty-nine for her, pointing out the probabilities.

"Of course, no one can tell what the precise effect will be," he qualified. "But in my opinion it is very likely to be destructive of dividends. Skipping the dry details, the new law, which is equitable enough on its face, can be made an engine of extortion in the hands of those who administer it. In fact, I happen to know that it was designed and carried through for that very purpose."

She smiled.

"I have understood you were in the opposition. Are you speaking politically?"

"I am stating the plain fact," said Kent, nettled a little by her coolness. "Decadent Rome never lifted a baser set of demagogues into office than we have here in this State at the present moment."

He spoke warmly, and she liked him best when he put her on the footing of an equal antagonist.

"I can't agree with your inference," she objected. "As a people we are neither obsequious nor stupid."

"Perhaps not. But it is one of the failures of a popular government that an honest majority may be controlled and directed by a small minority of shrewd rascals. That is exactly what has happened in the passage of this bill. I venture to say that not one man in ten who voted for it had the faintest suspicion that it was a 'graft'."

"If that be true, what chances there are for men with the gift of true leadership and a love of pure justice in their hearts!" she said half-absently; and he started forward and said: "I beg pardon?"

She let the blue-gray eyes meet his and there was a passing shadow of disappointment in them.

"I ought to beg yours. I'm afraid I was thinking aloud. But it is one of my dreams. If I were a man I should go into politics."

"To purify them?"

"To do my part in trying. The great heart of the people is honest and well-meaning: I think we all admit that. And there is intelligence, too. But human nature is the same as it used to be when they set up a man who *could* and called him a king. Gentle or simple, it must be led."

"There is no lack of leadership, such as it is," he hazarded.

"No; but there seems to be a pitiful lack of the right kind: men who will put self-seeking and un-

worthy ambition aside and lift the standard of justice
and right-doing for its own sake. Are there any such
men nowadays?"

"I don't know," he rejoined gravely. "Sometimes
I'm tempted to doubt it. It is a frantic scramble for
place and power for the most part. The kind of man
you have in mind isn't in it; shuns it as he would a
plague spot."

She contradicted him firmly.

"No, the kind of man I have in mind wouldn't shun
it; he would take hold with his hands and try to make
things better; he would put the selfish temptations
under foot and give the people a leader worth following—be the real mind and hand of the well-meaning
majority."

Kent shook his head slowly.

"Not unless we admit a motive stronger than the abstraction which we call patriotism."

"I don't understand," she said; meaning, rather, that
she refused to understand.

"I mean that such a man, however exalted his views
might be, would have to have an object more personal
to him than the mere dutiful promptings of patriotism
to make him do his best."

"But that would be self-seeking again."

"Not necessarily in the narrow sense. The old
knightly chivalry was a beautiful thing in its way, and

it gave an uplift to an age which would have been frankly brutal without it: yet it had its well-spring in what appeals to us now as being a rather fantastic sentiment."

"And we are not sentimentalists?" she suggested.

"No; and it's the worse for us in some respects. You will not find your ideal politician until you find a man with somewhat of the old knightly spirit in him. And I'll go further and say that when you do find him he will be at heart the champion of the woman he loves rather than that of a political constituency."

She became silent at that, and for a time the low sweet harmonies of the nocturne Penelope was playing filled the gap.

Kent left his chair and began to wish honestly for Ormsby's return. He was searing the wound again, and the process was more than commonly painful. They had been speaking in figures, as a man and a woman will; yet he made sure the mask of metaphor was transparent, no less to her than to him. As many times before, his heart was crying out to her; but now behind the cry there was an upsurging tidal wave of emotion new and strange; a toppling down of barriers and a sweeping inrush of passionate rebellion.

Why had she put it out of her power to make him her champion in the Field of the Lust of Mastery? Instantly, and like a revealing lightning flash, it dawned upon him that this was his awakening. Something of himself she had shown him in the former time: how he was rusting inactive in the small field when he should be doing a man's work, the work for which his training had fitted him, in the larger. But the glamour of sentiment had been over it all in those days, and to the passion-warped the high call is transmitted in terms of self-seeking.

He turned upon her suddenly.

"Did you mean to reproach me?" he asked abruptly.

"How absurd!"

"No, it isn't. You are responsible for me, in a certain sense. You·sent me out into the world, and somehow I feel as if I had disappointed you."

" 'But what went ye out for to see?' " she quoted softly.

"I know," he nodded, sitting down again. "You thought you were arousing a worthy ambition, but it was only avarice that was quickened. I've been trying to be a money-getter."

"You can be something vastly better."

"No, I am afraid not; it is too late."

Again the piano-mellowed silence supervened, and Kent put his elbows on his knees and his face in his hands, being very miserable. He believed now what he had been slow to credit before: that he had it in him to hew his way to the end of the line if only the motive were strong enough to call out all the reserves of battle-might and courage. That motive she alone, of all the women in the world, might have supplied, he told himself in keen self-pity. With her love to arm him, her clear-eyed faith to inspire him. . . . He sat up straight and pushed the cup of bitter herbs aside. There would be time enough to drain it farther on.

"Coming back to the stock market and the present crisis," he said, breaking the silence in sheer self-defense; "Ormsby and I—"

She put the resurrected topic back into its grave with a little gesture of apathetic impatience she used now and then with Ormsby.

"I suppose I ought to be interested, but I am not," she confessed. "Mother will do as she thinks best, and we shall calmly acquiesce, as we always do."

David Kent was not sorry to be relieved in so many words of the persuasive responsibility, and the talk drifted into reminiscence, with the Croydon summer for a background.

It was a dangerous pastime for Kent; perilous, and subversive of many things. One of his meliorating comforts had been the thought that however bitter his own disappointment was, Elinor at least was happy. But in this new-old field of talk a change came over her and he was no longer sure she was entirely happy.

She was saying things with a flavor akin to cynicism in them, as thus:

"Do you remember how we used.to go into raptures of pious indignation over the make-believe sentiment of the summer man and the summer girl? I recollect your saying once that it was wicked; a desecration of things which ought to be held sacred. It isn't so very long ago, but I think we were both very young that summer—years younger than we can ever be again. Don't you?"

"Doubtless," said David Kent. He was at a pass in which he would have agreed with her if she had asserted that black was white. It was not weakness; it was merely that he was absorbed in a groping search for the word which would fit her changed mood.

"We have learned to be more charitable since," she went on; "more charitable and less sentimental, perhaps. And yet we prided ourselves on our sincerity in that young time, don't you think?"

"I, at least, was sincere," he rejoined bluntly. He had found the mood-word at last: it was resentment; though, being a man, he could see no good reason why the memories of the Croydon summer should make her resentful.

She was not looking at him when she said: "No; sincerity is always just. And you were not quite just, I think."

"To you?" he demanded.

"Oh, no; to yourself."

Portia Van Brock's accusation was hammering itself into his brain. *You have marred her between you. . . . For your sake she can never be quite all she ought to be to him; for his sake she could never be quite the same to you.* A cold wave of apprehension submerged him. In seeking to do the most unselfish thing that offered, had he succeeded only in making her despise him?

The question was still hanging answerless when there came the sound of a door opening and closing, and Ormsby stood looking in upon them.

"We needn't keep these sleepy young persons out of bed any longer," he announced briefly; and the co-adjutor said good-night and joined him at once.

"What luck?" was David Kent's anxious query when they were free of the house and had turned their faces townward.

"Just as much as we might have expected. Mrs. Hepzibah refuses point-blank to sell her stock—won't talk about it. 'The idea of parting with it now, when it is actually worth more than it was when we bought it!'" he quoted, mimicking the thin-lipped, acidulous protest. "Later, in an evil minute, I tried to drag you in, and she let you have it square on the point of the jaw—intimated that it was a deal in which some of you inside people needed her block of stock to make you whole. She did, by Jove!"

Kent's laugh was mirthless.

"I was never down in her good books," he said, by way of accounting for the accusation.

If Ormsby thought he knew the reason why, he was magnanimous enough to steer clear of that shoal.

"It's a mess," he growled. "I don't fancy you had any better luck with Elinor."

"She seemed not to care much about it either way. She said her mother would have the casting vote."

"I know. What I don't know is, what remains to be done."

"More waiting," said Kent, definitively. "The fight is fairly on now—as between the Bucks crowd and the corporations, I mean—but there will probably be ups and downs enough to scare Mrs. Brentwood into letting go. We must be ready to strike when the iron is hot; that's all."

The New Yorker tramped a full square in thoughtful silence before he said: "Candidly, Kent, Mrs. Hepzibah's little stake in Western Pacific isn't altogether a matter of life and death to me, don't you know? If it comes to the worst, I can have my broker play the part of the god in the car. Happily, or unhappily, whichever way you like to put it, I sha'n't miss what he may have to put up to make good on her three thousand shares."

David Kent stopped short and wheeled suddenly upon his companion.

"Ormsby, that's a thing I've been afraid of, all along; and it's the one thing you must never do."

"Why not?" demanded the straightforward Ormsby.

Kent knew he was skating on the thinnest of ice, but his love for Elinor made him fearless of consequences.

"If you don't know without being told, it proves that your money has spoiled you to that extent. It is because you have no right to entrap Miss Brentwood into an obligation that would make her your debtor for the very food she eats and the clothes she wears. You will say she need never know: be very sure she would find out, one way or another; and she would never forgive you."

"Um," said Ormsby, turning visibly grim. "You are frank enough—to draw it mildly. Another man in my place might suggest that it isn't Mr. David Kent's affair."

Kent turned about and caught step again.

"I've said my say—all of it," he rejoined stolidly. "We've been decently modern up to now, and we won't go back to the elemental things so late in the day. All the same, you'll not take it amiss if I say that I know Miss Brentwood rather better than you do."

Ormsby did not say whether he would or would not, and the talk went aside to less summary ways and means preservative of the Brentwood fortunes. But at the archway of the Camelot Club, where Kent paused, Ormsby went back to the debatable ground in an out-spoken word.

"I know pretty well now what there is between us, Kent, and we mustn't quarrel if we can help it," he said. "If you complain that I didn't give you a fair show, I'll retort that I didn't dare to. Are you satisfied?"

"No," said David Kent; and with that they separated.

VIII

By the terms of its dating clause the new trust and corporation law became effective at once, "the public welfare requiring it"; and though there was an immediate sympathetic decline in the securities involved, there was no panic, financial or industrial, to mark the change from the old to the new.

Contrary to the expectations of the alarmists and the lawyers, and somewhat to the disappointment of the latter, the vested interests showed no disposition to test the constitutionality of the act in the courts. So far, indeed, from making difficulties, the various alien corporations affected by the new law wheeled promptly into line in compliance with its provisions, vying with one another in proving, or seeming to prove, the time-worn aphorism that capital can never afford to be otherwise than strictly law-abiding.

In the reorganization of the Western Pacific, David Kent developed at once and heartily into that rare and

(108)

much-sought-for quantity, a man for an emergency. Loring, also, was a busy man in this transition period, yet he found time to keep an appreciative eye on Kent, and, true to his implied promise, pushed him vigorously for the first place in the legal department of the localized company. Since the resident manager stood high in the Boston counsels of the company, the pushing was not without results; and while David Kent was still up to his eyes in the work of flogging the affairs of the newly named Trans-Western into conformity with the law, his appointment as general counsel came from the Advisory Board.

At one time, when success in his chosen vocation meant more to him than he thought it could ever mean again, the promoted subordinate would have had an attack of jubilance little in keeping with the grave responsibilities of his office. As it fell out, he was too busy to celebrate, and too sore on the sentimental side to rejoice. Hence, his recognition of the promotion was merely a deeper plunge into the flood of legalities and the adding of two more stenographers to his office force.

Now there is this to be said of such submersive battlings in a sea of work: while the fierce toil of the buffeting may be good for the swimmer's soul, it necessarily narrows his horizon, inasmuch as a man with his head in the sea-smother lacks the view-point of the captain who fights his ship from the conning tower.

So it befell that while the newly appointed general counsel of the reorganized Western Pacific was bolting his meals and clipping the nights at both ends in a strenuous endeavor to clear the decks for a possible battle-royal at the capital, events of a minatory nature were shaping themselves elsewhere.

To bring these events down to their focusing point in the period of transition, it is needful to go back a little; to a term of the circuit court held in the third year of Gaston the prosperous.

Who Mrs. Melissa Varnum was; how she came to be traveling from Midland City to the end of the track on a scalper's ticket; and in what manner she was given her choice of paying fare to the conductor or leaving the train at Gaston—these are details with which we need not concern ourselves. Suffice it to say that Kent, then local attorney for the company, mastered them; and when Mrs. Varnum, through Hawk, her counsel, sued for five thousand dollars damages, he was able to get a continuance, knowing from long experience that the jury would certainly find for the plaintiff if the case were then allowed to go to trial.

And at the succeeding term of court, which was the one that adjourned on the day of Kent's transfer to the capital, two of the company's witnesses had disappeared; and the one bit of company business Kent had been successful in doing that day was to postpone for a second time the coming to trial of the Varnum case.

It was while Kent's head was deepest in the flood of reorganization that a letter came from one Blashfield Hunnicott, his successor in the local attorneyship at Gaston, asking for instructions in the Varnum matter. Judge MacFarlane's court would convene in a week. Was he, Hunnicott, to let the case come to trial? Or should he—the witnesses still being unproducible—move for a further continuance?

Kent took his head out of the cross-seas long enough to answer. By all means Hunnicott was to obtain another continuance, if possible. And if, before the case were called, there should be any new developments, he was to wire at once to the general office, and further instructions would issue.

It was about this time, or, to be strictly accurate, on the day preceding the convening of Judge MacFarlane's court in Gaston, that Governor Bucks took a short vacation—his first since the adjournment of the Assembly.

One of the mysteries of this man—the only one for which his friends could not always account plausibly—was his habit of dropping out for a day or a week at irregular intervals, leaving no clue by which he could be traced. While he was merely a private citizen these

disappearances figured in the local notes of the Gaston
Clarion as "business trips," object and objective point
unknown or at least unstated; but since his election
the newspapers were usually more definite. On this
occasion, the public was duly informed that "Governor
Bucks, with one or two intimate friends, was taking a
few days' recreation with rod and gun on the headwaters
of Jump Creek"—a statement which the governor's
private secretary stood ready to corroborate to all and
sundry calling at the gubernatorial rooms on the second
floor of the capitol.

Now it chanced that, like all gossip, this statement
was subject to correction as to details in favor of the ex-
act fact. It is true that the governor, his gigantic figure
clad in sportsmanlike brown duck, might have been
seen boarding the train on the Monday evening; and in
addition to the ample hand-bag there were rod and
gun cases to bear out the newspaper notices. None the
less, it was equally true that the keeper of the Gun
Club shooting-box at the terminus of the Trans-Western's Jump Creek branch was not called upon to entertain so distinguished a guest as the State executive.
Also, it might have been remarked that the governor
traveled alone.

Late that same night, Stephen Hawk was keeping a
rather discomforting vigil with a visitor in the best
suite of rooms the Mid-Continent Hotel in Gaston af-

forded. The guest of honor was a brother lawyer—
though he might have refused to acknowledge the re-
lationship with the ex-district attorney—a keen-eyed,
business-like gentleman, whose name as an organizer of
vast capitalistic ventures had traveled far, and whose
present attitude was one of undisguised and angry contempt for Gaston and all things Gastonian.

"How much longer have we to wait?" he demanded
impatiently, when the hands of his watch pointed to the
quarter-hour after ten. "You've made me travel two
thousand miles to see this thing through: why didn't
you make sure of having your man here?"

Hawk wriggled uneasily in his chair. He was used
to being bullied, not only by the good and great, but by
the little and evil as well. Yet there was a rasp to the
great man's impatience that irritated him.

"I've been trying to tell you all the evening that I'm
only the hired man in this business, Mr. Falkland. I
can't compel the attendance of the other parties."

"Well, it's damned badly managed, as far as we've
gone," was the ungracious comment. "You say the
judge refuses to confer with me?"

"Ab-so-lutely."

"And the train—the last train the other man can
come on; is that in yet?"

Hawk consulted his watch.

"A good half-hour ago."

"You had your clerk at the station to meet it?"

"I did."

"And he hasn't reported?"

"Not yet."

Falkland took a cigar from his case, bit the end of it like a man with a grudge to satisfy, and began again.

"There is a very unbusinesslike mystery about all this, Mr. Hawk, and I may as well tell you shortly that my time is too valuable to make me tolerant of half-confidences. Get to the bottom of it. Has your man weakened?"

"No; he is not of the weakening kind. And, besides, the scheme is his own from start to finish, as you know."

"Well, what is the matter, then?"

Hawk rose.

"If you will be patient a little while longer, I'll go to the wire and try to find out. I am as much in the dark as you are."

This last was not strictly true. Hawk had a telegram in his pocket which was causing him more uneasiness than all the rasping criticisms of the New York attorney, and he was re-reading it by the light of the corridor bracket when a young man sprang from the ascending elevator and hurried to the door of the parlor suite. Hawk collared his Mercury before he could rap on the door.

"Well?" he queried sharply.

"It's just as you suspected—what Mr. Hendricks' telegram hinted at. I met him at the station and couldn't do a thing with him."

"Where has he gone?"

"To the same old place."

"You followed him?"

"Sure. That is what kept me so long."

Hawk hung upon his decision for the barest fraction of a second. Then he gave his orders concisely.

"Hunt up Doctor Macquoid and get him out to the club-house as quick as you can. Tell him to bring his hypodermic. I'll be there with all the help he'll need." And when the young man was gone, Hawk smote the air with a clenched fist and called down the Black Curse of Shielygh, or its modern equivalent, on all the fates subversive of well-laid plans.

A quarter of an hour later, on the upper floor of the club-house at the Gentlemen's Driving Park, four men burst in upon a fifth, a huge figure in brown duck, crouching in a corner like a wild beast at bay. A bottle and a tumbler stood on the table under the hanging lamp; and with the crash of breaking glass which followed the mad-bull rush of the duck-clothed giant, the reek of French brandy filled the room.

"Hold him still, if you can, and pull up that sleeve." It was Macquoid who spoke, and the three apparitors, breathing hard, sat upon the prostrate man and bared his arm for the physician. When the apomorphia began to do its work there was a struggle of another sort, out of which emerged a pallid and somewhat stricken reincarnation of the governor.

"Falkland is waiting at the hotel, and he and Mac-Farlane can't get together," said Hawk, tersely, when the patient was fit to listen. "Otherwise we shouldn't have disturbed you. It's all day with the scheme if you can't show up."

The governor groaned and passed his hand over his eyes.

"Get me into my clothes—Johnson has the grip—and give me all the time you can," was the sullen rejoinder; and in due course the Honorable Jasper G. Bucks, clothed upon and in his right mind, was enabled to keep his appointment with the New York attorney at the Mid-Continent Hotel.

But first came the whipping-in of MacFarlane. Bucks went alone to the judge's room on the floor above the parlor suite. It was now near midnight, but MacFarlane had not gone to bed. He was a spare man, with thin hair graying rapidly at the temples and a care-worn face; the face of a man whose tasks or responsibilities, or both, have overmatched him. He was walking the floor with his head down and his hands—thin, nerveless hands they were—tightly locked behind him, when the governor entered.

For a large man the Honorable Jasper was usually able to handle his weight admirably; but now he clung to the door-knob until he could launch himself at a chair and be sure of hitting it.

"What's this Hawk's telling me about you, MacFarlane?" he demanded, frowning portentously.

"I don't know what he has told you. But it is too flagrant, Bucks; I can't do it, and that's all there is about it." The protest was feebly fierce, and there was the snarl of a baited animal in the tone.

"It's too late to make difficulties now," was the harsh reply. "You've got to do it."

"I tell you I can not, and I will not!"

"A late attack of conscience, eh?" sneered the governor, who was sobering rapidly now. "Let me ask a question or two. How much was that security debt your son-in-law let you in for?"

"It was ten thousand dollars. It is an honest debt, and I shall pay it."

"But not out of the salary of a circuit judge," Bucks interposed. "Nor yet out of the fees you make your clerks divide with you. And that isn't all. Have you forgotten the gerrymander business? How would you like to see the true inwardness of that in the newspapers?"

The judge shrank as if the huge gesturing hand had struck him.

"You wouldn't dare," he began. "You were in that, too, deeper than—"

Again the governor interrupted him.

"Cut it out," he commanded. "I can reward, and I can punish. You are not going to do anything technically illegal; but, by the gods, you are going to walk the line laid down for you. If you don't, I shall give the documents in the gerrymander affair to the papers the day after you fail. Now we'll go and see Falkland."

MacFarlane made one last protest.

"For God's sake, Bucks! spare me that. It is nothing less than the foulest collusion between the judge, the counsel for the plaintiff—and the devil!"

"Cut that out, too, and come along," said the governor, brutally; and by the steadying help of the chair, the door-post and the wall of the corridor, he led the way to the parlor suite on the floor below.

The conference in Falkland's rooms was chiefly a monologue with the sharp-spoken New York lawyer in the speaking part. When it was concluded the judge took his leave abruptly, pleading the lateness of the hour and his duties for the morrow. When he was gone the New Yorker began again.

"You won't want to be known in this, I take it," he said, nodding at the governor. "Mr. Hawk here will answer well enough for the legal part, but how about the business end of it. Have you got a man you can trust?"

The governor's yellow eyebrows met in a meaning scowl.

"I've got a man I can hang, which is more to the purpose. It's Major Jim Guilford. He lives here; want to meet him?"

"God forbid!" said Falkland, fervently. He rose and whipped himself into his overcoat, turning to Hawk: "Have your young man get me a carriage, and see to it that my special is ready to pull east when I give the word, will you?"

Hawk went obediently, and the New Yorker had his final word with the governor alone.

"I think we understand each other perfectly," he said. "You are to have the patronage: we are to pay for all actual betterments for which vouchers can be shown at the close of the deal. All we ask is that the stock be depressed to the point agreed upon within the half-year."

"It's going to be done," said the governor, trying as he could to keep the eye-image of his fellow conspirator from multiplying itself by two.

"All right. Now as to the court affair. If it is managed exactly as I have outlined, there will be no trouble —and no recourse for the other fellows. When I say that, I'm leaving out your Supreme Court. Under certain conditions, if the defendant's hardship could be definitely shown, a writ of *certiorari* and *supersedeas* might issue. How about that?"

The governor closed one eye slowly, the better to check the troublesome multiplying process.

"The Supreme Court won't move in the matter. The ostensible reason will be that the court is now two years behind its docket."

"And the real reason?"

"Of the three justices, one of them was elected on our ticket; another is a personal friend of Judge Mac-Farlane. The goods will be delivered."

"That's all, then; all but one word. Your judge is a weak brother. Notwithstanding all the pains I took to show him that his action would be technically unassailable, he was ready to fly the track at any moment. Have you got him safe?"

Bucks held up one huge hand with the thumb and forefinger tightly pressed together.

"I've got him right there," he said. "If you and Hawk have got your papers in good shape, the thing will go through like a hog under a barbed-wire fence."

IX

THE SHOCKING OF HUNNICOTT

It was two weeks after the date of the governor's fishing trip, and by consequence Judge MacFarlane's court had been the even fortnight in session in Gaston, when Kent's attention was recalled to the forgotten Varnum case by another letter from the local attorney, Hunnicott.

"Varnum *vs.* Western Pacific comes up Friday of this week, and they are going to press for trial this time, and no mistake," wrote the local representative. "Hawk has been chasing around getting affidavits; for what purpose I don't know, though Lesher tells me that one of them was sworn by Houligan, the sub-contractor who tried to fight the engineer's estimates on the Jump Creek work.

"Also, there is a story going the rounds that the suit is to be made a blind for bigger game, though I guess this is all gossip, based on the fact that Mr. Semple Falkland's private car stopped over here two weeks ago,

(121)

from three o'clock in the afternoon till midnight of the
same day. Jason, of the *Clarion,* interviewed the New
Yorker, and Falkland told him he had stopped over to
look up the securities on a mortgage held by one of his
New York clients."

Kent read this unofficial letter thoughtfully, and
later on took it in to the general manager.

"Just to show you the kind of jackal we have to
deal with in the smaller towns," he said, by way of
explanation. "Here is a case that Stephen Hawk built
up out of nothing a year ago. The woman was put
off one of our trains because she was trying to travel
on a scalper's ticket. She didn't care to fight about it;
but when I had about persuaded her to compromise for
ten dollars and a pass to her destination, Hawk got
hold of her and induced her to sue for five thousand
dollars."

"Well?" said Loring.

"We fought it, of course—in the only way it could
be fought in the lower court. I got a continuance,
and we choked it off in the same way at the succeeding
term. The woman was tired out long ago, but Hawk
will hang on till his teeth fall out."

"Do you 'continue' again?" asked the general manager.

Kent nodded.

"I so instructed Hunnicott. Luckily, two of our most important witnesses are missing. They have always been missing, in point of fact."

Loring was glancing over the letter.

"How about this affidavit business, and the Falkland stop-over?" he asked.

"Oh, I fancy that's gossip, pure and simple, as Hunnicott says. Hawk is sharp enough not to let us know if he were baiting a trap. And Falkland probably told the *Clarion* man the simple truth."

Loring nodded in his turn. Then he broke away from the subject abruptly. "Sit down," he said; and when Kent had found a chair: "I had a caller this morning—Senator Duvall."

State Senator Duvall had been the father, or the ostensible father, of the Senate amendment to House Bill Twenty-nine. He was known to the corporations' lobby as a legislator who would sign a railroad's death-warrant with one hand and take favors from it with the other; and Kent laughed.

"How many did he demand passes for, this time? Or was it a special train he wanted?"

"Neither the one nor the other, this morning, as it happened," said the general manager. "Not to put too fine an edge upon it, he had something to sell, and he wanted me to buy it."

"What was it?" Kent asked quickly.

Loring was rubbing his eye-glasses absently with the corner of his handkerchief.

"I guess I made a mistake in not turning him over to you, David. He was too smooth for me. I couldn't find out just what it was he had for sale. He talked vaguely about an impending crisis and a man who had some information to dispose of; said the man had come to him because he was known to be a firm friend of the Trans-Western, and so on."

Kent gave his opinion promptly.

"It's a capitol-gang deal of some sort to hold us up; and Duvall is willing to sell out his fellow conspirators if the price is right."

"Have you any notion of what it is?"

Kent shook his head.

"Not the slightest. The ways have been tallowed for us, thus far, and I don't fully understand it. I presented our charter for re-filing yesterday, and Hendricks passed it without a word. As I was coming out of the secretary's office I met Bucks. We were pretty nearly open enemies in the old days in Gaston, but he went out of his way to shake hands and to congratulate me on my appointment as general counsel."

"That was warning in itself, wasn't it?"

"I took it that way. But I can't fathom his drift;

which is the more unaccountable since I have it on
pretty good authority that the ring is cinching the
other companies right and left. Some one was saying
at the Camelot last night that the Overland's reorganization of its within-the-State lines was going to
cost all kinds of money in excess of the legal fees."

Loring's smile was a wordless sarcasm.

"It's the reward of virtue," he said ironically. "We
were not in the list of subscribers to the conditional
fund for purchasing a certain veto which didn't ma-
terialize."

"And for that very reason, if for no other, we may
look out for squalls," Kent asserted. "Jasper G. Bucks
has a long memory; and just now the fates have given
him an arm to match. I am fortifying everywhere I
can, but if the junto has it in for us, we'll be made
to sweat blood before we are through with it."

"Which brings us back to Senator Duvall. Is it
worth while trying to do anything with him?"

"Oh, I don't know. I'm opposed to the method—the
bargain and sale plan—and I know you are. Turn him
over to me if he comes in again."

When Kent had dictated a letter in answer to Hunnicott's, he dismissed the Varnum matter from his
mind, having other and more important things to think
of. So, on the Friday, when the case was reached on

Judge MacFarlane's docket—but really, it is worth our while to be present in the Gaston court-room to see and hear what befalls.

When the Varnum case was called, Hunnicott promptly moved for a third continuance, in accordance with his instructions. The judge heard his argument, the old and well-worn one of the absence of important witnesses, with perfect patience; and after listening to Hawk's protest, which was hardly more than mechanical, he granted the continuance.

Then came the after-piece. Court adjourned, and immediately Hawk asked leave to present, "at chambers," an amended petition. Hunnicott was waylaid by a court officer as he was leaving the room; and a moment later, totally unprepared, he was in the judge's office, listening in some dazed fashion while Hawk went glibly through the formalities of presenting his petition.

Not until the papers were served upon him as the company's attorney, and the judge was naming three o'clock of the following afternoon as the time which he would appoint for the preliminary hearing, did the local attorney come alive.

"But, your Honor!—a delay of only twenty-four hours in which to prepare a rejoinder to this petition—to allegations of such astounding gravity?" he began, shocked into action by the very ungraspable magnitude of the thing.

"What more could you ask, Mr. Hunnicott?" said the judge, mildly. "You have already had a full measure of delay on the original petition. Yet I am willing to extend the time if you can come to an agreement with Mr. Hawk, here."

Hunnicott knew the hopelessness of that and did not make the attempt. Instead, he essayed a new line of objection.

"The time would be long enough if Gaston were the headquarters of the company, your Honor. But in such a grave and important charge as this amended petition brings, our general counsel should appear in person, and—"

"You are the company's attorney, Mr. Hunnicott," said the judge, dryly; "and you have hitherto been deemed competent to conduct the case in behalf of the defendant. I am unwilling to work a hardship to any one, but I can not entertain your protest. The preliminary hearing will be at three o'clock to-morrow."

Hunnicott knew when he was definitely at the string's end; and when he was out of the judge's room and the Court House, he made a dash for his office, dry-lipped and panting. Ten minutes sufficed for the writing of a telegram to Kent, and he was half-way down to the station with it when it occurred to him that it would never do to trust the incendiary thing to the wires in plain English. There was a little-used cipher code in his desk provided for just such emergencies, and back he went to labor sweating over the task of securing secrecy at the expense of the precious minutes of time. Wherefore, it was about four o'clock when he handed the telegram to the station operator, and adjured him by all that was good and great not to delay its sending.

It was just here he made his first and only slip, since he did not stay to see the thing done. It chanced that the regular day operator was off on leave of absence, and his substitute, a young man from the train-despatcher's office, was a person who considered the company wires an exclusive appanage of the train service department. At the moment of Hunnicott's assault he was taking an order for Number 17; and observing that the lawyer's cipher "rush" covered four closely written pages, he hung it upon the sending hook with a malediction on the legal department for burdening the wires with its mail correspondence, and so forgot it.

It was nine o'clock when the night operator came on duty; and being a careful man, he not only looked first to his sending hook, but was thoughtful enough to run over the accumulation of messages waiting to be transmitted, to the end that he might give precedence to the most important. And when he came to Hunnicott's cipher with the thrice-underlined "RUSH" written across its face, and had marked the hour of its handing in, he had the good sense to hang up the entire wire business of the railroad until the thing was safely out of his office.

It was half-past nine when the all-important cipher got itself written out in the headquarters office at the capital; and for two anxious hours the receiving operator tried by all means in his power to find the general counsel—tried and failed. For, to make the chain of mishaps complete in all its links, Kent and Loring were spending the evening at Miss Portia Van Brock's, having been bidden to meet a man they were both willing to cultivate—Oliver Marston, the lieutenant-governor. And for this cause it wanted but five minutes of midnight when Kent burst into Loring's bedroom on the third floor of the Clarendon, catastrophic news in hand.

"For heaven's sake, read that!" he gasped; and Loring sat on the edge of the bed to do it.

"So! they've sprung their mine at last: this is what Senator Duvall was trying to sell us," he said quietly, when he had mastered the purport of Hunnicott's war news.

Kent had caught his second wind in the moment of respite, and was settling into the collar in a way to strain the working harness to the breaking point.

"It's a put-up job from away back," he gritted. "If I'd had the sense of a pack-mule I should have been on the lookout for just such a trap as this. Look at the date of that message!"

The general manager did look, and shook his head. "'Received, 3 :45, P. M.; Forwarded, 9 :17, P. M.' That will cost somebody his job. What do we do?"

"We get busy at the drop of the hat. Luckily, we have the news, though I'll bet high it wasn't Hawk's fault that this message came through with no more than eight hours' delay. Get into your clothes, man! The minutes are precious, now!"

Loring began to dress while Kent walked the floor in a hot fit of impatience.

"The mastodonic cheek of the thing!" he kept repeating, until Loring pulled him down with another quiet remark.

"Tell me what we have to do, David. I am a little lame in law matters."

"Do? We have to appear in Judge MacFarlane's court to-morrow afternoon prepared to show that this thing is only a hold-up with a blank cartridge. Hawk meant to take a snap judgment. He counted on throwing the whole thing up against Hunnicott, knowing perfectly well that a little local attorney at a way-station couldn't begin to secure the necessary affidavits."

Loring paused with one end of his collar flying loose.

"Let me understand," he said. "Do we have to disprove these charges by affidavits?"

"Certainly; that is the proper rejoinder—the only one, in fact," said Kent; then, as a great doubt laid hold of him and shook him: "You don't mean to say there is any doubt about our ability to do it?"

"Oh, no; I suppose not, if it comes to a show-down. But I was thinking of your man Hunnicott. Doesn't it occur to you that he is in just about as good a fix to secure those affidavits in Gaston as we are here, David?"

"Good Lord! Do you mean that we have to send to Boston for our ammunition?"

"Haven't we? Don't you see how nicely the thing is timed? Ten days later our Trans-Western reorganization would be complete, and we could swear our own officers on the spot. These people know what they are about."

Kent was walking the floor again, but now the strength of the man was coming uppermost.

"Never mind: we'll wire Boston, and then we'll do what we can here. Could you get me to Gaston on a special engine in three hours?"

"Yes."

"Then we have till eleven o'clock to-morrow to prepare. I'll be ready by that time."

"David, you are a brick when it comes to the infighting," said the general manager; and then he finished buttoning his collar.

X

At ten forty-eight on the Saturday morning Kent was standing with the general manager on the Union Station track platform beside the engine which was to make the flying run to Gaston.

Nine hours of sharp work lay between the hurried conference in Loring's bedroom and the drive to the station at a quarter before eleven. Boston had been wired; divers and sundry friends of the railway company had been interviewed; some few affidavits had been secured; and now they were waiting to give Boston its last chance, with a clerk hanging over the operator in the station telegraph office to catch the first word of encouragement.

"If the Advisory Board doesn't send us something pretty solid, I'm going into this thing lame," said Kent, dubiously. "Of course, what Boston can send us will be only corroborative; unfortunately we can't wire

(133)

affidavits. But it will help. What we have secured here lacks directness."

"Necessarily," said Loring. "But I'm banking on the Board. If we don't get the ammunition before you have to start, I can wire it to you at Gaston. That gives us three hours more to go and come on."

"Yes; and if it comes to the worst—if the decision be unfavorable—it can only embarrass us temporarily. This is merely the preliminary hearing, and nothing permanent can be established until we have had a hearing on the merits, and we can go armed to that, at all events."

The general manager was looking at his watch, and he shut the case with a snap.

"Don't you let it come to that, as long as you have a leg to stand on, David," he said impressively. "An interregnum of ten days might make it exceedingly difficult for us to prove anything." Then, as the telegraph office watcher came to the door and shook his head as a sign that Boston was still silent: "Your time is up. Off with you, and don't let Oleson scare you when he gets 219 in motion. He is a good runner, and you have a clear track."

Kent clambered to the footplate of the smart eight-wheeler.

"Can you make it by two o'clock?" he asked, when

the engineer, a big-boned, blue-eyed Norwegian, dropped the reversing lever into the corner for the start.

"Ay tank maybe so, ain'd it? Yust you climb opp dat odder box, Mester Kent, and hol' you' hair on. Ve bane gone to maig dat time, als' ve preak some-dings, *ja!*" and he sent the light engine spinning down the yards to a quickstep of forty miles an hour.

Kent's after-memory of that distance-devouring rush was a blurred picture of a plunging, rocking, clamoring engine bounding over mile after mile of the brown plain; of the endless dizzying procession of oncoming telegraph poles hurtling like great side-flung projectiles past the cab windows; of now and then a lonely prairie station with waving semaphore arms, sighted, passed and left behind in a whirling sand-cloud in one and the same heart-beat. And for the central figure in the picture, the one constant quantity when all else was mutable and shifting and indistinct, the big, calm-eyed Norwegian on the opposite box, hurling his huge machine doggedly through space.

At 12:45 they stopped for water at a solitary tank in the midst of the brown desert. Kent got down stiffly from his cramped seat on the fireman's box and wetted his parched lips at the nozzle of the tender hose.

"Do we make it, Jarl?" he asked.

The engineer wagged his head.

"Ay tank so. Ve maig it all right iff dey haf bane got dose track clear."

"There are other trains to meet?"

"*Ja;* two bane comin' dis vay; ant Nummer Sam-teen ve pass opp by."

Oleson dropped off to pour a little oil into the speed-woundings while the tank was filling; and presently the dizzying race began again. For a time all things were propitious. The two trains to be met were found snugly withdrawn on the sidings at Mavero and Agri-culta, and the station semaphores beckoned the flying special past at full speed. Kent checked off the dodg-ing mile-posts: the pace was bettering the fastest run ever made on the Prairie Division—which was saying a good deal.

But at Juniberg, twenty-seven miles out of Gaston, there was a delay. Train Number 17, the east-bound time freight, had left Juniberg at one o'clock, having ample time to make Lesterville, the next station east, before the light engine could possibly overtake it. But Lesterville had not yet reported its arrival; for which cause the agent at Juniberg was constrained to put out his stop signal, and Kent's special came to a stand at the platform.

Under the circumstances, there appeared to be noth-ing for it but to wait until the delayed Number 17 was

heard from; and Kent's first care was to report to Loring, and to ask if there were anything from Boston.

The reply was encouraging. A complete denial of
everything, signed by the proper officials, had been received and repeated to Kent at Gaston—was there now
awaiting him. Kent saw in anticipation the nicely calculated scheme of the junto crumbling into small dust
in the precise moment of fruition, and had a sharp attack of ante-triumph which he had to walk off in turns
up and down the long platform. But as the waiting grew
longer, and the dragging minutes totaled the quarter-
hour and then the half, he began to perspire again.

Half-past two came and went, and still there was no
hopeful word from Lesterville. Kent had speech with
Oleson, watch in hand. Would the engineer take the
risk of a rear-end collision on a general manager's order? Oleson would obey orders if the heavens fell; and
Kent flew to the wire again. Hunnicott, at Gaston, was
besought to gain time in the hearing by any and all
means; and Loring was asked to authorize the risk of a
rear-end smash-up. He did it promptly. The light
engine was to go on until it should "pick up" the delayed train between stations.

The Juniberg man gave Oleson his release and the
order to proceed with due care while the sounder was
still clicking a further communication from headquarters. Loring was providing for the last contingency by

sending Kent the authority to requisition Number 17's engine for the completion of the run in case the track should be blocked, with the freight engine free beyond the obstruction.

Having his shackles stricken off, the Norwegian proceeded "with due care," which is to say that he sent the eight-wheeler darting down the line toward Lesterville at the rate of a mile a minute. The mystery of the delay was solved at a point half-way between the two stations. A broken flange had derailed three cars of the freight, and the block was impassable.

Armed with the general manager's mandatory wire, Kent ran forward to the engine of the freight train and was shortly on his way again. But in the twenty-mile run to Gaston more time was lost by the lumbering freight locomotive, and it was twenty minutes past three o'clock when the county seat came in sight and Kent began to oscillate between two sharp-pointed horns of a cruel dilemma.

By dropping off at the street-crossing nearest the Court House, he might still be in time to get a hearing with such documentary backing as he had been able to secure at the capital. By going on to the station he could pick up the Boston wire which, while it was not strictly evidence, might create a strong presumption in his favor; but in this case he would probably be too late to use it. So he counted the rail-lengths, watch in hand, with a curse to the count for his witlessness in failing to have Loring repeat the Boston message to him during the long wait at Juniberg; and when the time for the decision arrived he signaled the engineer to slow down, jumped from the step at the nearest crossing and hastened up the street toward the Court House.

In the mean time, to go back a little, during this day of hurryings to and fro Blashfield Hunnicott had been having the exciting experiences of a decade crowded into a corresponding number of hours. Early in the morning he had begun besieging the headquarters wire office for news and instructions, and, owing to Kent's good intentions to be on the ground in person, had got little enough of either.

At length, to his unspeakable relief, he had news of the coming special; and with the conviction that help was at hand he waited at the station with what coolness there was in him to meet his chief. But as the time for the hearing drew near he grew nervous again; and all the keen pains of utter helplessness returned with renewed acuteness when the operator, who had overheard the Juniberg-Lesterville wire talk, told him that the special was hung up at the former station.

"O my good Lord!" he groaned. "I'm in for it with empty hands!" None the less, he ran to the baggage-room end of the building and, capturing an express wagon, had himself trundled out to the Court House.

The judge was at his desk when Hunnicott entered, and Hawk was on hand, calmly reading the morning paper. The hands of the clock on the wall opposite the judge's desk pointed to five minutes of the hour, and for five minutes Hunnicott sat listening, hoping against hope that he should hear the rush and roar of the incoming special.

Promptly on the stroke of three the judge tapped upon his desk with his pencil.

"Now, gentlemen, proceed with your case; and I must ask you to be as brief as possible. I have an appointment at four which can not be postponed," he said quietly; and Hawk threw down his paper and began at once.

Hunnicott heard his opponent's argument mechanically, having his ear attuned for whistle signals and wheel drummings. Hawk spoke rapidly and straight to his point, as befitted a man speaking to the facts and with no jury present to be swayed by oratorical effort. When he came to the summarizing of the allegations in the amended petition, he did it wholly without heat, piling up the accusations one upon another with the careful method of a bricklayer building a wall. The wall-building simile thrust itself upon Hunnicott with irresistible force as he listened. If the special engine should not dash up in time to batter down the wall—

Hawk closed as dispassionately as he had begun, and

the judge bowed gravely in Hunnicott's direction. The local attorney got upon his feet, and as he began to speak a telegram was handed in. It was Kent's wire from Juniberg, beseeching him to gain time at all hazards, and he settled himself to the task. For thirty dragging minutes he rang the changes on the various steps in the suit, knowing well that the fatal moment was approaching when—Kent still failing him—he would be compelled to submit his case without a scrap of an affidavit to support it.

The moment came, and still there was no encouraging whistle shriek from the dun plain beyond the open windows. Hawk was visibly disgusted, and Judge MacFarlane was growing justly impatient. Hunnicott began again, and the judge reproved him mildly.

"Much of what you are saying is entirely irrelevant, Mr. Hunnicott. This hearing is on the plaintiff's amended petition."

No one knew better than the local attorney that he was wholly at the court's mercy; that he had been so from the moment the judge began to consider his purely formal defense, entirely unsupported by affidavits or evidence of any kind. None the less, he strung his denials out by every amplification he could devise, and, having fired his last shot, sat down in despairing breathlessness to hear the judge's summing-up and decision.

Judge MacFarlane was mercifully brief. On the part

of the plaintiff there was an amended petition fully fortified by uncontroverted affidavits. On the part of the defendant company there was nothing but a formal denial of the allegations. The duty of the court in the premises was clear. The prayer of the plaintiff was granted, the temporary relief asked for was given, and the order of the court would issue accordingly.

The judge was rising when the still, hot air of the room began to vibrate with the tremulous thunder of the sound for which Hunnicott had been so long straining his ears. He was the first of the three to hear it, and he hurried out ahead of the others. At the foot of the stair he ran blindly against Kent, dusty, travel-worn and haggard.

"You're too late!" he blurted out. "We're done up. Hawk's petition has been granted and the road is in the hands of a receiver."

Kent dashed his fist upon the stair-rail.

"Who is the man?" he demanded.

"Major Jim Guilford," said Hunnicott. Then, as footfalls coming stairward were heard in the upper corridor, he locked arms with Kent, faced him about and thrust him out over the door-stone. "Let's get out of this. You look as if you might kill somebody."

XI

THE LAST DITCH

It was a mark of the later and larger development of David Kent that he was able to keep his head in the moment of catastrophes. In boyhood his hair had been a brick-dust red, and having the temperament which belongs of right to the auburn-hued, his first impulse was to face about and make a personal matter of the legal robbery with Judge MacFarlane.

Happily for all concerned, Hunnicott's better counsels prevailed, and when the anger fit passed Kent found himself growing cool and determined. Hunnicott was crestfallen and disposed to be apologetic; but Kent did him justice.

"Don't blame yourself: there was nothing else you could have done. Have you a stenographer in your office?"

"Yes."

"A good one?"

"It's young Perkins: you know him."

(143)

"He'll do. 'Phone him to run down to the station and get what telegrams there are for me, and we'll talk as we go."

Once free of the Court House, Kent began a rapid-fire of questions.

"Where is Judge MacFarlane stopping?"

"At the Mid-Continent."

"Have you any idea when he intends leaving town?"

"No; but he will probably take the first train. He never stays here an hour longer than he has to after adjournment."

"That would be the Flyer east at six o'clock. Is he going east?"

"Come to think of it, I believe he is. Somebody said he was going to Hot Springs. He's in miserable health."

Kent saw more possibilities, and worse, and quickened his pace a little.

"I hope your young man won't let the grass grow under his feet," he said. "The minutes between now and six o'clock are worth days to us."

"What do we do?" asked Hunnicott, willing to take a little lesson in practice as he ran.

"The affidavits I have brought with me and the telegrams which are waiting at the station must convince MacFarlane that he has made a mistake. We shall prepare a motion for the discharge of the receiver and for the vacation of the order appointing him, and ask the judge to set an early day for the hearing on the merits of the case. He can't refuse."

Hunnicott shook his head.

"It has been all cut and dried from 'way back," he objected. "They won't let you upset it at the last moment."

"We'll give them a run for their money," said Kent. "A good bit of it depends upon Perkins' speed as a stenographer."

As it befell, Perkins did not prove a disappointment, and by five o'clock Kent was in the lobby of the Mid-Continent, sending his card up to the judge's room. Word came back that the judge was in the café fortifying the inner man in preparation for his journey, and Kent did not stand upon ceremony. From the archway of the dining-room he marked down his man at a small table in the corner, and went to him at once, plunging promptly into the matter in hand.

"The exigencies of the case must plead my excuse for intruding upon you here, Judge MacFarlane," he began courteously. "But I have been told that you were leaving town—"

The judge waved him down with a deprecatory fork.

"Court is adjourned, Mr. Kent, and I must decline to discuss the case *ex parte*. Why did you allow it to go by default?"

"That is precisely what I am here to explain," said Kent, suavely. "The time allowed us was very short; and a series of accidents—"

Again the judge interrupted.

"A court can hardly take cognizance of accidents, Mr. Kent. Your local attorney was on the ground and he had the full benefit of the delay."

"I know," was the patient rejoinder. "Technically, your order is unassailable. None the less, a great injustice has been done, as we are prepared to prove. I am not here to ask you to reopen the case at your dinner-table, but if you will glance over these papers I am sure you will set an early day for the hearing upon the merits."

Judge MacFarlane forced a gray smile.

"You vote yea and nay in the same breath, Mr. Kent. If I should examine your papers, I should be reopening the case at my dinner-table. You shall have your hearing in due course."

"At chambers?" said Kent. "We shall be ready at any moment; we are ready now, in point of fact."

"I can not say as to that. My health is very precarious, and I am under a physician's orders to take a complete rest for a time. I am sorry if the delay shall work a hardship to the company you represent; but under the circumstances, with not even an affidavit offered by your side, it is your misfortune. And now I

shall have to ask you to excuse me. It lacks but a few
minutes of my train time."

The hotel porter was droning out the call for the
east-bound Flyer, and Kent effaced himself while Judge
MacFarlane was paying his bill and making ready for
his departure. But when the judge set out to walk to the
station, Kent walked with him. There were five squares
to be measured, and for five squares he hung at MacFarlane's elbow and the plea he made should have won him
a hearing. Yet the judge remained impassible, and at
the end of the argument turned him back in a word to
his starting point.

"I can not recall the order at this time, if I would,
Mr. Kent; neither can I set a day for the hearing on the
merits. What has been done was done in open court and
in the presence of your attorney, who offered no evidence
in contradiction of the allegations set forth in the plaintiff's amended petition, although they were supported
by more than a dozen affidavits; and it can not be undone in the streets. Since you have not improved your
opportunities, you must abide the consequences. The
law can not be hurried."

They had reached the station and the east-bound train
was whistling for Gaston. Kent's patience was nearly
gone, and the auburn-hued temperament was clamoring
hotly for its innings.

"This vacation of yours, Judge MacFarlane: how

long is it likely to last?" he inquired, muzzling his wrath yet another moment.

"I can not say; if I could I might be able to give you a more definite answer as to the hearing on the merits. But my health is very miserable, as I have said. If I am able to return shortly, I shall give you the hearing at chambers at an early date."

"And if not?"

"If not, I am afraid it will have to go over to the next term of court."

"Six months," said Kent; and then his temper broke loose. "Judge MacFarlane, it is my opinion, speaking as man to man, that you are a scoundrel. I know what you have done, and why you have done it. Also, I know why you are running away, now that it is done. So help me God, I'll bring you to book for it if I have to make a lifetime job of it! It's all right for your political backers; they are thieves and bushwhackers, and they make no secret of it. But there is one thing worse than a trickster, and that is a trickster's tool!"

For the moment while the train was hammering in over the switches they stood facing each other fiercely, all masks flung aside, each after his kind; the younger man flushed and battle-mad; the elder white, haggard, tremulous. Kent did not guess, then or ever, how near he came to death. Two years earlier a judge had been shot and maimed on a western circuit and since then,

MacFarlane had taken a coward's precaution. Here was
a man that knew, and while he lived the cup of trembling might never be put aside.

It was the conductor's cry of "All aboard!" that broke
the homicidal spell. Judge MacFarlane started guiltily,
shook off the angry eye-grip of his accuser, and went to
take his place in the Pullman. One minute later the
east-bound train was threading its way out among the
switches of the lower yard, and Kent had burst into the
telegraph office to wire the volcanic news to his chief.

XII

THE MAN IN POSSESSION

Appraised at its value in the current coin of street gossip, the legal seizure of the Trans-Western figured mainly as an example of the failure of modern business methods when applied to the concealment of a working corporation's true financial condition.

This unsympathetic point of view was sufficiently defined in a bit of shop-talk between Harnwicke, the cold-blooded, and his traffic manager in the office of the Overland Short Line the morning after the newspaper announcement of the receivership.

"I told you they were in deep water," said the lawyer, confidently. "They haven't been making any earnings —net earnings—since the Y. S. & F. cut into them at Rio Verde, and the dividends were only a bluff for stock-bracing purposes. I surmised that an empty treasury was what was the matter when they refused to join us in the veto affair."

"That is one way of looking at it," said the traffic

manager. "But some of the papers are claiming that it
was a legal hold-up, pure and simple."

"Nothing of the kind," retorted the lawyer, whose respect for the law was as great as his contempt for
the makers of the laws. "Judge MacFarlane had no discretion in the matter. Hawk had a perfect right to file
an amended petition, and the judge was obliged to act
upon it. I'm not saying it wasn't a devilish sharp trick
of Hawk's. It was. He saw a chance to smite them
under the fifth rib, and he took it."

"But how about his client: the woman who was put
off the train? Is she any better off than she was before?"

"Oh, she'll get her five thousand dollars, of course,
if they don't take the case out of court. It has served
its turn. It's an ugly crusher for the Loring management. Hawk's allegations charge all sorts of crooked-
ness, and neither Loring nor Kent seemed to have a
word to say for themselves. I understand Kent was in
court, either in person or by attorney, when the receivership order was made, and that he hadn't a word to say
for himself."

This view of Harnwicke's, colored perhaps by the
fact that the Trans-Western was a business competitor
of the Short Line, was the generally accepted one in railroad and financial circles at the capital. Civilization
apart, there is still a deal of the primitive in human

nature, and wolves are not the only creatures that are prone to fall upon the disabled member of the pack and devour him.

But in the State at large the press was discussing the event from a political point of view; one section, small but vehement, raising the cry of trickery and judicial corruption, and prophesying the withdrawal of all foreign capital from the State, while the other, large and complacent, pointed eloquently to the beneficent working of the law under which the cause of a poor woman, suing for her undoubted right, might be made the whip to flog corporate tyranny into instant subjection.

As for the dispossessed stock-holders in the far-away East, they were slow to take the alarm, and still slower to get concerted action. Like many of the western roads, the Western Pacific had been capitalized largely by popular subscription; hence there was no single holder, or group of holders, of sufficient financial weight to enter the field against the spoilers.

But when Loring and his associates had fairly got the wires hot with the tale of what had been done, and the much more alarming tale of what was likely to be done, the Boston inertness vanished. A pool of the stock was formed, with the members of the Advisory Board as a nucleus; money was subscribed, and no less a legal light than an ex-attorney-general of the state of Massachusetts was despatched to the seat of war to advise

with the men on the ground. None the less, disaster
out-travels the swiftest of "limited" trains. Before the
heavily-feed consulting attorney had crossed the Hud-
son in his westward journey, Wall Street had taken notice, and there was a momentary splash in the troubled
pool of the Stock Exchange and a vanishing circle of
ripples to show where Western Pacific had gone down.

In the meantime Major James Guilford, somewhile
president of the Apache National Bank of Gaston, and
antecedent to that the frowning autocrat of a twenty-
five-mile logging road in the North Carolina mountains,
had given bond in some sort and had taken possession
of the company's property and of the offices in the Quintard Building.

His first official act as receiver was to ask for the
resignations of a dozen heads of departments, beginning
with the general manager and pausing for the moment
with the supervisor of track. That done, he filled the
vacancies with political troughsmen; and with these as
assistant decapitators the major passed rapidly down the
line, striking off heads in daily batches until the over-
flow of the Bucks political following was provided for
on the railroad's pay-rolls to the wife's cousin's nephew.

This was the work of the first few administrative days
or weeks, and while it was going on, the business attitude of the road remained unchanged. But once seated
firmly in the saddle, with his awkward squad well in

hand, the major proceeded to throw a bomb of consternation into the camp of his competitors.

Kent was dining with Ormsby in the grill-room of the Camelot Club when the waiter brought in the evening edition of the *Argus,* whose railroad reporter had heard the preliminary fizzing of the bomb fuse. The story was set out on the first page, first column, with appropriate headlines.

WAR TO THE KNIFE AND THE KNIFE TO THE HILT!

TRANS-WESTERN CUTS COMMODITY RATE.

Great Excitement in Railroad Circles. Receiver Guilford's Hold-up.

Kent ran his eye rapidly down the column and passed the paper across to Ormsby.

"I told you so," he said. "They didn't find the road insolvent, but they are going to make it so in the shortest possible order. A rate war will do it quicker than anything else on earth."

Ormsby thrust out his jaw.

"Have we got to stand by and see 'em do it?"

"The man from Massachusetts says yes, and he knows, or thinks he does. He has been here two weeks

now, and he has nosed out for himself all the dead-
walls. We can't appeal, because there is no decision to
appeal from. We can't take it out of the lower court
until it is finished in the lower court. We can't enjoin
an officer of the court; and there is no authority in the
State that will set aside Judge MacFarlane's order
when that order was made under technically legal conditions."

"You could have told him all that in the first five
minutes," said Ormsby.

"I did tell him, and was mildly sat upon. To-day he
came around and gave me back my opinion, clause for
clause, as his own. But I have no kick coming. Somebody will have to be here to fight the battle to a finish
when the judge returns, and our expert will advise the
Bostonians to retain me."

"Does he stay?" Ormsby asked.

"Oh, no; he is going back with Loring to-night.
Loring has an idea of his own which may or may not be
worth the powder it will take to explode it. He is going
to beseech the Boston people to enlarge the pool until
it controls a safe majority of the stock."

"What good will that do?"

"None, directly. It's merely a safe preliminary to anything that may happen. I tell Loring he is like all the
others: he knows when he has enough and is willing to
stand from under. I'm the only fool in the lot."

Ormsby's smile was heartening and good for sore nerves.

"I like your pluck, Kent; I'll be hanged if I don't. And I'll back you to win, yet."

Kent shook his head unhopefully.

"Don't mistake me," he said. "I am fighting for the pure love of it, and not with any great hope of saving the stock-holders. These grafters have us by the nape of the neck. We can't make a move till MacFarlane comes back and gives us a hearing on the merits. That may not be till the next term of court. Meanwhile, the temporary receiver is to all intents and purposes a permanent receiver; and the interval would suffice to wreck a dozen railroads."

"And still you won't give up?"

"No."

"I hope you won't have to. But to a man up a tree it looks very much like a dead cock in the pit. As I have said, if there is any backing to do, I'm with you, first, last, and all the time, merely from a sportsman's interest in the game. But is there any use in a little handful of us trying to buck up against a whole state government?"

The coffee had been served, and Kent dropped a lump of sugar into his cup.

"Ormsby, I'll never let go while I'm alive enough to fight," he said slowly. "One decent quality I have—

and the only one, perhaps: I don't know when I'm
beaten. And I'll down this crowd of political plunderers
yet, if Bucks doesn't get me sand-bagged."

His listener pushed back his chair.

"If you stood to lose anything more than your job
I could understand it," he commented. "As it is, I
can't. Any way you look at it, your stake in the game
isn't worth the time and effort it will take to play the
string out. And I happen to know you're ambitious to
do things—things that count."

"What is it you don't understand—the motive?"

"That's it."

Kent laughed.

"You are not as astute as Miss Van Brock. She
pointed it out to me last night—or thought she did—
in two words."

Ormsby's eyes darkened, and he did not affect to mis-
understand.

"It would be a grand-stand play," he said half-
musingly, "if you should happen to worry it through,
I mean. I believe Mrs. Hepzibah would be ready to fall
on your neck and forgive you, and turn me down."
Then, half-jestingly: "Kent, what will you take to drop
this thing permanently and go away?"

David Kent's smile showed his teeth.

"The one thing you wouldn't be willing to give. You

asked me once when we had fallen over the fence upon this forbidden ground if I were satisfied, and I told you I wasn't. Do we understand each other?"

"I guess so," said Ormsby. "But— Say, Kent, I like you too well to see you go up against a stone fence blindfolded. I'm like Guilford: I am the man in possession. And possession is nine points of the law."

Kent rose and took the proffered cigar from Ormsby's case.

"It depends a good bit upon how the possession is gained—and held—doesn't it?" he rejoined coolly. "And your figure is unfortunate in its other half. I am going to beat Guilford."

XIII

Just why Receiver Guilford, an officer of the court who was supposed to be nursing an insolvent railroad to the end that its creditors might not lose all, should begin by declaring war on the road's revenue, was a question which the managers of competing lines strove vainly to answer. But when, in defiance of all precedent, he made the cut rates effective to and from all local stations on the Trans-Western, giving the shippers at intermediate and non-competitive points the full benefit of the reductions, the railroad colony denounced him as a madman and gave him a month in which to find the bottom of a presumably empty treasury.

But the event proved that the major's madness was not altogether without method. It is an axiom in the carrying trade that low rates make business; create it, so to speak, out of nothing. Given an abundant crop, low prices, and high freight rates in the great cereal belt, and, be the farmers never so poor, much of the

(159)

grain will be stored and held against the chance of better conditions.

So it came about that Major Guilford's relief measure was timed to a nicety, and the blanket cut in rates opened a veritable flood-gate for business in Trans-Western territory. From the day of its announcement the traffic of the road increased by leaps and bounds. Stored grain came out of its hiding places at every country cross-roads to beg for cars; stock feeders drove their market cattle unheard-of distances, across the tracks of competing lines, over and around obstacles of every sort, to pour them into the loading corrals of the Trans-Western.

Nor was the traffic all outgoing. With the easing of the money burden, the merchants in the tributary towns began thriftily to take advantage of the low rates to renew their stocks; long-deferred visits and business trips suddenly became possible; and the saying that it was cheaper to travel than to stay at home gained instant and grateful currency.

In a short time the rolling stock of the road was taxed to its utmost capacity, and the newly appointed purchasing agent was buying cars and locomotives right and left. Also, to keep pace with the ever-increasing procession of trains, a doubled construction force wrought night and day installing new side tracks and passing points.

Under the fructifying influence of such a golden shower of prosperity, land values began to rise again, slowly at first, as buyers distrusted the continuance of the golden shower; more rapidly a little later, as the Guilford policy defined itself in terms of apparent permanence.

Towns along the line—hamlets long since fallen into the way-station rut of desuetude—awoke with a start, bestirring themselves joyfully to meet the inspiriting conditions. At Midland City, Stephen Hawk, the new right-of-way agent, ventured to ask municipal help to construct a ten-mile branch to Lavabee: it was forthcoming promptly; and the mass meeting, at which the bond loan was anticipated by public subscription shouted itself hoarse in enthusiasm.

At Gaston, where Hawk asked for a donation of land whereon the company might build the long-promised division repair-shops, people fought with one another to be first among the donors. And at Juniberg, where the company proposed to establish the first of a series of grain subtreasuries—warehouses in which the farmers of the surrounding country could store their products and borrow money on them from the railroad company at the rate of three per cent. per annum—at Juniberg enough money was subscribed to erect three such depots as the heaviest tributary crop could possibly fill.

It was while the pendulum of prosperity was in full swing that David Kent took a day off from sweating over his problem of ousting the receiver and ran down to Gaston. Single-eyed as he was in the pursuit of justice, he was not unmindful of the six lots standing in his name in the Gaston suburb, and from all accounts the time was come to dispose of them.

He made the journey in daylight, with his eyes wide open and the mental pencil busy at work noting the changes upon which the State press had been dilating daily, but which he was now seeing for the first time. They were incontestable—and wonderful. He admitted the fact without prejudice to a settled conviction that the sun-burst of prosperity was merely another brief period of bubble-blowing. Towns whose streets had been grass-grown since the day when each in turn had surrendered its right to be called the terminus of the westward-building railroad, were springing into new life. The song of the circular saw, the bee-boom of the planing-mill and the tapping of hammers were heard in the land, and the wayside hamlets were dotted with new roofs. And Gaston—

But Gaston deserved a separate paragraph in the mental note-book, and Kent accorded it, marveling still more. It was as if the strenuous onrush of the climaxing Year Three had never been interrupted. The ma-

terial for the new company shops was arriving by train-
loads, and an army of men was at work clearing the
grounds. On a siding near the station a huge grain elevator was rising. In the streets the hustling activity of
the "terminus" period was once more in full swing; and
at the Mid-Continent Kent had some little difficulty in
securing a room.

He was smoking his after-dinner cigar in the lobby of
the hotel and trying as he might to orient himself when
Blashfield Hunnicott drifted in. Kent gave the sometime local attorney a cigar, made room for him on the
plush-covered settee, and proceeded to pump him dry of
Gaston news. Summed up, the inquiries pointed themselves thus: was there any basis for the Gaston revival
other than the lately changed attitude of the railroad?
In other words, if the cut rates should be withdrawn
and the railroad activities cease, would there not be a
second and still more disastrous collapse of the Gaston
bubble?

Pressed hardly, Hunnicott admitted the probability;
given another turn, the screw of inquiry squeezed out
an admission of the fact, slurred over by the revivalist,
that the railway company's treasury was really the alms-
box into which all hands were dipping.

"One more question and I'll let up on you," said
Kent. "It used to be said of you in the flush times that

you kept tab on the real estate transfers when everybody else was too busy to read the record. Do you still do it?"

Hunnicott laughed uneasily.

"Rather more than ever just now, as you'd imagine."

"It is well. Now you know the members of the old gang, from his Excellency down. Tell me one thing: are they buying or selling?"

Hunnicott sprang up and slapped his leg.

"By Jupiter, Kent! They are selling—every last man of them!"

"Precisely. And when they have sold all they have to sell?"

"They'll turn us loose—drop us—quit booming the town, if your theory is the right one. But say, Kent, I can't believe it, you know. It's too big a thing to be credited to Jim Guilford and his handful of subs in the railroad office. Why, it's all along the line, everywhere."

"I'm telling you that Guilford isn't the man. He is only a cog in the wheel. There is a bigger mind than his behind it."

"I can't help it," Hunnicott protested. "I don't believe that any man or clique could bring this thing about unless we were really on the upturn."

"Very good; believe what you please, but do as I tell you. Sell every foot of Gaston dirt that stands in your name; and while you are about it, sell those six lots for me in Subdivision Five. More than that, do it pretty soon."

Hunnicott promised, in the brokerage affair, at least. Then he switched the talk to the receivership.

"Still up in the air, are you, in the railroad grab case?"

Kent nodded.

"No news of MacFarlane?"

"Plenty of it. His health is still precarious, and will likely remain so until the spoilsmen have picked the skeleton clean."

Hunnicott was silent for a full minute. Then he said:

"Say, Kent, hasn't it occurred to you that they are rather putting meat on the bones instead of taking it off? Their bills for betterments must be out of sight."

It had occurred to Kent, but he gave his own explanation of Major Guilford's policy in a terse sentence.

"It is a part of the bluff; fattening the thing a little before they barbecue it."

"I suppose so. It's a pity we don't live a little farther back in the history of the world: say at a time when we could hire MacFarlane's doctor to obliterate the judge, and no questions asked."

Who can explain how it is that some jesting word, trivial and purposeless it may be, will fire a hidden train of thought which was waiting only for some chance spark? "Obliterate the judge," said Hunnicott in grim jest; and straightway Kent saw possibilities; saw a thing to be done, though not yet the manner of its doing.

"If you'll excuse me," he said abruptly to his companion, "I believe I'll try to catch the Flyer back to the capital. I came down to see about selling those lots of mine, but if you will undertake it for me—"

"Of course," said Hunnicott; "I'll be only too glad. You've ten minutes: can you make it?"

Kent guessed so, and made the guess a certainty with two minutes to spare. The through sleeper was lightly loaded, and he picked out the most unneighbored section of the twelve, being wishful only for undisturbed thinking ground. But before the train had swung past the suburb lights of Gaston, the smoker's unrest seized him and the thought-wheels demanded tobacco. Kent fought it as long as he could, making sure that the smoking-compartment liars' club would be in session; but when the demand became a nagging insistence, he found his pipe and tobacco and went to the men's room.

The little den behind the drawing-room had but one occupant besides the rear-end brakeman—a tall, saturnine man in a gray grass-cloth duster who was smoking a Porto Rican stogie. Kent took a second look and held out his hand.

"This is an unexpected pleasure, Judge Marston. I was counting on three hours of solitary confinement."

The lieutenant-governor acknowledged the hand-clasp,

nodded, and made room on the leather-covered divan for the new-comer. Hildreth, the editor of the *Argus*, put it aptly when he said that the grim-faced old cattle king had "blown" into politics. He was a compromise on the People's Party ticket; was no part of the Bucks programme, and had been made to feel it. Tradition had it that he had been a terror to the armed and organized cattle thieves of the early days; hence the brevet title of "Judge." But those that knew him best did not know that he had once been the brightest man upon the Supreme Bench of his native state: this before failing health had driven him into exile.

As a mixer, the capital had long since voted Oliver Marston a conspicuous failure. A reticent, reserved man by temperament and habit, and with both temperament and habit confirmed by his long exile on the cattle ranges, he had grown rather less than more talkative after his latest plunge into public life; and even Miss Van Brock confessed that she found him impossible on the social side. None the less, Kent had felt drawn toward him from the first; partly because Marston was a good man in bad company, and partly because there was something remindful of the elder Kent in the strong face, the slow smile and the introspective eye of the old man from the hill country.

For a time the talk was a desultory monologue, with Kent doing his best to keep it from dying outright.

Later, when he was fairly driven in upon his reserves, he began to speak of himself, and of the hopeless fight for enlargement in the Trans-Western struggle. Marston lighted the match-devouring stogie for the twentieth time, squared himself on the end of the divan and listened attentively. At the end of the recounting he said:

"It seems to be a failure of justice, Mr. Kent. Can you prove your postulate?"

"I can. With fifteen minutes more on the day of the preliminary hearing I should have shown it to any one's satisfaction."

Marston went into a brown study with his eyes fixed upon the stamped-leather devil in the panel at the opposite end of the compartment. When he spoke again, Kent wondered at the legal verbiage, and still more at the clear-cut, judicial opinion.

"The facts in the case, as you state them, point to judicial connivance, and we should always be slow to charge that, Mr. Kent. Technically, the court was not at fault. Due notice was served on the company's attorney of record, and you admit, yourself, that the delay, short as it was, would have been sufficient if you had not been accidentally detained. And, since there were no contravening affidavits submitted, Judge MacFarlane was technically warranted in granting the prayer for a temporary receiver."

"I'm not trying to refute that," said Kent. "But

afterward, when I called upon the judge with the evidence in hand—"

"He was under no absolute obligation to retry the case out of court, as you know, Mr. Kent. Neither was he obliged to give you an unofficial notice of the day upon which he would hear your motion for the discharge of the receiver and the vacation of his order appointing him."

"Under no absolute legal obligation, perhaps," retorted Kent. "But the moral obligation—"

"We are coming to that. I have been giving you what would probably be a minority opinion of an appellate court, if you could take an appeal. The majority opinion might take higher ground, pointing to the manifest injustice done to the defendant company by the shortness of the delay granted; by Judge MacFarlane's refusal to continue the hearing for one hour, though your attorney was present and pleading for the same; and lastly for the indefinite postponement of the hearing on the merits on insufficient grounds, since the judge was not at the time, and has not since been, too ill to attend to the routine duties of his office."

Kent looked up quickly.

"Judge Marston, do you know that last assertion to be true?" he demanded.

The slow smile came and went in the introspective eyes of the older man.

"I have been giving you the opinion of the higher court," he said, with his nearest approach to jocoseness. "It is based upon the supposition that your allegations would be supported by evidence."

Kent smoked on in silence while the train measured the rail-lengths between two of the isolated prairie stations. When he spoke again there was honest deference in his manner.

"Mr. Marston, you have a far better right to your courtesy title of 'Judge' than that given by the Great American Title Company, Unlimited," he said. "Will you advise me?"

"As plain Oliver Marston, and a man old enough to be your father, yes. What have you been doing? Trying to oust the receiver, I suppose."

"Yes; trying to find some technical flaw by which he could be ousted."

"It can't be done. You must strike higher. Are you fully convinced of Judge MacFarlane's venality?"

"As fully as I can be without having seen with my own eyes and heard with my own ears."

Marston opened his watch and looked at it. Then he lighted another of the villainous little cigars.

"We have an hour yet," he said. "You have been giving me the legal points in the case: now give me the inferences—all of them."

Kent laughed.

"I'm afraid I sha'n't be able to forget the lieutenant-governor. I shall have to call some pretty hard names."

"Call them," said his companion, briefly; and Kent went deep into the details, beginning with the formation of the political gang in Gaston the dismantled.

The listener in the gray dust-coat heard him through without comment. When Kent reached the end of the inferences, telling the truth without scruple and letting the charge of political and judicial corruption lie where it would, the engineer was whistling for the capital.

"You have told me some things I knew, and some others that I only suspected," was all the answer he got until the train was slowing into the Union Station. Then as he flung away the stump of the little cigar the silent one added: "If I were in your place, Mr. Kent, I believe I should take a supplementary course of reading in the State law."

"In what particular part of it?" said Kent, keen anxiety in every word.

"In that part of the fundamental law which relates to the election of circuit judges, let us say. If I had your case to fight, I should try to obliterate Judge MacFarlane."

Kent had but a moment in which to remark the curious coincidence in the use of precisely the same word by both Hunnicott and his present adviser.

"But, my dear sir! we should gain nothing by Mac-

Farlane's removal when his successor would be appointed by the executive!"

Marston turned in the doorway of the smoking-compartment and laid a fatherly hand on the younger man's shoulder.

"My boy, I didn't say 'remove'; I said 'obliterate'. Good night."

XIV

THE GERRYMANDER

With Judge Marston's hint partly to point the way, Kent was no long time in getting at work on the new lead.

Having been at the time a practitioner in one of the counties affected, he knew the political deal by which MacFarlane had been elected. Briefly described, it was a swapping of horses in midstream. In the preliminary canvass it was discovered that in all probability Judge MacFarlane's district, as constituted, would not reëlect him. But the adjoining district was strong enough to spare a county without loss to the party; and that county added to MacFarlane's voting strength would tip the scale in his favor. The Assembly was in session, and the remedy was applied in the shape of a bill readjusting the district lines to fit the political necessity.

While this bill was still in the lower house an obstacle presented itself in the form of a vigorous protest from Judge Whitcomb, whose district was the one to suffer loss. The county in question was a prosperous one, and the court fees—which a compliant clerk might secretly divide with the judge appointing him—were large: wherefore Whitcomb threatened political reprisals if Kiowa County should be taken away from him. The outcome was a compromise. For elective purposes the two districts were gerrymandered as the bill proposed; but it was expressly provided that the transferred county should remain judicially in Whitcomb's district until the expiration of Whitcomb's term of office.

Having refreshed his memory as to the facts, Kent spent a forenoon in the State library. He stayed on past the luncheon hour, feeding on a dry diet of Digests; and it was not until hunger began to sharpen his faculties that he thought of going back of the statutory law to the fountain-head in the constitution of the State. Here, after he had read carefully section by section almost through the entire instrument, his eye lighted upon a clause which gradually grew luminous as he read and re-read it.

"That is what Marston meant; it must be what he meant," he mused; and returning the book to its niche in the alcove he sat down to put his face in his hands and sum up the status in logical sequence.

The conclusion must have been convincing, since he presently sprang up and left the room quickly to have himself shot down the elevator shaft to the street level. The telegraph office in the capitol was closed, but there was another in the Hotel Brunswick, two squares distant, and thither he went.

"Hold the pool in fighting trim at all hazards. Think I have found weak link in the chain," was his wire to Loring, at Boston; and having sent it, he went around to Cassatti's and astonished the waiter by ordering a hearty luncheon at half-past three o'clock in the afternoon.

It was late in the evening before he left the tiny office on the fifth floor of the Quintard Building where one of his former stenographers had set up in business for herself. Since five o'clock the young woman had been steadily driving the type-writer to Kent's dictation. When the final sheet came out with a whirring rasp of the ratchet, he suddenly remembered that he had promised Miss Van Brock to dine with her. It was too late for the dinner, but not too late to go and apologize, and he did the thing that he could, stopping at his rooms on the way to dress while his cab-driver waited.

He found Portia alone, for which he was glad; but her greeting was distinctly accusative.

"If I should pretend to be deeply offended and tell Thomas to show you the door, what could you say for yourself?" she began, before he could say a word in exculpation.

"I should say every sort of excuseful thing I could think of, knowing very well that the most ingenious lie would fall far short of atoning for the offense," he replied humbly.

"Possibly it would be better to tell the truth—had you thought of that?" she suggested, quite without malice.

"Yes, I had; and I shall, if you'll let me begin back a bit." He drew up a chair to face her and sat on the edge of it. "You know I told you I was going to Gaston to sell my six lots while Major Guilford's little boom is on?"

"I'm trying to remember: go on."

"Well, I went yesterday morning and returned late last night. Do you know, it's positively marvelous!"

"Which—the six lots, the boom, or the celerity of your movements?" she asked, with a simulation of the deepest interest.

"All three, if you please; but I meant the miraculous revival of things along the Trans-Western. But that is neither here nor there—"

"I think it is very much here and there," she interrupted.

"I see you don't want me to tell the truth—the whole truth; but I am determined. The first man I met after dinner was Hunnicott, and when I had made him my broker in the real estate affair we fell to talking about the railroad steal. Speaking of MacFarlane's continued absence, Hunnicott said, jokingly, that it was a pity we couldn't go back to the methods of a few hundred years ago and hire the Hot Springs doctor to 'obliterate' him. The word stuck in my mind, and I broke away and took the train chiefly to have a chance to think out the new line. In the smoking-room of the sleeper I found —whom, do you suppose?"

"Oh, I don't know: Judge MacFarlane, perhaps, coming back to give you a chance to poison him at short range?"

"No; it was Marston."

"And he talked so long and so fast that you couldn't get here in time for dinner this evening? That would be the most picturesque of the little fictions you spoke of."

Kent laughed.

"For the first hour he wouldn't talk at all; just sat there wooden-faced, smoking vile little cigars that made me think I was getting hay-fever. But I wouldn't give up; and after I had worn out all the commonplaces I began on the Trans-Western muddle. At that he woke up all at once, and before I knew it he was giving me an expert legal opinion on the case; meaty and sound and judicial. Miss Van Brock, that man is a lawyer, and an exceedingly able one, at that."

"Of course," she said coolly. "He was one of the

justices of the Supreme Court of his own state at forty-two: that was before he had to come West for his health. I found that out a long time ago."

"And you never told me!" said Kent, reproachfully. "Well, no matter; I found out for myself that he is a man to tie to. After we had canvassed the purely legal side of the affair, he wanted to know more, and I went in for the details, telling him all the inferences which involve Bucks, Meigs, Hendricks, MacFarlane and the lot of them."

Miss Portia's eyes were flashing.

"Good, good, good!" she said. "David, I'm proud of you. That took courage—heaps of it."

"I did have to forget pretty hard that he was the lieutenant-governor and nominally one of the gang. But if he is not with us, neither is he against us. He took it all in quietly, and when I was through, he said: 'You have told me some things that I knew, and some others that I only suspected.'"

"Was that all?" asked Miss Van Brock, eagerly.

"No; I took a good long breath and asked his advice."

"Did he give it?"

"He did. He said in sober earnest just what Hunnicott had said in a joke: 'If I had your case to fight, I should try to obliterate Judge MacFarlane.' I began to say that MacFarlane's removal wouldn't help us so long as Bucks has the appointing of his successor, and then

he turned on me and hammered it in with a last word
just as we were leaving the train : 'I didn't say remove ;
I said obliterate.' I caught on, after so long a time, and
I've been hard at work ever since."

"You are obliterating me," said Miss Portia. "I
haven't the slightest idea what it is all about."

"It's easy from this on," said Kent, consolingly. "You
know how MacFarlane secured his reëlection ?"

"Everybody knows that."

"Well, to cut a long story short, the gerrymander deal
won't stand the light. The constitution says—"

"Oh, please don't quote law books at me. Put it in
English—woman-English, if you can."

"I will. The special act of the Assembly is void ;
therefore there was no legal election, and, by consequence, there is no judge and no receiver."

Miss Van Brock was silent for a reflective minute.
Then she said :

"On second thought, perhaps you would better tell
me what the constitution says, Mr. David. Possibly I
could grasp it."

"It is in the section on elections. It says : 'All circuit
or district judges, and all special judges, shall be elected
by the qualified voters of the respective circuits or districts in which they are to hold their court.' Kiowa
County was cut out of Judge Whitcomb's circuit and
placed in Judge MacFarlane's for electoral purposes

only. In all other respects it remains a part of Judge
Whitcomb's circuit, and will so continue until Whitcomb's term expires. Without the vote of Kiowa, Mac-
Farlane could not have been elected; with it he was il-
legally elected, or, to put it the other way about, he was
not elected at all. Since he is not lawfully a judge,
his acts are void, among them this appointment of
Major Guilford as receiver for the Trans-Western."

She was not as enthusiastic as he thought she ought
to be. In the soil prepared for it by the political confidences of the winter there had grown up a many-branch-
ing tree of intimacy between these two; a frank, sexless
friendship, as Kent would have described it, in which a
man who was not very much given to free speech with
any one unburdened himself, and the woman made him
believe that her quick, apprehending sympathy was the
one thing needful—as women have done since the world
began.

Since the looting of the railroad which had taken
him out of the steadying grind of regular work, Kent
had been the prey of mixed motives. From the first he
had thrown himself heartily into the problem of retrieval, but the pugnacious professional ambition to
break the power of the machine had divided time pretty
equally with sentiment. Elinor had said little about the
vise-nip of hardship which the stock-smashing would

impose upon three unguardianed women; but Penelope
had been less reticent. Wanting bare justice at the
hands of the wreckers, Elinor would go to her wedding
with Ormsby as the beggar maid went to King Co-
phetua; and all the loyalty of an unselfish love rose up
in Kent to make the fight with the grafters a personal
duel.

At every step in the hitherto discouraging struggle
Portia Van Brock had been his keen-sighted adviser,
prompter, ally of proof. He told himself now and again
in a flush of gratitude that he was coming to owe her
more than he had ever owed any woman; that where
other men, more—or less—fortunate, were not denied
the joy of possession, he, the disappointed one, was finding a true and loyal comradeship next best, if not quite
equal to the beatitudes of passion.

In all of which David Kent was not entirely just to
himself. However much he owed to Portia—and the
debt was large—she was not his only creditor. Something he owed to the unsatisfied love; more, perhaps, to
the good blood in his veins; but most of all to the battle
itself. For out of the soul-harrowings of endeavor was
emerging a better man, a stronger man, than any his
friends had known. Brutal as their blind gropings
were, the Flagellants of the Dark Ages plied their whips
to some dim purpose. Natures there be that rise only

to the occasion; and if there be no occasion, no floggings of adversity or bone-wrenchings upon the rack of things denied, there will be no awakening—no victory.

David Kent was suffering in both kinds, and was the better man for it. From looking forward to success in the narrow field of professional advancement, or in the scarcely broader one of the righting of one woman's financial wrongs, he was coming now to crave it in the name of manhood; to burn with an eager desire to see justice done for its own sake.

So, when he had come to Portia with the scheme of effacing Judge MacFarlane and his receiver at one shrewd blow, the first of the many plans which held out a fair promise of success as a reward for daring, he was disappointed at her lack of enthusiasm.

"What is the matter with it?" he demanded, when he had given her five full minutes for reflection.

"I don't know, David," she said gravely. "Have I ever thrown cold water on any of your schemes thus far?"

"No, indeed. You have been the loyalest partizan a man ever had, I think; the only one I have to whom I can talk freely. And I have told you more than I have all the others put together."

"I know you have. And it hurts me to pull back now when you want me to push. But I can't help it. Do you believe in a woman's intuition?"

"I suppose I do: all men do, don't they?"

She was tying little knots in the fringe of the table scarf, but the prophetess-eyes, as Penelope called them, were not following the deft intertwinings of the slender fingers.

"You mean to set about 'obliterating' Judge MacFarlane forthwith?" she asked.

"Assuredly. I have been whipping the thing into shape all afternoon: that is what kept me from dining with you."

"It involves some kind of legal procedure?"

"Yes; a rather complicated one."

"Could you explain it so that I could understand it?"

"I think so. In the first place the question is raised by means of an information or inquiry called a *quo warranto*. This is directed to the receiver, and is a demand to know by what authority he holds. Is it clear thus far?"

"Pellucidly," she said.

"In reply the receiver cites his authority, which is the order from Judge MacFarlane; and in our turn we proceed to show that the authority does not exist—that the judge's election was illegal and that therefore his acts are void. Do I make it plain?"

"You make it seem as though it were impossible to fail. And yet I know you will fail."

"How do you know it?"

"Don't ask me; I couldn't begin to tell you that. But in some spiritual or mental looking-glass I can see you coming to me with the story of that failure—coming to ask my help."

He smiled.

"You don't need to be the prophetess Penelope says you are to foresee part of that. I always come to you with my woes."

"Do you?—oftener than you go to Miss Brentwood?"

This time his smile was a mere tightening of the lips.

"You do love to grind me on that side, don't you?" he said. "I and my affairs are less than nothing to Miss Brentwood, and no one knows it any better than you do."

"But you want to go to her," she persisted. "I am only the alternative."

He looked her full in the eyes.

"Miss Van Brock, what is it you want me to say? What can I say more than I said a moment ago—that you are the truest friend a man ever had?"

The answering look out of the brown eyes was age-old in its infinite wisdom.

"How little you men know when you think you know the most," she said half-musingly; then she broke off abruptly. "Let us talk about something else. If Major Guilford is wrecking the railroad, why is he spending so much money on improvements? Have you thought to ask yourself that question?"

"A good many times," he admitted, following her promptly back to first principles.

"And you have not found the answer?"

"Not one that fully satisfies me—no."

"I've found one."

"Intuitively?" he smiled.

"No; it's pure logic, this time. Do you remember showing me a letter that Mr. Hunnicott wrote you just before the explosion—a letter in which he repeated a bit of gossip about Mr. Semple Falkland and his mysterious visit to Gaston?"

"Yes, I remember it."

"Do you know who Mr. Falkland is?"

"Who doesn't?" he queried. "He has half of Wall Street in his clientele."

"Yes; but particularly he is the advisory counsel of the Plantagould System. Ever since you showed me that letter I have been trying to account for his presence in Gaston on the day before Judge MacFarlane's spring term of court. I should never have found out but for Mrs. Brentwood."

"Mrs. Brentwood!"

Miss Van Brock nodded.

"Yes; the mother of my—of the young person for whom I am the alternative, is in a peck of trouble; I quote her *verbatim*. She and her two daughters hold some three thousand shares of Western Pacific stock. It was purchased at fifty-seven, and it is now down to twenty-one."

"Twenty and a quarter to-day," Kent corrected.

"Never mind the fractions. The mother of the incomparable—Penelope, has heard that I am a famous business woman; a worthy understudy for Mrs. Hetty Green; so she came to me for advice. She had a letter from a New York broker offering her a fraction more than the market price for her three thousand shares of Western Pacific."

"Well?" said Kent.

"Meaning what did I do? I did what you did not do—what you are not doing even now; I put two and two together in the twinkling of a bedstaff. Why should a New York broker be picking up outlying Western Pacific at a fraction more than the market when the stock is sinking every day? I was curious enough to pass the 'why' along to a friend of mine in Wall Street."

"Of course he told you all about it," said Kent, incredulously.

"He told me what I needed to know. The broker in question is a Plantagould man."

"Still I fail to 'connect up,' as the linemen say."

"Do you? Ah, David, David! will you leave it for a woman to point out what you should have suspected the moment you read that bit of gossip in Mr. Hunnicott's letter?"

Her hand was on the arm of her chair. He covered it with his own.

"I'll leave it for you, Portia. You are my good angel."

She withdrew the hand quickly, but there was no more than playful resentment in her retort.

"Shame on you!" she scoffed. "What would Miss Brentwood say?"

"I wish you would leave her out of it," he frowned. "You are continually ignoring the fact that she has promised to be the wife of another man."

"And has thereby freed you from all obligations of loyalty? Don't deceive yourself: women are not made that way. Doubtless she will go on and marry the other man in due season; but she will never forgive you if you smash her ideals. But we were talking about the things you ought to have guessed. Fetch me the atlas from the book-case—lower shelf; right-hand corner; that's it."

He did it; and in further obedience opened the thin quarto at the map of the United States. There were heavy black lines, inked in with a pen, tracing out the various ramifications of a great railway system. The nucleus of the system lay in the middle West, but there was a growing network of the black lines reaching out toward the Pacific. And connecting the trans-Mississippi network with the western was a broad red line paralleling the Trans-Western Railway.

She smiled at his sudden start of comprehension.

"Do you begin to suspect things?" she asked.

He nodded his head.

"You ought to be a man. If you were, I should never give you a moment's peace until you consented to take a partnership with me. It's as plain as day, now."

"Is it? Then I wish you would make it appear so to me. I am not half as subtile as you give me credit for being."

"Yet you worked this out."

"That was easy enough; after I had seen Mrs. Brentwood's letter, and yours from Mr. Hunnicott. The Plantagould people want your railroad, and the receivership is a part of a plan for acquiring it. But why is Major Guilford spending so much money for improvements?"

"His reasons are not far to seek now that you have shown me where to look. His instructions are to run the stock down so that the Plantagould can buy it in. Cut rates and big expenditures will do that—have done it. On the other hand, it is doubtless a condition of the deal that the road shall be turned over whole as to its property values—there is to be no wrecking in the general acceptance of the word. The Plantagould doesn't want a picked skeleton."

Miss Portia's eyes narrowed.

"It's a skilful bit of engineering, isn't it?" she said.

"You'd admire it as artistic work yourself if your point of view were not so hopelessly personal."

"You don't know half the artistic skill of it yet," he went on. "Besides all these different ends that are being conserved, the gang is taking care of its surplus heelers on the pay-rolls of the company. More than that, it is making immense political capital for itself. Everybody knows what the policy of the road was under the old régime: 'All the tariff the traffic will stand.' But now a Bucks man has hold of it, and liberality is the word. Every man in Trans-Western territory is swearing by Bucks and Guilford. Ah, my dear friend, his Excellency the governor is a truly great man!"

She nodded.

"I've been trying to impress you with that fact all along. The mistake you made was in not joining the People's Party early in the campaign, David."

But Kent was following out his own line of thought and putting it in words as it came.

"Think of the brain-work it took to bring all these things into line. There was no hitch, no slip, and nothing was overlooked. They picked their time, and it was a moment when we were absolutely helpless. I had filed our charter, but our local organization was still incomplete. They had their judge and the needful case in his court, pending and ready for use at the precise moment.

They had Hawk on the ground, armed and equipped; and they knew that unless a miracle intervened they would have nobody but an unprepared local attorney to obstruct them."

"Is that all?" she asked.

"No. The finest bit of sculpture is on the capstone of the pyramid. Since we have had no hearing on the merits, Guilford is only a temporary receiver, subject to discharge if the allegations in Hawk's amended petition are not sustained. After the major has sufficiently smashed the stock, Judge MacFarlane will come back, the hearing on the merits will be given, we shall doubtless make our point, and the road will revert to the stock-holders. But by that time enough of the stock will have changed hands on the 'wreck' price to put the Plantagould people safely in the saddle, and the freeze-out will be a fact accomplished."

Miss Van Brock drew a long breath that was more than half a sigh.

"You spoke the simple truth, David, when you said that his Excellency is a great man. It seems utterly hopeless now that we have cleared up all the little mysteries."

Kent rose to take his leave.

"No; that is where they all go out and I stay in," he said cheerfully. "The shrewder he is, the more credit

there will be in making him let go. And you mark my
words: I am going to make him let go. Good night."

She had gone with him to the door; was in the act of
closing it behind him, when he turned back for a belated question.

"By the way, what did you tell Mrs. Brentwood to
do?"

"I told her not to do anything until she had consulted
you and Mr. Loring and Brookes Ormsby. Was that
right?"

"Quite right. If it comes up again, rub it in some
more. We'll save her alive yet, if she will let us. Did
you say I might come to dinner to-morrow evening?
Thank you: you grow sweeter and more truly compas-
sionate day by day. Good night again."

XV

When Receiver Guilford took possession of the properties, appurtenances and appendages of the sequestered Trans-Western Railway, one of the luxuries to which he fell heir was private car "Naught-seven," a commodious hotel on wheels originally used as the directors' car of the Western Pacific, and later taken over by Loring to be put in commission as the general manager's special.

In the hands of a friendly receiver this car became a boon to the capitol contingent; its observation platform served as a shifting rostrum from which a deep-chested executive or a mellifluous Hawk often addressed admiring crowds at way stations, and its dining saloon was the moving scene of many little relaxative feasts, at which *Veuve Cliquot* flowed freely, priceless cigars were burned, and the members of the organization unbent, each after his kind.

But to the men of the throttle and oil-can, car Naught-seven, in the gift of a hospitable receiver, short-

(192)

ly became a nightmare. Like most private cars, it was heavier than the heaviest Pullman; and the engineer who was constrained to haul it like a dragging anchor at the tail end of a fast train was prone to say words not to be found in any vocabulary known to respectable philologists.

It was in the evening of a wind-blown day, a week after Kent's visit to Gaston, that Engineer "Red" Callahan, oiling around for the all-night run with the Flyer on the Western Division, heard above the din and clamor of Union Station noises the sullen thump betokening the addition of another car to his train.

"Now fwhat the divvle will that be?" he rasped, pausing, torch in hand, to apostrophize his fireman.

The answer came up out of the shadows to the rear on the lips of M'Tosh, the train-master.

"You have the Naught-seven to-night, Callahan, and a pretty severe head wind. Can you make your time?"

"Haven't thim bloody fools in the up-town office anything betther to do than to tie that sivinty-ton ball-an'-chain to my leg such a night as this?" This is not what Callahan said: it is merely a printable paraphrase of his rejoinder.

M'Tosh shook his head. He was a hold-over from the Loring administration, not because his place was not worth taking, but because as yet no political heeler had turned up with the requisite technical ability to hold it.

"I don't blame you for cussing it out," he said; and the saying of it was a mark of the relaxed discipline which was creeping into all branches of the service. "Mr. Loring's car is anybody's private wagon these days. Can you make your time with her?"

"Not on yer life," Callahan growled. "Is it the owld potgutted thafe iv a rayceiver that's in her?"

"Yes; with Governor Bucks and a party of his friends. I take it you ought to feel honored."

"Do I?" snapped Callahan. "If I don't make thim junketers think they're in the scuff iv a cyclone whin I get thim on the crooks beyant Dolores ye can gimme time, Misther M'Tosh. Where do I get shut iv thim?"

"At Agua Caliente. They are going to the hotel at Breezeland, I suppose. There is your signal to pull out."

"I'll go whin I'm dommed good an' ready," said Callahan, jabbing the snout of his oiler into the link machinery. And again M'Tosh let the breach of discipline go without reproof.

Breezeland Inn, the hotel at Agua Caliente, is a year-round resort for asthmatics and other health seekers, with a sanatorium annex which utilizes the waters of the warm springs for therapeutic purposes. But during the hot months the capital and the plains cities to the eastward send their quota of summer idlers and the house fills to its capacity.

It was for this reason that Mr. Brookes Ormsby, looking for a comfortable resort to which he might take Mrs. Brentwood and her daughters for an outing, hit upon the expedient of going first in person to Breezeland, partly to make sure of accommodations, and partly to check up the attractions of the place against picturesque descriptions in the advertisements.

When he turned out of his sleeper in the early morning at Agua Caliente station, car Naught-seven had been thrown in on a siding a little farther up the line, and Ormsby recognized the burly person of the governor and the florid face and pursy figure of the receiver, in the group of men crossing from the private car to the waiting Inn tally-ho. Being a seasoned traveler, the clubman lost no time in finding the station agent.

"Isn't there some way you can get me up to the hotel before that crowd reaches?" he asked; adding: "I'll make it worth your while."

The reply effaced the necessity for haste.

"The Inn auto will be down in a few minutes, and you can go up in that. Naught-seven brought Governor Bucks and the receiver and their party, and they're going down to Megilp, the mining camp on the other side of the State line. They've chartered the tally-ho for the day."

Ormsby waited, and a little later was whisked away to the hotel in the tonneau of the guests' automobile.

Afterward came a day which was rather hard to get through. Breakfast, a leisurely weighing and measuring of the climatic, picturesque and health-mending conditions, and the writing of a letter or two helped him wear out the forenoon; but after luncheon the time dragged dispiteously, and he was glad enough when the auto-car came to take him to the station for the evening train.

As it happened, there were no other passengers for the east-bound Flyer; and finding he still had some minutes to wait, Ormsby lounged into the telegraph office. Here the bonds of ennui were loosened by the gradual development of a little mystery. First the telephone bell rang smartly, and when the telegraph operator took down the ear-piece and said "Well?" in the imperious tone common to his kind, he evidently received a communication that shocked him.

Ormsby overheard but a meager half of the wire conversation; and the excitement, whatever its nature, was at the other end of the line. None the less, the station agent's broken ejaculations were provocative of keen interest in a man who had been boring himself desperately for the better part of a day.

"Caught him doing it, you say? . . . Great Scott! . . . Oh, I don't believe that, you know . . . yes—uh-huh—I hear. . . But who did the shooting?" Whether the information came or not, Ormsby did not know, for at this conjuncture the telegraph instruments on the table set up a furious chattering, and the railway man dropped the receiver and sprang to his key.

This left the listener out of it completely, and Ormsby strolled out to the platform, wondering what had happened and where it had happened. He glanced up at the telephone wires: two of them ran up the graveled driveway toward Breezeland Inn; the poles of the other two sentineled the road to the west down which the tally-ho had driven in the early morning.

In the reflective instant the telegraph operator dashed out of his bay-windowed retreat and ran up the track to the private car. In a few minutes he was back again, holding an excited conference with the chauffeur of the Inn automobile, who was waiting to see if the Flyer should bring him any fares for the hotel.

Curiosity is said to be peculiarly a foible feminine. It is not, as every one knows. But of the major masculine allotment, Ormsby the masterful had rather less than his due share. He saw the chauffeur turn his car in the length of it and send it spinning down the road and across the line into the adjoining State; heard the mellow whistle of the incoming train, and saw the station man nervously setting his stop signal; all with no more than a mild desire to know the reason for so much excitement and haste—a desire which was content to wait on the explanation of events.

The explanation, such as it was, did not linger. The heavy train thundered in from the west; stopped barely long enough to allow the single passenger to swing up the steps of the Pullman; and went on again to stop a second time with a jerk when it had passed the side-track switch.

Ormsby put his head out of the window and saw that the private car was to be taken on; remarked also that the thing was done with the utmost celerity. Once out on the main line with car Naught-seven coupled in, the train was backed swiftly down to the station and the small mystery of hurryings was sufficiently solved. The governor and his party were returning, and they did not wish to miss connections.

Ormsby had settled back into the corner of his section when he heard the spitting explosions of the automobile and the crash of hoofs and iron-tired wheels on the sharp gravel. He looked out again and was in time to see the finish of the race. Up the road from the westward came the six-horse tally-ho, the horses galloping in the traces and the automobile straining in the lead at the end of an improvised tow-line. In a twinkling the coach was abreast of the private car, the transfer of passengers was effected, and Ormsby was near enough at his onlooking window to remark several things: that there was pell-mell haste and suppressed excitement; that the governor was the coolest man in the group; and that the receiver had to be helped across from the coach to the car. Then the train moved out, gathering speed with each added wheel-turn.

The onlooker leaned from his window to see what became of the tangle of horses and auto-car precipitated by the sudden stop of the tally-ho. Mirage effects are common on the western plains, and if Ormsby had not been familiar with them he might have marveled at the striking example afforded by the backward look. In the rapidly increasing perspective the six horses of the tally-ho were suddenly multiplied into a troop; and where the station agent had stood on the platform there seemed to be a dozen gesticulating figures fading into indistinctness, as the fast train swept on its way eastward.

The club-man saw no more of the junketing party that night. Once when the train stopped to cut out the dining-car, and he had stepped down for a breath of fresh air on the station platform, he noticed that the private car was brilliantly lighted, and that the curtains and window shades were closely drawn. Also, he heard the popping of bottle corks and the clink of glass, betokening that the governor's party was still celebrating its successful race for the train. Singularly enough,

Ormsby's reflections concerned themselves chiefly with the small dishonesty.

"I suppose it all goes into the receiver's expense account and the railroad pays for it," he said to himself. "So and so much for an inspection trip to Megilp and return. I must tell Kent about it. It will put another shovelful of coal into his furnace—not that he is especially needing it."

At the moment of this saying—it was between ten and eleven o'clock at night—David Kent's wrath-fire was far from needing an additional stoking. Once more Miss Van Brock had given proof of her prophetic gift, and Kent had been moodily filling in the details of the picture drawn by her woman's intuition. He had gone late to the house in Alameda Square, knowing that Portia had dinner guests. And it was imperative that he should have her to himself.

"You needn't tell me anything but the manner of its doing," she was saying. "I knew they would find a way to stop you—or make one. And you needn't be spiteful at me," she added, when Kent gripped the arms of his chair.

"I don't mind your saying 'I told you so'," he fumed. "It's the fact that I didn't have sense enough to see what an easy game I was dealing them. It didn't take Meigs five minutes to shut me off."

"Tell me about it," she said; and he did it crisply.

"The *quo warranto* inquiry is instituted in the name of the State; or rather the proceedings are brought by some person with the approval of the governor or the attorney-general, one or both. I took to-day for obtaining this approval because I knew Bucks was out of town and I thought I could bully Meigs."

"And you couldn't?" she said.

"Not in a thousand years. At first he said he would take the matter under advisement: I knew that meant a consultation with Bucks. Then I put the whip on; told him a few of the things I know, and let him imagine a lot more; but it was no good. He was as smooth as oil, admitting nothing, denying nothing. And what grinds me worst is that I let him put me in fault; gave him a chance to show conclusively how absurd it was for me to expect him to take up a question of such magnitude on the spur of the moment."

"Of course," she said sympathetically. "I knew they would find a way. What are you doing?"

Kent laughed in spite of his sore *amour-propre*.

"At this present moment I am doing precisely what you said I should: unloading my woes upon you."

"Oh, but I didn't say that. I said you would come to me for help. Have you?"

"I'd say yes, if I didn't know so well just what I am up against."

Miss Van Brock laughed unfeelingly.

"Is it a man's weakness to fight better in the dark?"

"It is a man's common sense to know when he is knocked out," he retorted.

She held him with her eyes while she said:

"Tell me what you want to accomplish, David; at the end of the ends, I mean. Is it only that you wish to save Miss Brentwood's little marriage portion?"

He told the simple truth, as who could help, with Portia's eyes demanding it.

"It was that at first; I'll admit it. But latterly—"

"Latterly you have begun to think larger things?" She looked away from him, and her next word seemed to be part of an unspoken thought. "I have been wondering if you are great enough, David."

He shook his head despondently.

"Haven't I just been showing you that I am not?"

"You have been showing me that you can not always out-plan the other person. That is a lack, but it is not fatal. Are you great enough to run fast and far when it is a straight-away race depending only upon mere man-strength and indomitable determination?"

Her words fired him curiously. He recalled the little thrill of inspiration which a somewhat similar appeal from Elinor had once given him, and tried to compare the two sensations. There was no comparison. The one was a call to moral victory; the other to material success. None the less, he decided that the present was the more potent spell, perhaps only because it was the present.

"Try me," he said impulsively.

"If I do . . David, no man can serve two masters—or two mistresses. If I do, will you agree to put the sentimental affair resolutely in the background?"

He took his head in his hands and was a long minute making up his mind. But his refusal was blunt enough when it came.

"No; at least, not until they are married."

It would have taken a keener discernment than Kent's or any man's to have fathomed the prompting of her laugh.

"I was only trying you," she said. "Perhaps, if you had said yes I should have deserted you and gone over to the other side."

He got up and went to sit beside her on the pillowed divan.

"Don't try me again, please—not that way. I am only a man."

"I make no promises—not even good ones," she retorted. And then: "Would you like to have your *quo warranto* blind alley turned into a thoroughfare?"

"I believe you can do it if you try," he admitted, brightening a little.

"Maybe I can; or rather maybe I can put you in the

way of doing it. You say Mr. Meigs is obstinate, and the governor is likely to prove still more obstinate. Have you thought of any way of softening them?"

"You know I haven't. It's a stark impossibility from my point of view."

"Nothing is impossible; it is always a question of ways and means." Then, suddenly: "Have you been paying any attention to the development of the Belmount oil field?"

"Enough to know that it is a big thing; the biggest since the Pennsylvania discoveries, according to all accounts."

"And the people of the State are enthusiastic about it, thinking that now the long tyranny of the oil monopoly will be broken?"

"That is the way most of the newspapers talk, and there seems to be some little ground for it, granting the powers of the new law."

She laid the tips of her fingers on his arm and knotted the thread of suggestion in a single sentence.

"In the present state of affairs—with the People's Party as yet on trial, and the public mind ready to take fire at the merest hint of a foreign capitalistic monopoly in the State—tell me what would happen to the man who would let the Universal Oil Company into the Belmount field in defiance of the new trust and corporation law?"

"By Jove!" Kent exclaimed, sitting up as if the shapely hand had given him a buffet. "It would ruin him politically, world without end! Tell me; is Bucks going to do that?"

She laughed softly.

"That is for you to find out, Mr. David Kent; not by hearsay, but in good, solid terms of fact that will appeal to a level-headed, conservative newspaper editor like—well, like Mr. Hildreth, of the *Argus,* let us say. Are you big enough to do it?"

"I am desperate enough to try," was the slow-spoken answer.

"And when you have the weapon in your hands; when you have found the sword and sharpened it?"

"Then I can go to his Excellency and tell him what will happen if he doesn't instruct his attorney-general in the *quo warranto* affair."

"That will probably suffice to save your railroad— and Miss Brentwood's marriage portion. But after, David; what will you do afterward?"

"I'll go on fighting the devil with fire until I have burned him out. If this is to be a government of dictators, I can be one of them, too."

She clapped her hands enthusiastically.

"There spoke the man David Kent; the man I have been trying to discover deep down under the rubbish of ill-temper and hesitancy and—yes, I will say it—of sentiment. Have you learned your lesson, David mine?"

It was a mark of another change in him that he rose and stood over her, and that his voice was cool and dispassionate when he said:

"If I have, it is because I have you for an inspired text-book, Portia dear."

And with that he took his leave.

XVI

SHARPENING THE SWORD

In the beginning of the new campaign of investigation David Kent wisely discounted the help of paid professional spies—or rather he deferred it to a later stage—by taking counsel with Jeffrey Hildreth, night editor of the *Argus*. Here, if anywhere, practical help was to be had; and the tender of it was cheerfully hearty and enthusiastic.

"Most assuredly you may depend on the *Argus*, horse, foot and artillery," said the editor, when Kent had guardedly outlined some portion of his plan. "We are on your side of the fence, and have been ever since Bucks was sprung as .a candidate on the convention. But you've no case. Of course, it's an open secret that the Universal people are trying to break through the fence of the new law and establish themselves in the Belmount field without losing their identity or any of their monopolistic privileges. And it is equally a matter of course to some of us that the Bucks ring will

sell the State out if the price is right. But to impli-
cate Bucks and the capitol gang in printable shape is
quite another matter."

"I know," Kent admitted. "But it isn't impossible; it has got to be possible."

The night editor sat back in his chair and chewed his
cigar reflectively. Suddenly he asked:

"What's your object, Kent? It isn't purely *pro
bono publico,* I take it?"

Kent could no longer say truthfully that it was, and
he did not lie about it.

"No, it's purely personal, I guess. I need to get a
grip on Bucks and I mean to do it."

Hildreth laughed.

"And, having got it, you'll telephone me to let up—
as you did in the House Bill Twenty-nine fiasco. Where
do we come in?"

"No; you shall come in on the ground floor this
time; though I may ask you to hold your hand until I
have used my leverage. And if you'll go into it to stay,
you sha'n't be alone. Giving the *Argus* precedence in
any item of news, I'll engage to have every other opposition editor in the State ready to back you."

"Gad! you're growing, Kent. Do you mean to down
the Bucks crowd ded-definitely?" demanded the editor, who stammered a little under excitable provocation. "Bigger men than you have tried it—and failed."

"But no one of them with half my obstinacy, Hildreth. It can be done, and I am going to do it."

The night editor laughed again.

"If you can show that gang up, Kent, nothing in this State will be too good for you."

"I've got it to do," said Kent. "Afterward, perhaps I'll come around for some of the good things. I am not in this for health or pleasure. Can I count on you after the mud-slinging begins?"

Hildreth reflected further, disregarding the fore-man's reproachful calls for copy.

"I'll go you," he said at last; "and I'll undertake to swing the chief into line. But I am going to disagree with you flat on the project of a sudden exposé. Right or wrong, Bucks has pup-popular sentiment on his side. Take the Trans-Western territory, for example: at the present speaking these grafters—or their man Guilford; it's all the same—own those people down there body and soul. You couldn't pry Bucks out of their affections with a crowbar—suddenly, I mean. We'll have to work up to it gradually; educate the people as we go along."

"I concede that much," said Kent. "And you may as well begin on this same Trans-Western deal,"—wherewith he pieced together the inferences which pointed to the stock-smashing project behind the receivership.

"Don't use too much of it," he added, in conclusion.

"It is all inference and deduction as yet, as I say. But you will admit it's plausible."

The editor was sitting far back in his chair again, chewing absently on the extinct cigar.

"Kent, did you fuf-figure all that out by yourself?"

"No," said Kent, briefly. "There is a keener mind than mine behind it—and behind this oil field business, as well."

"I'd like to give that mind a stunt on the *Argus*," said the editor. "But about the Belmount mix-up: you will give us a stickful now and then as we go along, if you unearth anything that the public would like to read?"

"Certainly; any and everything that won't tend to interfere with my little intermediate scheme. As I have intimated, I must bring Bucks to terms on my own account before I turn him over to you and the people of the State. But I mean to be in on that, too."

Hildreth wagged his head dubiously.

"I may be overcautious; and I don't want to seem to scare you out, Kent. You ought to know your man better than I do—better than any of us; but if I had your job, I believe I should want to travel with a bodyguard. I do, for a fact."

David Kent's laugh came easily. Fear, the fear of man, was not among his weaknesses.

"I am taking all the chances," he said; and so the conference ended.

Two days later the "educational" campaign was opened by an editorial in the *Argus* setting forth some hitherto unpublished matter concerning the manner in which the Trans-Western had been placed in the hands of a receiver. In its next issue the paper named the receivership after its true author, showing by a list of the officials that the road under Major Guilford had been made a hospital for Bucks politicians, and hinting pointedly that it was to be wrecked for the benefit of a stock-jobbing syndicate of eastern capitalists.

Having thus reawakened public interest in the Trans-Western affair, Hildreth sounded a new note of alarm pitched upon the efforts of the Universal Oil Company to establish itself in the Belmount oil region; a cry which was promptly taken up by other State editors. This editorial was followed closely by others in the same strain, and at the end of a fortnight Kent was fain to call a halt.

"Not too fast, Hildreth," he cautioned, dropping into the editor's den late one night. "You are doing mighty good work, but you are making it infinitely harder for me—driving the game to deeper cover. One of my men had a clue: Bucks and Meigs were holding conferences with a man from the Belmount field whose record runs back to New York. But they have taken the alarm and thrown us off the track."

"The secretary of State's office is the place you want to watch," said Hildreth. "New oil companies are incorporating every day. Pretty soon one of these will swallow up all the others: that one will be the Universal under another name, and in its application for a charter you'll find askings big enough to cover all the rights and privileges of the original monopoly."

"That is a good idea," said Kent, who already had a clerk in the secretary of State's office in his pay. "But how are we coming on in the political field?"

"We are doing business there, and you have the *Argus* to thank for it. You—or your idea, I should say— has a respectable following all over the State now; as it didn't have until we began to leg for it."

Again Kent acquiesced, making no mention of sundry journeys he had made for the sole purpose of enlisting other editors, or of the open house Miss Van Brock was keeping for out-of-town newspaper men visiting the capital.

"Moreover, we've served your turn in the Trans-Western affair," Hildreth went on. "Public interest is on the *qui vive* for new developments in that. By the way, has the capitol gang any notion of your part in all this upstirring?"

Kent smiled and handed the editor an open letter. It

was from Receiver Guilford. The post of general counsel for the Trans-Western was vacant, and the letter was a formal tender of the office to the "Hon. David Kent."

"H'm," said the editor. "I don't understand that a little bit."

"Why?"

"If they could get you to accept a general agency in Central Africa or New Zealand, or some other antipodean place where you'd be safely out of the way, it would be evident enough. But here they are proposing to take you right into the heart of things."

Kent got a match out of the editor's desk and relighted his cigar.

"You've got brain-fag to-night, Hildreth. It's a bribe, pure and simple. They argue that it is merely a matter of dollars and cents to me, as it would be to one of them; and they propose to retain me just as they would any other attorney whose opposition they might want to get rid of. Don't you see?"

"Sure. I was thinking up the wrong spout. Have you replied to the major?"

"Yes. I told him that my present engagements preclude the possibility of considering his offer; much to my regret."

"Did you say that? You're a cold-plucked one, Kent, and I'm coming to admire you. But now is the time **for** you to begin to look out. They have spotted you, and their attempt to buy you has failed. I don't know how deeply you have gone into Bucks' tinkering with the Universal people, but if you are in the way of getting the grip you spoke of—as this letter seems to indicate —you want to be careful."

Kent promised and went his way. One of his saving graces was the ability to hold his tongue, even in a confidential talk with as good a friend as Hildreth. As for example: he had let the suggestion of watching the secretary of State's office come as a new thing from the editor, whereas in fact it was one of the earliest measures he had taken.

And on that road he had traveled far, thanks to a keen wit, to Portia Van Brock's incessant promptings, and to the help of the leaky clerk in Hendricks' office; so far, indeed, that he had found the "stool pigeon" oil company, to which Hildreth's hint had pointed—a company composed, with a single exception, of men of "straw," the exception being the man Rumford, whose conferences with the governor and the attorney-general had aroused his suspicions.

It was about this time that Hunnicott reported the sale of the Gaston lots at a rather fancy cash figure, and the money came in good play.

"Two things remain to be proved," said Portia, in one of their many connings of the intricate course;

"two things that must be proved before you can attack openly: that Rumford is really representing the Universal Oil Company; and that he is bribing the junto to let the Universal incorporate under the mask of his 'straw' company. Now is the time when you can not afford to be economical. Have you money?"

Since it was the day after the Hunnicott remittance, Kent could answer yes with a good conscience.

"Then spend it," she said; and he did spend it like a millionaire, lying awake nights to devise new ways of employing it.

And for the abutments of the arch of proof the money-spending sufficed. By dint of a warm and somewhat costly wire investigation of Rumford's antecedents, Kent succeeded in placing the Belmount promoter unquestionably as one of the trusted lieutenants of the Universal; and the leaky clerk in the secretary of State's office gave the text of the application for the "straw" company charter, showing that the powers asked for were as despotic as the great monopoly could desire.

But for the keystone of the arch, the criminal implication of the plotters themselves, he was indebted to a fit of ill-considered anger and to a chapter of accidents.

XVII

THE CONSPIRATORS

It was chiefly due to Portia's urgings that Kent took Ormsby into his confidence when the campaign was fairly opened. She put it diplomatically on the ground of charity to an exiled millionaire, temporarily out of a job; but her real reason went deeper. From its inception as a one-man fight against political chicanery in high places, the criticism of the Bucks formula was beginning to shape itself in a readjustment of party lines in the field of State politics; and Miss Van Brock, whose designs upon Kent's future ran far in advance of her admissions to him, was anxiously casting about for a managerial promoter.

A little practice-play in municipal politics made the need apparent. It came in the midst of things, basing itself upon the year-gone triumph of agrarianism in the State. In the upheaval, the capital city had participated to the extent of electing a majority of the aldermen on the People's Party ticket; and before long it

HE JAMMED THE FIRE END OF HIS CIGAR AMONG THE FINGERS
OF THE GRASPING HAND

developed that a majority of this aldermanic majority
could be counted among the spoilsmen—was in fact a
creature of the larger ring.

Late in the summer an ordinance was proposed by
the terms of which a single corporation was to be given
a franchise granting a complete monopoly of the streets
for gas and water mains and transit rights of way.
Thereupon a bitter struggle ensued. Party lines were
obliterated, and men who shunned the primaries and
otherwise shirked their political duties raised the cry
of corruption, and a Civic League was formed to fight
the ring.

Into this struggle, as giving him the chance to front
the enemy in a fair field, David Kent flung himself with
all the ardor of a born fighter. Mass meetings were
held, with Kent as spokesman for the League, and the
outcome was a decency triumph which brought Kent's
name into grateful public prominence. Hildreth played
an able second, and by the time the obnoxious ordinance
had been safely tabled, Kent had a semi-political following which was all his own. Men who had hitherto known him only as a corporation lawyer began to
prophesy large things of the fiery young advocate, whose
arguments were as sound and convincing as his invec-
tive was keen and merciless.

Figuratively speaking, Portia stood in the wings and
applauded. Also, she saw that her protégé had reached

the point where he needed grooming for whatever race lay before him. Hence her urgings, which made a triumvirate out of the council of two, with Brookes Ormsby as the third member.

"You understand, I'm not interested a little bit in the merits of the case," said the newly elected chairman, in his first official interview with Miss Van Brock. "So far as the internal politics of this particularly wild and woolly State are concerned, I'm neither in them nor of them. But I am willing to do what I can for Kent."

"Owing him a good turn?" said Portia, with malice aforethought.

Ormsby's laugh was an Englishman's deep-chested haw-haw.

"So he has been making you his confidante in that, too, has he?"

"There was no confidence needed," she retorted. "I have eyes; and, to use one of your own pet phrases, I was not born yesterday. But let that go: you are willing to help us?"

"I said I was willing to help Kent. If you bracket yourself with him, I am more than willing. But I am rather new to the game. You will have to tell me the moves."

"We are only in the opening," she said, continuing the figure. "You will learn as you go along. By and by you will have to spend money; but just now the need is for a cool head to keep our young firebrand out of the personalities. Where is he to-night?"

Ormsby's smile was a grin.

"I left him at 124 Tejon Avenue half an hour ago. Do you think he is likely to get into trouble there?"

On the porch of the Brentwood apartment house David Kent was answering that question measurably well for himself. With the striking of the City Hall clock at nine Mrs. Brentwood had complained of the glare of the electric crossing-lamp and had gone in, leaving the caller with Penelope in the hammock on one side of him and Elinor in a basket chair on the other.

Their talk had been of the late municipal struggle, and of Kent's part in it; and, like Miss Van Brock, Penelope was applausive. But Elinor's congratulations were tempered with deprecation.

"I am glad you won for the League, of course; everybody must be glad of that," she said. "But I hope the *Argus* didn't report your speeches correctly. If it did, you have made a host of bitter enemies."

"What does a man—a real man—care for that?" This from the depths of the hammock.

"I, at least, can afford to be careless," said Kent. "I am not running for office, and I have nothing to lose, politically or otherwise."

"Can any man say that truthfully?" Elinor queried.

"I think I can. I have given no hostages to fortune."

Penelope lifted the challenge promptly.

"Lord Bacon said that, didn't he?—about men marrying. If he were alive now he wouldn't need to say it. Men don't have to be discouraged."

"Don't they?" said Kent.

"No, indeed; they are too utterly selfish for any matrimonial use, as it is. No, don't argue with me, please. I'm fixed—irrevocably fixed."

Elinor overtook the runaway conversation and drove it back into the path of her own choosing.

"But I do think you owe it to yourself to be more careful in your public utterances," she insisted. "If these men on the other side are only half as unprincipled as your accusations make them out to be, they would not stop short of personal violence."

"I am not hunting clemency or personal immunity just now," laughed Kent. "On the contrary, I am only anxious to make the score as heavy as possible. And so far from keeping prudently in the background, I'll confess that I went into this franchise fight chiefly to let the capitol gang know who I am and where I stand."

A sudden light came into Elinor's eyes and burned there steadily. She was of those who lay votive offerings upon the shrine of manly courage.

"One part of me approves as much as another part

disapproves," she said after a time. "I suppose it isn't possible to avoid making political enemies; but is it needful to turn them into personal enemies?"

He looked at her curiously.

"I am afraid I don't know any middle path, not being a politician," he objected. "And as for the enmity of these men, I shall count it an honor to win it. If I do not win it, I shall know I am not succeeding."

Silence for another little space, which Miss Brentwood broke by saying:

"Don't you want to smoke? You may."

Kent felt in his pocket.

"I have no cigar."

She looked past him to the hammock. "Penelope!" she called softly; and when there was no response she went to spread the hammock rug over her sister.

"You may smoke your pipe," she said; and when she had passed behind him to her chair she made another concession: "Let me fill it for you—you used to."

He gave her the pipe and tobacco, and by a curious contradiction of terms began to wonder if he ought not to go. Notwithstanding his frank defiance of Brookes Ormsby, and his declaration of intention in the sentimental affair, he had his own notions about the sanctity of a betrothal. Mrs. Brentwood had vanished, and Penelope was asleep in the hammock. Could he trust himself to be decently loyal to Ormsby if he should stay?

Nice questions of conscience had not been troubling him much of late; but this was new ground—or if not new, so old that it had the effect of being new.

He let the question go unanswered—and stayed. But he was minded to fling the biggest barrier he could lay hands on in the way of possible disloyalty by saying good things of Ormsby.

"I owe you much for my acquaintance with him," he said, when the subject was fairly introduced. "He has been all kinds of a good friend to me, and he promises to be more."

"Isn't your debt to Penelope, rather than to me?" she returned.

"No, I think not. You are responsible, in the broader sense, at all events. He did not come West for Penelope's sake." Then he took the plunge: "May I know when it is to be—or am I to wait for my bidding with the other and more formally invited guests?"

She laughed, a low little laugh that somehow grated upon his nerves.

"You shall know—when I know."

"Forgive me," he said quickly. "But from something Ormsby said—"

"He should not have spoken of it; I have given him no right," she said coldly.

"You make me twice sorry: once if I am a trespasser,

and again if I have unwittingly broken a confidence. But as a friend—a very old friend—I ventured—"

She interrupted him again, but this time her laugh did not hurt him.

"Yes; our friendship antedates Mr. Ormsby; it is old enough to excuse anything you said—or were going to say."

"Thank you," he rejoined, and he meant it. "What I was going to say touches a matter which I believe you haven't confided to any one. May I talk business for a few minutes?"

"If you will light your pipe and go on smoking. It makes me nervous to have people hang on the brink of things."

He lighted the pipe, wondering what other thing he might do to allay her nervousness. None the less, he would not go back from his purpose, which was barrier-building.

"I have thought, wholly without warrant, perhaps, that your loss in this railroad steal has had something to do with the postponement of your happiness—and Ormsby's. Has it?"

"And if it should have?"

"I merely wanted to say that we still have a fighting chance. But one of the hard and fast conditions is that every individual stockholder shall hang on to his or her holdings like grim death."

She caught her breath with a little gasp.

"The encouragement comes too late for us. We have parted with our stock."

Kent turned cold and hot and cold again while she was saying it. Then the lawyer in him came uppermost.

"Is it gone beyond recall? How much too late am I?" he demanded.

"My mother wrote the letter to-day. She had an offer from some one in New York."

Kent was on his feet instantly.

"Has that letter been mailed? Because if it has, it must be stopped by wire!"

Miss Brentwood rose.

"It was on the hall table this afternoon; I'll go and see," and in a moment she returned with the letter in her hand.

Kent took it from her as if it had been an edged weapon or a can of high explosives.

"Heavens! what a turn you gave me!" he said, sitting down again. "Can I see your mother?"

"I think she has gone to bed. What do you want to do?"

"I want to tell her that she mustn't do any such suicidal thing as this."

"You don't know my mother," was the calm reply. "Mr. Ormsby said everything he could think of."

"Then we must take matters into our own hands. Will you help me?"

"How?" she asked.

"By keeping your own counsel and trusting me. Your mother supposes this letter has gone: it has gone—this way." He tore the sealed envelope across and across and dropped the pieces into his pocket. "Now we are safe—at least until the man at the other end writes again."

It shocked her a little, and she did not promise to be a party to the subterfuge. But neither did she say she would not.

"I am willing to believe that you have strong reasons for taking such strong measures," she said. "May I know them?"

Kent's gift of reticence came to his rescue in time to prevent the introduction of another and rather uncertain factor into his complicated problem.

"I can explain it more intelligibly a little later on; or if I don't, Ormsby will. In the mean time, you must take my word for it that we shall have our railroad back in due season."

It is a question for the psychologists to answer if there be or be not crises in a man's life when the event, weighty or trivial, turns upon that thing which, for the want of a better name, is called a premonition.

In the silence that followed his dismissal of the subject, Kent became aware of a vague prompting which was urging him to cut his visit short. There was no definable reason for his going. He had finally brought himself to the point of speaking openly to Elinor of her engagement, and they were, as he fondly believed, safely beyond the danger point in that field. Moreover, Penelope was stirring in her hammock and the perilous privacy was at an end. Nevertheless, he rose and said good-night, and was half-way to the next corner before he realized how inexcusably abrupt his leave-taking had been.

When he did realize it, he was of two minds whether to go back or to let the apology excuse another call the following evening. Then the insistent prompting seized him again; and when next he came to a competent sense of things present he was standing opposite the capitol building, staring fixedly up at a pair of lighted windows in the second story.

They were the windows of the governor's room; and David Kent's brain cleared suddenly. In the earliest beginnings of the determinate plan to wrest the Trans-Western out of the grasp of the junto he had known that it must come finally to some desperate duel with the master-spirit of the ringsters. Was Jasper Bucks behind those lighted windows—alone?

Kent had not meant to make the open attack until he should have a weapon in his hands which would arm him to win. But now as he stood looking up at the beckoning windows a mad desire to have it out once for all with the robber-in-chief sent the blood tingling to his finger-tips. True, he had nothing as yet in the oil-field conspiracy that the newspapers or the public would accept as evidence of fraud and corruption. But on the other hand, Bucks was only a man, after all; a man with a bucaneer's record, and by consequence vulnerable beneath the brazen armor of assurance. If the attack were bold enough—

Kent did not stop to argue it out. When a man's blood is up the odds against him shrink and become as naught. Two minutes later he was in the upper corridor of the capitol, striding swiftly to the door of the lighted room.

Recalling it afterward he wondered if the occult prompting which had dragged him out of his chair on the Brentwood porch saw to it that he walked upon the strip of matting in the tile-paved corridor and so made his approach noiseless. Also, if the same silent monitor bade him stop short of the governor's office: at the door, namely, of the public anteroom, which stood ajar?

A low murmur of voices came from beyond, and for a moment he paused listening. Then he went boldly within, crossing the anteroom and standing fairly in the broad beam of light pouring through the open door of communication with the private office.

Four men sat in low-toned conference around the governor's writing-table, and if any one of them had looked up the silent witness must have been discovered. Kent marked them down one by one: the governor; Hendricks, the secretary of State; Rumford, the oil man; and Senator Duvall. For five pregnant minutes he stood looking on, almost within arm's reach of the four; hearing distinctly what was said; seeing the papers which changed hands across the table. Then he turned and went away, noiselessly as he had come, the thick-piled carpet of the anteroom muffling his footfalls.

It was midnight when he reached his quarters in the Clarendon and flung himself full length upon the bed, sodden with weariness. For two hours he had tramped the deserted streets, striving in sharp travail of soul to fit the invincible, chance-given weapon to his hand. When he came in the thing was done, and he slept the sleep of an outworn laborer.

XVIII

DOWN, BRUNO!

For six days after the night of revelations Kent dived deep, personally and by paid proxy, in a sea of secrecy which, but for the five pregnant minutes in the doorway of the governor's office, might easily have proved fathomless.

On the seventh day the conflagration broke out. The editor of the Belmount *Refiner* was the first to smell smoke and to raise the cry of "Fire!" but by midnight the wires were humming with the news and the entire State was ablaze.

The story as it appeared under the scare headlines the next morning was crisply told. An oil company had been formed with Senator Duvall at its head. After its incorporation it was ascertained that it not only held options on all the most valuable wells in the Belmount region, but that its charter gave it immunity from the law requiring all corporations to have their organizations, officers, and operating headquarters in

(229)

the State. By the time the new company was three days old it had quietly taken up its options and was the single big fish in the pool by virtue of its having swallowed all the little ones.

Then came the finishing stroke which had set the wires to humming. On the sixth day it was noised about that Senator Duvall had transferred his controlling interest to Rumford—otherwise to the Universal Oil Company; that he had served only as a figurehead in the transaction, using his standing, social and political, to secure the charter which had been denied Rumford and his associates.

It had all been managed very skilfully; the capping of the wells by the Universal's agent, the practical sealing up of the entire district, being the first public intimation of the result of Duvall's treachery and the complete triumph of a foreign monopoly.

The storm that swept the State when the facts came out was cyclonic, and it was reported, as it needed to be, that Senator Duvall had disappeared. Never in the history of the State had public feeling risen so high; and there were not lacking those who said that if Duvall showed himself his life would not be safe in the streets of the capital.

It was after the *Argus* had gone to press on the night of explosions that Editor Hildreth sought and found

David Kent in his rooms at the Clarendon, and poured out the vials of his wrath.

"Say, I'd like to know if you cuc-call this giving me a fair show!" he demanded, flinging into Kent's sitting-room and dropping into a chair. "Did I, or did I not understand that I was to have the age on this oil business when there was anything fit to print?"

Kent gave the night editor a cigar and was otherwise exasperatingly imperturbable.

"Keep your clothes on, and don't accuse a man of disloyalty until you have all the documents in the case," he said. "I didn't know, until I saw your bulletin a few hours ago, that the thing had been pulled off. In fact, I've been too busy with other things to pay much attention to the Belmount end of it."

"The ded-devil you have!" sputtered Hildreth, chewing savagely on the gift cigar. "I'd like to know what business you had to mix up in other things to the detriment of my news column. You were the one man who knew all about it; or at least you did a week or two ago."

"Yes; but other and more important things have intervened. I have been desperately busy, as I say."

"Well, you've lost your chance to get your grip on the capitol gang, anyway; that is one comfort," growled the editor, getting what consolation he could out of

Kent's apparent failure. "They played it too fuf-fine for you."

"Did they?" said Kent.

"It looks pretty much that way, doesn't it? Duvall is the scapegoat, and the only one. About day after to-morrow Bucks' organ, the *Tribune*, will come out with an 'inspired' editorial whitewashing the entire capitol outfit. It will show how Rumford's application for the charter was refused, and how a truly good and beneficent state government has been hoodwinked and betrayed by one of its most trusted supporters."

Kent threw off his street coat and went to get his dressing-gown from the wardrobe in the bedroom. When he came back he said: "Hildreth, you have taken me at my word thus far, and you haven't had occasion to call me either a knave or a fool. Do it a little longer and I'll put you in the way of touching off a set-piece of pyrotechnics that will double discount this mild little snap-cracker of the Belmount business."

"Can't you do it now?"

"No; the time isn't ripe yet. We must let the *Tribune's* coat of whitewash dry in first."

Hildreth wriggled in his chair.

"Kent, if I thought it would do any good, I'd cuc-curse you out; I would for a fact. You are too blamed close-mouthed for any ordinary newspaper use."

But Kent only laughed at him. Now that the strain

was in some measure relaxed he could stand any amount of abuse from so good a friend as the night editor.

"Turn on the hot water if you want to, and if it will relieve the pressure. I know about how you feel; and I'd be as sore as you are if I didn't know that I am going to make it up to you a little later on. But about this oil blaze and to-morrow's—or to-day's—issue of the *Argus*. I hope you haven't said too much."

"I haven't sus-said anything. The stuff trickled in by Associated wire at the last minute, and we had to cut and slash for space and run it pretty much as it came—the bare story."

"All right; that's better. Now suppose you hint darkly that only half of the truth has come out; that more—and more startling—developments may be safely predicted in the immediate hence. Hit it up hard toward the capitol, and don't be afraid of libeling anybody."

Hildreth's eyes narrowed.

"Say, Kent; you have grown a lot in these last few weeks: what is your diet?"

"Hard work—and a determination to make my brag good."

"To down the ring, you mean?"

"Yes; to down the ring."

"Are you any nearer to it than you were when you began?"

"A good many parasangs."

"By Jove! I more than half believe you've got hold of something ded-definite at last!"

"I have, indeed. Hildreth, I have evidence—printable evidence—enough to dig a dozen political graves, one of them big enough to hold Jasper G. Bucks' six-feet-two."

"Let me see it!" said the night editor, eagerly; but Kent laughed and pushed him toward the door.

"Go home and go to bed. I wouldn't show it to you to-night if I had it here—as I have not. I don't go around with a stick of dynamite in my pocket."

"Where is it?" Hildreth asked.

"It is in a safety-deposit box in the vault of the Security Bank; where it is going to stay until I am ready to use it. Go home, I say, and let me go to bed. I'm ragged enough to sleep the clock around."

In spite of his weariness, which was real enough, Kent was up betimes the next morning. He had a wire appointment with Blashfield Hunnicott and two others in Gaston, and he took an early train to keep it. The ex-local attorney met him at the station with a two-seated rig; and on the way to the western suburbs they picked up Frazee, the county assessor, and Orton, the appraiser of the Apache Building and Loan Association.

"Hunnicott has told you what I am after," said Kent,

when the surrey party was made up. "We all know the property well enough, but to have it all fair and above-board, we'll drive out and look it over.so that our knowledge may be said to be fully up to date."

Twenty minutes afterward the quartet was locating the corners of a square in Gaston's remotest suburb; an "addition" whose only improvements were the weathered and rotting street and lot stakings on the bare, brown plain.

" 'Lots 1 to 56 in Block 10, Guilford & Hawk's Addition,' " said Kent, reading from a memorandum in his note-book. "It lies beautifully, doesn't it?"

"Yes; for a chicken farm," chuckled the assessor.

"Well, give me your candid opinion, you two: what is the property worth?"

The Building and Loan man scratched his chin.

"Say fifty dollars for the plot—if you'll fence it."

"No, put it up. You are having a little boom here now: give it the top boom price, if you like."

The two referees drew apart and laid their heads together.

"As property is going here just now, fifty dollars for the inside lots, and one hundred dollars apiece for the corners; say three thousand for the plot. And that is just about three times as much as anybody but a land-crazy idiot would give for it." It was Frazee who announced the decision.

"Thank you both until you are better paid. Now we'll go back to town and you can write me a joint letter stating the fact. If you think it will get you disliked here at home, make the figure higher; make it high enough so that all Gaston will be dead sure to approve."

"You are going to print it?" asked the Building and Loan appraiser.

"I may want to. You may shape it to that end."

"I'll stand by my figures," said Frazee. "It will give me my little chance to get back at the governor. I had it assessed as unimproved suburban property at so much the lot, but he made a kick to the board of equalization and got it put in as unimproved farm land at fifty dollars an acre." Then, looking at his watch: "We'd better be getting back, if you have to catch the Accommodation. Won't you stay over and visit with us?"

"I can't, this time; much obliged," said Kent; and they drove to the Building and Loan office where the joint letter of appraisal was written and signed.

Kent caught his train with something to spare, and was back at the capital in good time to keep a dinner engagement at Miss Van Brock's. He had understood that Ormsby would be the only other guest. But Portia had a little surprise in store for him. Loring had dropped in, unannounced, from the East; and Portia, having first ascertained that Mrs. Brentwood's asthma was prohibitive of late dinings-out, had instructed Ormsby to bring Elinor and Penelope.

Kent had been saving the results of his deep-sea divings in the oil-field investigation to spread them out before Miss Van Brock and Ormsby "in committee," but he put a padlock on his lips when he saw the others.

Portia gave him Elinor to take out, and he would have rejoiced brazenly if the table talk, from the bouillon to the ices, had not been persistently general, turning most naturally upon the Universal Oil Company's successful *coup* in the Belmount field. Kent kept out of it as much as he could, striving manfully to monopolize Elinor for his own especial behoof; but finally Portia laid her commands upon him.

"You are not to be allowed to maroon yourself with Miss Brentwood any longer," she said dictatorially. "You know more about the unpublished part of this Belmount conspiracy than any one else excepting the conspirators themselves, and you are to tell us all about it."

Kent looked up rather helplessly.

"Really, I—I'm not sure that I know anything worth repeating at your dinner-table," he protested.

But Miss Van Brock made a mock of his caution.

"You needn't be afraid. I pledged everybody to secrecy before you came. It is understood that we are in 'executive session.' And if you don't know much, you may tell us what you know now more than you knew before you knew so little as you know now."

"Hold on," said Kent; "will you please say that over again and say it slowly?"

"Never mind," laughed Ormsby. "Miss Portia has a copyright on that. But before you begin, I'd like to know if the newspapers have it straight as far as they have gone into it?"

"They have, all but one small detail. They are saying that Senator Duvall has left the city and the State."

"Hasn't he?" Loring asked.

"He hadn't yesterday."

"My-oh!" said Portia. "They will mob him if he shows himself."

Kent nodded assent.

"He knows it: he is hiding out. But I found him."

"Where?" from the three women in chorus.

"In his own house, out in Pentland Place. The family has been away since April, and the place has been shut up. I took him the first meal he'd had in thirty-six hours."

Portia clapped her hands. The butler came in with the coffee and she dismissed him and bade him shut the doors.

"Now begin at the very tip end of the beginning," she commanded.

Kent had a sharp little tussle with his inborn reticence, thrust it to the wall and told a plain tale.

"It begins in a piece of reckless folly. Shortly after I left Mrs. Brentwood's last Thursday evening I had a curious experience. The shortest way down-town is diagonally through the capitol grounds, but some undefinable impulse led me to go around on the Capitol Avenue side. As I was passing the right wing of the building I saw lights in the governor's room, and in a sudden fit of desperation resolved to go up and have it out with Bucks. It was abnormally foolish, I'll confess. I had nothing definite to go on; but I—well, I was keyed up to just about the right pitch, and I thought I might bluff him."

"Mercy me! You do need a guardian angel worse than anybody I know!" Portia cut in. "Do go on."

Kent nodded.

"I had one that night; angel or demon, whichever you please. I was fairly dragged into doing what I did. When I reached the upper corridor the door of the public anteroom was ajar, and I heard voices. The outer room was not lighted, but the door between it and the governor's private office was open. I went in and stood in that open doorway for as much as five minutes, I think, and none of the four men sitting around the governor's writing-table saw me."

He had his small audience well in hand by this time, and Ormsby's question was almost mechanical.

"Who were the four?"

"After the newspaper rapid-fire of this morning you might guess them all. They were his Excellency, Grafton Hendricks, Rumford, and Senator Duvall. They were in the act of closing the deal as I became an onlooker. Rumford had withdrawn his application for a charter, and another 'straw' company had been formed with Duvall at its head. I saw at once what I fancy Duvall never suspected; that he was going to be made the scapegoat for the ring. They all promised to stand by him—and you see how that promise has been kept."

"Good heavens!" ejaculated Loring. "What a despicable lot of scoundrels! But the bribe: did you learn anything about that?"

"I saw it," said Kent, impressively. "It was a slip of paper passed across the table by Rumford to Bucks, face down. Bucks glanced at it before he thrust it into his pocket, and I had my glimpse, too. It was a draft on a Chicago bank, but I could not read the figures, and I doubt if either of the other conspirators knew the amount. Then the governor tossed a folded paper over to the oil man, saying, 'There is your deed to the choicest piece of property in all Gaston, and you've got it dirt cheap.' I came away at that."

Elinor's sigh was almost a sob; but Miss Van Brock's eyes were dancing.

"Go on, go on," she exclaimed. "That is only the beginning."

Kent's smile was of reminiscent weariness.

"I found it so, I assure you. So far as any usable evidence was concerned, I was no better off than before; it was merely my assertion against their denial—one man against four. But I have had a full week, and it has not been wasted. I needn't bore you with the mechanical details. One of my men followed Bucks' messenger to Chicago—he wouldn't trust the banks here or the mails—and we know now, know it in black on white, with the proper affidavits, that the draft was for two hundred thousand dollars, payable to the order of Jasper G. Bucks. The ostensible consideration was the transfer from Bucks to Rumford of a piece of property in the outskirts of Gaston. I had this piece of land appraised for me to-day by two disinterested citizens of Gaston, and they valued it at a possible, but highly improbable, three thousand."

"Oh, how clumsy!" said Portia, in fine scorn. "Does his Excellency imagine for a moment that any one would be deceived by such a primitive bit of dust-throwing?" and Ormsby also had something to say about the fatal mistakes of the shrewdest criminals.

"It was not so bad," said Kent. "If it should ever be charged that he took money from Rumford, here is a plain business transaction to account for it. The deed, as recorded, has nothing to say of the enormous price paid. The phrasing is the common form used when the parties to the transfer do not wish to make the price public: 'For one dollar to me in hand paid, and other valuable considerations.' Luckily, we are able to establish conclusively what the 'other valuable considerations' were."

"It seems to me that these documents arm and equip you for anything you want to do," said Loring, polishing his eye-glasses after his ingrained habit.

Kent shook his head.

"No; thus far the evidence is all circumstantial, or rather inferential. But I picked up the final link in the chain—the human link—yesterday. One of the detectives had been dogging Duvall. Two days ago the senator disappeared, unaccountably. I put two and two together, and late last evening took the liberty of breaking into his house."

"Alone?" said Elinor, with the courage-worshiping light in the blue-gray eyes.

"Yes; it didn't seem worth while to double the risk. I did it rather clumsily, I suppose, and my greeting was a shot fired at random in the darkness—the senator mistaking me for a burglar, as he afterward explained.

There was no harm done, and the pistol welcome effect-
ually broke the ice in what might otherwise have been
a rather difficult interview. We had it out in an upper
room, with the gas turned low and the window curtains
drawn. To cut a long story short, I finally succeeded in
making him understand what he was in for; that his
confederates had used him and thrown him aside. Then
I went out and brought him some supper."

Ormsby smote softly upon the edge of the table with
an extended forefinger.

"Will he testify?" he asked.

Kent's rejoinder was definitive.

"He has put himself entirely in my hands. He is a
ruined man, politically and socially, and he is desperate.
While I couldn't make him give me any of the details
in the Trans-Western affair, he made a clean breast of
the oil field deal, and I have his statement locked up
with the other papers in the Security vaults."

It was Penelope who gave David Kent his due meed
of praise.

"I am neither a triumphant politician nor a successful detective, but I recognize both when they are pointed
out to me," she said. "Mr. Kent, will you serve these
gentlemen up hot for dinner, or cold for luncheon?"

"Yes," Portia chimed in. "You have outrun your
pace-setters, and I'm proud of you. Tell us what you
mean to do next."

Kent laughed.

"You want to make me say some melodramatic thing about having the shackles forged and snapping them upon the gubernatorial wrists, don't you? It will be prosaic enough from this on. I fancy we shall have no difficulty now in convincing his Excellency of the justice of our proceedings to quash Judge MacFarlane and his receiver."

"But how will you go about it? Surely you can not go personally and threaten the governor of the State!" this from Miss Brentwood.

"Can't I?" said Kent. "Having the score written out and safely committed to memory, that will be quite the easiest number on the programme, I assure you."

But Loring had something to say about the risk.

"Thus far you have not considered your personal safety—haven't had to, perhaps. But you are coming to that now. You are dealing with a desperate man, David; with a gang of them, in fact."

"That is so," said Ormsby. "And, as chairman of the executive committee, I shall have to take steps. We can't afford to bury you just yet, Kent."

"I think you needn't select the pall-bearers yet a while," laughed the undaunted one; and then Miss Van Brock gave the signal and the "executive committee" adjourned to the drawing-room. Here the talk, already so deeply channeled in the groove political, ran

easily to forecastings and predictions for another electoral year; and when Penelope began to yawn behind
her fan, Ormsby took pity on her and the party broke
up.

It was at the moment of leave-taking that Elinor
sought and found her chance to extract a promise from
David Kent.

"I must have a word with you before you do what
you say you are going to do," she whispered hurriedly.
"Will you come to see me?"

"Certainly, if you wish it. But you mustn't let Loring's nervousness infect you. There is no danger."

"There is a danger," she insisted, "a much greater
danger than the one Mr. Loring fears. Come as soon as
you can, won't you?"

It was a new thing for her to plead with him, and he
promised in an access of tumultuous hope reawakened
by her changed attitude. But afterward, when he was
walking down-town with Loring, the episode troubled
him a little; would have troubled him more if he had
not been so deeply interested in Loring's story of the
campaign in the East.

Taking it all in all, the ex-manager's report was encouraging. The New Englanders were by no means
disposed to lie down in the harness, and since the Western Pacific proper was an interstate line, the Advisory
Board had taken its grievance to Washington. Many

of the small stockholders were standing firm, though there had been panicky defections in spite of all that could be done. Loring had no direct evidence to sustain the stock deal theory; but it was morally certain that the Plantagould brokers were picking up Western Pacific by littles wherever they could find it.

"I am inclined to believe we haven't much time to lose," was Kent's comment. "Things will focus here long before Washington can get action. The other lines are bringing a tremendous pressure to bear on Guilford, whose cut rates are demoralizing business frightfully. The fictitious boom in Trans-Western traffic is about worked out; and for political reasons Bucks can't afford to have the road in the hands of his henchmen when the collapse comes. The major is bolstering things from week to week now until the Plantagould people get what they are after—a controlling majority of the stock—and then Judge MacFarlane will come back."

They were within two squares of the Clarendon, and the cross-street was deserted save for a drunken cowboy in shaps and sombrero staggering aimlessly around the corner.

"That's curious," Loring remarked. "Don't you know, I saw that same fellow, or his double, lurching across the avenue as we came out of Alameda Square, and I wondered what he was doing out in that region."

"It was his double, I guess," said Kent. "This one is many pegs too drunk to have covered the distance as fast as we have been walking."

But drunk or sober, the cow-boy turned up again most unexpectedly; this time at the entrance of the alley half-way down the block. In passing he stumbled heavily against Kent; there was a thick-tongued oath, and Loring struck out smartly with his walking-stick. By consequence the man's pistol went off harmlessly in the air: The shot brought a policeman lumbering heavily up from the street beyond, and the skirling of relief whistles shrilled on the night. But the man with a pistol had twisted out of Kent's grasp and was gone in a flash.

"By Jove!" said Loring, breathing hard; "he wasn't as drunk as he seemed to be!"

Kent drew down his cuffs and shook himself straight in his coat.

"No; he wasn't drunk at all; I guess he was the man you saw when we came out of the square." Then, as the policeman came up puffing: "Let me do the talking; the whisky theory will be good enough for the newspapers."

XIX

DEEP-SEA SOUNDINGS

"*Oof!* I feel as if I had been dipped in a warm bath of conspiracy and hung up to dry in the cold storage of nihilism! If you take me to any more meetings of your committee of safety, I shall be like the man without music in his soul—'fit for treasons, stratagems and spoils.'"

Thus Penelope, after the breaking up of the Van Brock dinner party. Elinor had elected to walk the few blocks intervening between Alameda Square and Tejon Avenue, and Ormsby had dismissed his chauffeur with the motor-car.

"I told you beforehand it was going to be a political confab," said the club-man in self-defense. "And you mustn't treat it lightly, either. Ten prattling words of what you have heard to-night set afloat on the gossip pool of this town might make it pretty difficult for our David."

"We are not very likely to babble," retorted Penelope.

"We are not so rich in intimates in this aboriginal desert." But Elinor spoke to the penal clause in his warning.

"Then Mr. Kent's danger is more real than he admitted?" she said.

"It's real enough, I fancy; more real for him than it might be for another man in his place. He is a curious combination, is David: keen and sharp-witted and as cold as an icicle in the planning part; but when it comes to the in-fighting he hasn't sense enough to pound sand, as his New Hampshire neighbors would say."

"I like that side of him best," Penelope averred. "Deliver me from a man of the cold and calculating sort who sits on his impulses, sleeps on his injuries, and takes money-revenge for an insult. Mr. Loring tells a story of a transplanted Vermonter in South America. A hot-headed Peruvian called him a liar, and he said: 'Oh, pshaw! you can't prove it.' "

"What a merciless generalizer you are!" said Ormsby, laughing. "The man who marries you will have his work cut out for him if he proposes to fill the requirements."

"Won't he?" said Penelope. "I can fancy him sitting up nights to figure it all out."

They had reached the Tejon Avenue apartment house, and to Elinor's "Won't you come in?" Ormsby said:

"It's pretty late, but I'll smoke a cigar on the porch, if you'll let me."

Penelope took the hammock, but she kept it only during the first inch of Ormsby's cigar. After her sister had gone in, Elinor went back to the lapsed topic.

"I am rather concerned about Mr. Kent. You described him exactly; and—well, he is past the planning part and into the fighting part. Do you think he will take ordinary precautions?"

"I hope so, I'm sure," rejoined the amateur chairman. "As his business manager I am responsible for him, after a fashion. I was glad to see Loring to-night —glad he has come back. Kent defers to him more than he does to any one else; and Loring is a solid, sober-minded sort."

"Yes," she agreed; "I was glad, too."

After that the talk languished, and the silence was broken only by the distant droning of an electric car, the fizz and click of the arc light over the roadway, and the occasional *dap* of one the great beetles darting hither and thither in the glare.

Ormsby was wondering if the time was come for the successful exploiting of an idea which had been growing on him steadily for weeks, not to say months.

It was becoming more and more evident to him that he was not advancing in the sentimental siege beyond

the first parallel thrown up so skilfully on the last night
of the westward journey. It was not that Elinor was
lacking in loyalty or in acquiescence; she scrupulously
gave him both as an accepted suitor. But though he
could not put his finger upon the precise thing said or
done which marked the loosening of his hold, he knew
he was receding rather than advancing.

Now to a man of expedients the interposition of an
obstacle suggests only ways and means for overcoming
it. Ormsby had certain clear-cut convictions touching
the subjugation of women, and as his stout heart gave
him resolution he lived up to them. When he spoke
again it was of the matter which concerned him most
deeply; and his plea was a gentle repetition of many
others in the same strain.

"Elinor, I have waited patiently for a long time, and
I'll go on doing it, if that is what will come the nearest
to pleasing you. But it would be a prodigious comfort
if I might be counting the days or the weeks. Are you
still finding it impossible to set the limit?"

She nodded slowly, and he took the next step like
a man feeling his way in the dark.

"That is as large an answer as you have ever given
me, I think. Is there any speakable reason?"

"You know the reason," she said, looking away from
him.

"I am not sure that I do. Is it because the money-

gods have been unpropitious—because these robber
barons have looted your railroad?"

"No; that is only part of it—the smallest part."

"I hoped so: if you have too little, I have a good
bit too much. But that corners it in a way to make
me sorry. I am not keeping my promise to win what
you weren't able to give me at first."

"Please don't put it that way. If there be any fault,
it is mine. You have left nothing undone."

The man of expedients ran over his cards reflectively
and decided that the moment for playing his long suit
was fully come.

"Your goodness of heart excuses me where I am to
blame," he qualified. "I am coming to believe that I
have defeated my own cause."

"By being too good to me?" she suggested.

"No; by running where I should have been content
to walk; by shackling you with a promise, and so in
a certain sense becoming your jailer. That is putting
it rather clumsily, but isn't it true?"

"I had never thought of it in that light," she said
unresponsively.

"You wouldn't, naturally. But the fact remains.
It has wrenched your point of view hopelessly aside,
don't you think? I have seen it and felt it all along,
but I haven't had the courage of my convictions."

"In what way?" she asked.

"In the only way the thing can be stood squarely upon its feet. It's hard—desperately hard; and hardest of all for a man of my peculiar build. I am no longer what you would call a young man, Elinor, and I have never learned to turn back and begin all over again with any show of heartiness. They used to say of me in the Yacht Club that if I gained a half-length in a race, I'd hold it if it took the sticks out of my boat."

"I know," she assented absently.

"Well, it's the same way now. But for your sake— or rather for the sake of my love—I am going to turn back for once. You are free again, Elinor. All I ask is that you will let me begin where I left off somewhere on the road between here and Boston last fall."

She sat with clasped hands looking steadily at the darkened windows of the opposite house, and he let her take her own time. When she spoke there was a thrill in her voice that he had never heard before.

"I don't deserve it—so much consideration, I mean," she said; and he made haste to spare her.

"Yes, you do; you deserve anything the best man in the world could do for you, and I'm a good bit short of that."

"But if I don't want you to go back?"

He had gained something—much more than he knew;

and for a tremulous instant he was near to losing it
again by a passionate retraction of all he had been saying. But the cool purpose came to his rescue in time.

"I should still insist on doing it. You gave me what
you could, but I want more, and I am willing to do
what is necessary to win it."

Again she said: "You are too good to me," and again
he contradicted her.

"No; it is hardly a question of goodness; indeed, I
am not sure that it escapes being selfish. But I am
very much in earnest, and I am going to prove it.
Three years ago you met a man whom you thought you
could love—don't interrupt me, please. He was like
some other men we know: he didn't have the courage of
his convictions, lacking the few dollars which might
have made things more nearly equal. May I go on?"

"I suppose you have earned the right to say what
you please," was the impassive reply.

It was the old struggle in which they were so evenly
matched—of the woman to preserve her poise; of the
man to break it down. Another lover might have given
up in despair, but Ormsby's strength lay in holding
on in the face of all discouragements.

"I believe, as much as I believe anything in this
world, that you were mistaken in regard to your feeling for the other man," he went on calmly. "But I

want you to be sure of that for yourself, and you can't
be sure unless you are free to choose between us."

"Oh, don't!—you shouldn't say such things to me,"
she broke out; and then he knew he was gaining ground.

"Yes, I must. We have been stumbling around in
the dark all these months, and I mean to be the lan-
tern-bearer for once in a way. You know, and I know,
and Kent is coming to know. That man is going to
be a success, Elinor: he has it in him, and he sha'n't
lack the money-backing he may need. When he arrives—"

She turned on him quickly, and the blue-gray eyes
were suspiciously bright.

"Please don't bury me alive," she begged.

He saw what he had done; that the nicely calculated
purpose had carried straight and true to its mark; and
for a moment the mixed motives, which are at the bottom of most human sayings and doings, surged in him
like the sea at the vexed tide-line of an iron-bound
coast. But it was the better Brookes Ormsby that
struggled up out of the elemental conflict.

"Don't mistake me," he said. "I am neither better nor worse than other men, I fancy. My motives,
such as they are, would probably turn out to be purely
selfish in the last analysis. I am proceeding on the theory that constraint breeds the desire for the thing it for-

bids; therefore I remove it. Also, it is a part of that theory that the successful David Kent will not appeal to you as the unspoiled country lawyer did. No, I'm not going to spoil him; if I were, I shouldn't be telling you about it. But—may I be brutally frank?—the David Kent who will come successfully out of this political prize-fight will not be the man you have idealized."

There was a muttering of thunder in the air, and the cool precursory breeze of a shower was sweeping through the tree-tops.

"Shall we go into the house?" she asked; and he took it as his dismissal.

"You may; I have kept you up long enough." And then, taking her hand: "Are we safely ashore on the new continent, Elinor? May I come and go as heretofore?"

"You were always welcome, Brookes; you will be twice welcome, now."

It was the first time she had ever called him by his Christian name and it went near to toppling down the carefully reared structure of self-restraint. But he made shift to shore the tottering walls with a playful retort.

"If that is the case, I'll have to think up some more self-abnegations. Good night."

XX

THE WINNING LOSER

Editor Hildreth's prophecy concerning the probable attitude of the administration newspapers in the discussion of the oil field affair waited but a day for its fulfilment. On the Friday morning there appeared in the *Capital Tribune,* the *Midland City Chronicle,* the *Range County Maverick* and the *Agriculta Ruralist* able editorials exonerating the People's Party, its policy and the executive, and heaping mountains of obloquy on the name of Duvall. These editorials were so similar in tone, tenor and texture, as pointedly to suggest a common model—a coincidence which was not allowed to pass unremarked by Hildreth and other molders of public opinion on the opposite side of the political fence.

But Hildreth did not pause at generalities. Two days after the *Universal's* triumph in the Belmount field, the *Argus* began to "hit it up" boldly toward the capitol, and two things came of it. The first was an attempt by some party or parties unknown to buy up a controlling interest in the *Argus*. The second was the waylaying of David Kent in the lobby of the Clarendon Hotel by no less a personage than the Honorable Melton Meigs, attorney-general of the State.

In his first conversation with Ormsby, Kent had spoken of the three leading spirits of the junto as from personal knowledge; but of the three, Bucks, Hendricks and Meigs, the attorney-general was the least known to him. Prior to his nomination on the State ticket Meigs had been best known as the most astute criminal lawyer in the State, his astuteness lying not so much in his ability as a pleader as in a certain oratorical gift by which he was able to convince not only a jury but the public of the entire innocence of his client.

He was a small man physically, with womanish hands and feet, and a beardless face of that prematurely aged cast which is oftenest seen in dwarfs and precocious infants; and his distinguishing characteristic, the one which stuck longest in the mind of a chance acquaintance or a casual observer, was a smile of the congealed sort which served to mask whatever emotion there might be behind it.

Kent had seen little of Meigs since the latter had turned him down in the *quo warranto* matter; and his guard went up quickly when the attorney-general ac-

costed him in the lobby of the hotel and asked for a
private interview.

"I am very much occupied just now, Mr. Meigs," he
demurred; "but if it is a matter of importance—"

"It is; a matter of the greatest importance," was the
smooth-toned reply. "I am sure you will not regret
it if you will give me a few moments, Mr. Kent."

Kent decided quickly. Being forewarned, there was
nothing to fear.

"We will go up to my rooms, if you please," he said,
leading the way to the elevator; and no other word
was spoken until they were behind closed doors on the
fourth floor.

"A prefatory remark may make my business with
you seem a little less singular, Mr. Kent," Meigs began,
when Kent had passed his cigar-case and the attorney-
general had apologized for a weak digestive tract. "On
wholly divergent lines and from wholly different motives we are both working toward the same end, I believe, and it has occurred to me that we might be of
some assistance to each other."

Kent's rejoinder was a mute signal to the effect that
he was attending.

"Some little time ago you came to me as the legal
representative of the stock-holders of the Trans-Western Railway Company, and I did not find it possible
at that time to meet your wishes in the matter of a

quo warranto information questioning Judge MacFarlane's election and status. You will admit, I presume,
that your demand was a little peremptory?"

"I admit nothing," said Kent, curtly. "But for the
sake of expediting present matters—"

"Precisely," was the smiling rejoinder. "You will
note that I said 'at that time.' Later developments—
more especially this charge made openly by the public press of juggling with foreign corporations—have
led me to believe that as the public prosecutor I may
have duties which transcend all other considerations—
of loyalty to a party standard—of—"

Kent took his turn at interrupting.

"Mr. Meigs, there is nothing to be gained by indi-
rection. May I ask you to come to the point?"

"Briefly, then: the course pursued by Senator Duvall in the Belmount affair leaves an unproved charge
against others; a charge which I am determined to
sift to the bottom—you see, I am speaking quite frankly.
That charge involves the reputation of men high in
authority; but I shall be strong to do my sworn duty,
Mr. Kent; I ask you to believe that."

Kent nodded and waved him on.

"You will readily understand the delicacy of the task,
and how, in the nature of things, I am handicapped and
hedged up on every side. Evidence—of a kind to enable

me to assail a popular idol—is exceedingly difficult to procure."

"It is," said Kent, grimly.

"Exactly. But in revolving the matter in my own mind, I thought of you. You are known at the capitol, Mr. Kent, and I may say throughout the State, as the uncompromising antagonist of the State administration. I have asked myself this: Is it possible that a cool-headed, resolute attorney like Mr. David Kent would move so far and so determinedly in this matter of antagonism without substantially paving the ground under his feet with evidence as he went along?"

Kent admitted that it was possible, but highly improbable.

"So I decided," was the smile-tempered rejoinder. "In that case it only remains for me to remind you of your public duty, Mr. Kent; to ask you in the name of justice and of the people of the State, to place your information in the hands of the public prosecutor."

Kent's face betrayed nothing more than his appreciation of the confidence reposed in him by the man whose high sense of official honor was making him turn traitor to the party leader who had dragged him through a successful election.

"I have what evidence I need, Mr. Meigs," he declared. "But if I make no secret of this, neither do I conceal the fact that the motive *pro bono publico* has had little to do with its accumulating. I want justice first for what might be called a purely private end, and I mean to have it."

"Pre-cisely," smiled the attorney-general. "And now we are beginning to see our way a little clearer. It is not too late for us to move in the *quo warranto* proceedings. If you will call at my office I shall be glad to reopen the matter with you."

"And the price?" said Kent, shortly.

"Oh, my dear sir! must we put it upon the ground of a *quid pro quo?* Rather let us say that we shall help each other. You are in a position to assist me very materially: I may be in a position to serve your turn. Come to my office to-morrow morning prepared to do your duty as an honest, loyal citizen, and you will find me quite willing to meet you half-way."

Kent rose and opened his watch.

"Mr. Meigs, I have given you your opportunity, and you have seemed to give me mine," he said coolly. "Will you pardon me if I say that I can paddle my own canoe—if I ask you to assure his Excellency that one more device of his to escape punishment has been tried and found wanting?"

For a flitting moment the cast-iron smile faded from the impassive face of the attorney-general and an unrelenting devil came to peer out of the colorless eyes. Then Meigs rose cat-like and laid his hand on the door-knob.

"Do I understand that you refuse to move in a matter which should be the first duty of a good citizen, Mr. Kent?" he asked purringly.

"I certainly do refuse to fall into any such clumsy trap as you have been trying to bait for me, Mr. Meigs," said David Kent, dropping back into his former curtness.

The door opened slowly under the impulse of the slender womanish hand.

"You have a task of some magnitude before you, Mr. Kent. You can scarcely hope to accomplish it alone."

"Meaning that you would like to know if the fight will go on if I should chance to meet another drunken cow-boy with a better aim? It will."

The door closed softly behind the retreating figure of the attorney-general, and Kent released the spring of the night-latch. Then he went to the dropped portière at the farther end of the room, drew it aside and looked in on a man who was writing at a table pushed out between the windows.

"You heard him, Loring?" he asked.

The ex-manager nodded.

"They are hard pressed," he said. Then, looking up quickly: "You could name your price if you wanted to close out the stock of goods in hand, David."

"I shall name it when the time comes. Are you ready to go over to the *Argus* office with me? I want to have a three-cornered talk with Hildreth."

"In a minute. I'll join you in the lobby if you don't want to wait."

It was in the afternoon of the same day that Kent found a note in his key-box at the Clarendon asking him to call up 124 Tejon Avenue by telephone. He did it at once, and Penelope answered. The key-box note had been placed at Elinor's request, and she, Miss Penelope, could not say what was wanted; neither could she say definitely when her sister would be in. Elinor had gone out an hour earlier with Mr. Ormsby and Miss Van Brock in Mr. Ormsby's motor-car. When was he, David Kent, coming up? Did he know they were talking of spending the remainder of the summer at Breezeland Inn? And where was Mr. Loring all this time?

Kent made fitting answers to all these queries, hung up the ear-piece and went away moodily reflective. He was due at a meeting of the executive committee of the Civic League, but he let the public business wait while

he speculated upon the probable object of Elinor's telephoning him.

Now there is no field in which the inconsistency of
human nature is so persistent as in that which is bound-
ed by the sentimentally narrowed horizon of a man in
love. With Ormsby at the nodus of his point of view,
David Kent made no secret of his open rivalry of the
millionaire, declaring his intention boldly and taking
no shame therefor. But when he faced about toward
Elinor he found himself growing hotly jealous for her
good faith; careful and fearful lest she should say or
do something not strictly in accordance with the letter
and spirit of her obligations as Ormsby's *fiancée*.

For example: at the "conspiracy dinner," as Loring
dubbed it, Ormsby being present to fight for his own
hand, Kent, as we have seen, had boldly monopolized
Miss Brentwood, and would have committed himself
still more pointedly had the occasion favored him. None
the less, when Elinor had begged him privately to see
her before moving in the attack on the junto, he had almost resented the implied establishing of confidential
relations with her lover's open rival.

For this cause he had been postponing the promised
visit, and thereby postponing the taking of the final
step in the campaign of intimidation. The unexplained
telephone call decided him, however. He would go and
see Elinor and have the ordeal over with.

But as a preliminary he dined that evening with Ormsby at the Camelot Club, and over the coffee had it out with him.

"I am going out to see Miss Brentwood to-night," he announced abruptly. "Have you any objection?"

The millionaire gave him the shrewdest of overlooks, ending with a deep-rumbling laugh.

"Kent, you are the queerest lot I have ever discovered, and that is saying a good bit. Why, in the name of all the proprieties, should I object?"

"Your right is unchallenged," Kent admitted.

"Is it? Better ask Miss Brentwood about that. She might say it isn't."

"I don't understand," said Kent, dry-tongued.

"Don't you? Perhaps I'd better explain: she might find it a little difficult. You have been laboring under the impression that we are engaged, haven't you?"

"Laboring under the—why, good heavens, man! it's in everybody's mouth!"

"Curious, isn't it, how such things get about," commented the player of long suits. "How do you suppose they get started?"

"I don't suppose anything about it, so far as we two are concerned; I have your own word for it. You said you were the man in possession."

Ormsby laughed again.

"You are something of a bluffer yourself, David. Did you let my little stagger scare you out?"

David Kent pushed his chair back from the table and nailed Ormsby with a look that would have made a younger man betray himself.

"Do you mean to tell me that there is no engagement between you and Miss Brentwood?"

"Just that." Ormsby put all the nonchalance he could muster into the laconic reply, but he was anticipating the sequent demand which came like a shot out of a gun.

"And there never has been?"

Ormsby grinned.

"When you are digging a well and have found your stream of water, it's folly to go deeper, David. Can't you let 'good enough' alone?"

Kent turned it over in his mind, frowning thoughtfully into his coffee-cup. When he spoke it was out of the mid-heart of manliness.

"I wish you would tell me one thing, Ormsby. Am I responsible for—for the present state of affairs?"

Ormsby stretched the truth a little; partly for Elinor's sake; more, perhaps, for Kent's.

"You have done nothing that an honorable rival—and incidentally a good friend of mine—might not do. Therefore you are not responsible."

"That is putting it very diplomatically," Kent mused. "I am afraid it does not exonerate me wholly."

"Yes, it does. But it doesn't put me out of the running, you understand. I'm 'forninst' you yet; rather more stubbornly than before, I fancy."

Kent nodded.

"That, of course; I should think less of you if you were not. And you shall have as fair a show as you are giving me—which is saying a lot. Shall we go and smoke?"

XXI

It was still early in the evening when Kent mounted
the steps of the Brentwood apartment house. Mother
and daughters were all on the porch, but it was Mrs.
Brentwood who welcomed him.

"We were just wondering if you would imagine the
message which Elinor was going to send, and didn't,
and come out to see what was wanted," she said. "I
am in need of a little legal advice. Will you give me
a few minutes in the library?"

Kent went with her obediently, but not without
wondering why she had sent for him, of all the retain-
able lawyers in the capital. And the wonder became
amazement when she opened her confidence. She had
received two letters from a New York broker who
offered to buy her railroad stock at a little more than
the market price. To the second letter she had replied,
asking a price ten points higher than the market. At
this the broker had apparently dropped the attempted
negotiation, since there had been no more letters. What
would Mr. Kent advise her to do—write again?

Kent smiled inwardly at the good lady's definition of "legal advice," but he rose promptly to the occasion. If he were in Mrs. Brentwood's place, he would not write again; nor would he pay any attention whatever to any similar proposals from any source. Had there been any others?

Mrs. Brentwood confessed that there had been; that a firm of Boston brokers had also written her. Did Mr. Kent know the meaning of all this anxiety to buy in Western Pacific when the stock was going down day by day?

Kent took time for reflection before he answered. It was exceedingly difficult to eliminate the personal factor in the equation. If all went well, if by due process of law the Trans-Western should be rescued out of the hands of the wreckers, the property would be a long time recovering from the wounds inflicted by the cut rates and the Guilford bad management. In consequence, any advance in the market value of the stock must be slow and uncertain under the skilfullest handling. But, while it might be advisable for Mrs. Brentwood to take what she could get, the transfer of the three thousand shares at the critical moment might be the death blow to all his hopes in the fight for retrieval.

Happily, he hit upon the expedient of shifting the responsibility for the decision to other shoulders.

"I scarcely feel competent to advise you in a matter

which is personal rather than legal," he said at length. "Have you talked it over with Mr. Ormsby?"

Mrs. Brentwood's reply was openly contemptuous.

"Brookes Ormsby doesn't know anything about dollars. You have to express it in millions before he can grasp it. He says for me not to sell at any price."

Kent shook his head.

"I shouldn't put it quite so strongly. At the same time, I am not the person to advise you."

The shrewd eyes looked up at him quickly.

"Would you mind telling me why, Mr. Kent?"

"Not in the least. I am an interested party. For weeks Mr. Loring and I have been striving by all means to prevent transfers of the stock from the hands of the original holders. I don't want to advise you to your hurt; but to tell you to sell might be to undo all that has been done."

"Then you are still hoping to get the railroad out of Major Guilford's hands?"

"Yes."

"And in that case the price of the stock will go up again?"

"That is just the difficulty. It may be a long time recovering."

"Do you think the sale of my three thousand shares would make any difference?" she asked.

"There is reason to fear that it would make all the difference."

She was silent for a time, and when she spoke again Kent realized that he was coming to know an entirely unsuspected side of Elinor's mother.

"It makes it pretty hard for me," she said slowly. "This little drib of railroad stock is all that my girls have left out of what their father willed them. I want to save it if I can."

"So do I," said David Kent, frankly; "and for the same reason."

Mrs. Brentwood confined herself to a dry "Why?"

"Because I have loved your elder daughter well and truly ever since that summer at the foot of Old Croydon, Mrs. Brentwood, and her happiness and well-being concern me very nearly."

"You are pretty plain-spoken, Mr. Kent. I suppose you know Elinor is to be married to Brookes Ormsby?" Mrs. Brentwood was quite herself again.

Kent dexterously equivocated.

"I know they have been engaged for some time," he said; but the small quibble availed him nothing.

"Which one of them was it told you it was broken off?" she inquired.

He smiled in spite of the increasing gravity of the situation.

"You may be sure it was not Miss Elinor."

"Humph!" said Mrs. Brentwood. "She didn't tell me, either. 'Twas Brookes Ormsby, and he said he wanted to begin all over again, or something of that sort. He is nothing but a foolish boy, for all his hair is getting thin."

"He is a very honorable man," said Kent.

"Because he is giving you another chance? I don't mind telling you plainly that it won't do any good, Mr. Kent."

"Why?" he asked in his turn.

"For several reasons: one is that Elinor will never marry without my consent; another is that she can't afford to marry a poor man."

Kent rose.

"I am glad to know how you feel about it, Mrs. Brentwood: nevertheless, I shall ask you to give your consent some day, God willing."

He expected an outburst of some sort, and was telling himself that he had fairly provoked it, when she cut the ground from beneath his feet.

"Don't you go off with any such foolish notion as that, David Kent," she said, not unsympathetically. "She's in love with Brookes Ormsby, and she knows it now, if she didn't before." And it was with this arrow rankling in him that Kent bowed himself out and went to join the young women on the porch.

XXII

The conversation on the Brentwood porch was chiefly
of Breezeland Inn as a health and pleasure resort, until
an outbound electric car stopped at the corner below
and Loring came up to make a quartet of the trio behind the vine-covered trellis.

Later, the ex-manager confessed to a desire for music
—Penelope's music—and the twain went in to the sitting-room and the piano, leaving Elinor and Kent to
make the best of each other as the spirit moved them.

It was Elinor's chance for free speech with Kent—the
opportunity she had craved. But now it was come, the
simplicity of the thing to be said.had departed and an
embarrassing complexity had taken its place. Under
other conditions Kent would have been quick to see her
difficulty, and would have made haste to efface it; but
he was fresh from the interview with Mrs. Brentwood,
and the Parthian arrow was still rankling. None the
less, he was the first to break away from the commonplaces.

"What is the matter with us this evening?" he queried. "We have been sitting here talking the vaguest trivialities ever since Penelope and Loring side-tracked us. I haven't been doing anything I am ashamed of; have you?"

"Yes," she confessed, looking away from him.

"What is it?"

"I asked a certain good friend of mine to come to see me when there is good reason to believe he didn't want to come."

"What makes you think he didn't want to come?"

"Why—I don't know; did he?" She had turned upon him swiftly with an outflash of the playful daring which had been one of his major fetterings in time past—the ecstatic little charm that goes with quick repartee and instant and sympathetic apprehension.

"You have never yet asked anything of him that he wasn't glad enough to give," he rejoined, keeping up the third person figurative.

"Is that saying very much—or very little?"

"Very little, indeed. But it is only your askings that have been lacking—not his good will."

"That was said like the David Kent I used to know. Are you really quite the same?"

"I hope not," he protested gravely. "People used to say of me that I matured late, and year by year as I look back I can see that it was a true saying. I have done some desperately boyish things since I was a man grown; things that make me tingle when I recall them."

"Like wasting a whole summer exploring Mount Croydon with a—a somebody who did not mature late?"

"No; I wasn't counting that among my lapses. An older man than I ever hope to be might find excuses for the Croydon summer. I meant in other ways. For one thing, I have craved success as I think few men have ever craved it; and yet my plowings in that field have been ill-timed and boyish to a degree."

She shook her head.

"I don't know how you measure success; it is a word of so many, many meanings. But I think you are your own severest critic."

"That may be; but the fact remains. It is only within the past few months that I have begun to get a true inkling of things; to know, for example, that opportunities are things to be compelled—not waited for."

She was looking away from him again.

"I am not sure that I like you better for your having discovered yourself. I liked the other David Kent."

He smiled rather joylessly.

"Somebody has said that for every new point of view gained we have to sacrifice all the treasures of the old. I am sorry if I am disappointing you."

"I don't know that you are. And yet, when you were sitting at Miss Van Brock's table the other evening telling us about your experience with the politicians, I kept saying to myself that I didn't know you—that I had never known you."

"I wish I knew just how to take that," he said dubiously.

"I wish I knew how to make you understand," she returned; and then: "I could have made the other David Kent understand."

"You are in duty bound to try to make this one understand, don't you think? You spoke of a danger which was not the violent kind, such as Loring fears. What is it?"

"You have had two whole days," she rejoined. "Haven't you discovered it?"

"I haven't found anything to fear but failure," was his reply.

"That is it; you have given it a name—its only true name—failure."

"But I am not going to fail."

"You mean you are going to take our railroad away from these men who have stolen it?"

"That is what I mean."

"And you will do it by threatening to expose them?"

"I shall tell Governor Bucks what I know about the oil field deal, assuring him that I shall publish the facts if he doesn't let the law take its course in ousting Judge MacFarlane and the receiver."

She rose and stood before him, leaning against one of the vine-clad porch pillars with her hands behind her.

"David Kent, are there any circumstances in which you would accept a bribe?"

He answered her in all seriousness.

"They say every man has his price: mine is higher than any bid they have yet made—or can make, I hope."

"Why don't you let *them* bribe *you?*" she asked coolly. "Is it because it is inexpedient—because there is more 'success' the other way?"

He tried to emulate her coolness and made a failure of it.

"Have I ever done anything to make you think I had thrown common honesty and self-respect overboard?" he demanded.

Her answer was another question, sharp-edged and well thrust home.

"Is it any worse to take a bribe than it is to give one? You have just admitted that you are going to buy the governor's neutrality, you know."

"I don't see it in that light at all."

"The other David Kent would have seen it. He would have said: These men are public criminals. If I can not bring them to justice, I can at least expose them to the scorn of all good men. Therefore I have no right to bargain with them."

Kent was silent for a long time. When he spoke it was
to say:

"Why have you done this, Elinor?"

"Because I had to, David. Could I do less?"

"I suppose not. It's in the blood—in your blood and
mine. Other folk call it the Puritan virus of over-
righteousness, and scoff at it. I don't know: sometimes
I think they have the best of the argument."

"I can't believe you are quite sincere when you say
that," she asserted.

"Yes, I am. One can not compromise with conscience; that says itself. But I have come to believe
latterly that one's conscience may be morbidly acute, or
even diseased. I'll admit I've been taking treatment."

"That sounds very dreadful," she rejoined.

"It does, doesn't it? Yet it had to be done. As I intimated a few minutes ago, my life has hitherto been a
sort of unostentatious failure. I used to think it was
because I was outclassed: I know now it has been because I wouldn't do as other men do. It has been a
rather heart-breaking process—to sort out the scruples,
admitting the just and overriding the others—but I
have been given to see that it is the price of success."

"I want you to succeed," she said.

"Pardon me; I don't think you do. You have reopened the door to doubt, and if I admit the doubt I
shall fail."

The sonata Penelope was playing was approaching its finale, and Elinor was suddenly shaken with a trembling fit of fear—the fear of consequences which might involve this man's entire future. She knew Kent was leaning on her, and she saw herself as one who has ruthlessly thrust an iron bar among the wheels of a delicate mechanism. Who was she to be his conscience-keeper— to stand in the way and bid him go back? Were her own motives always so exalted? Had she not once deliberately debated this same question of expediency, to the utter abasement of her own ideals?

Penelope had left the piano, and Loring was looking at his watch. Kent saw them through the open window and got upon his feet.

"Grantham is saying he had no idea it was so late," he hazarded. "If I thank you for what you have said I am afraid it must be as the patient thanks the surgeon for the knife-stroke which leaves him a cripple for life."

It was the one word needed to break her resolution.

"Oh, forget it; please forget it!" she said. "I had no right . . You are doing a man's work in the world, and it must be done in a man's way. If I can not help, you must not let me hinder. If you let anything I have said discourage you, I shall never cease regretting it."

His smile was a mere indrawing of the lips.

"Having opened the door, you would try to shut it again, would you? How like a woman! But I am

afraid it can't be done. I had been trying to keep away
from that point of view. . . There is much to be
said on both sides. There was a time when I wouldn't
have gone into such a thing as this fight with the junto;
but being in, I should have seen it through regardless of
the public welfare—ignoring that side of it. I can't
do it now; you have shown me that I can't."

"But I don't want to be a stumbling-block," she insisted. "Won't you believe that I wanted to help?"

"I believe that your motive was all it should be; yes.
But the result is the same."

Loring and Penelope were coming out, and the end
of their privacy was at hand.

"What will you do?" she asked.

"I don't know: nothing that I had meant to do. It
was a false start and I am back under the wire again."

"But you must not turn back unless you are fully
convinced of the wrong of going on," she protested.

"Didn't you mean to convince me?"

"No—yes—I don't know. I—it seems very clear to
me; but I want it to seem clear to you. Doesn't your
conscience tell you that you ought to turn back?"

"No," he said shortly; but he immediately qualified
the denial. "You may be right: I am afraid you are
right. But I shall have to fight it out for myself. There
are many things to consider. If I hold my hand, these
bucaneers will triumph over the stockholders, and a

host of innocent people will suffer loss." Then, seeing the quick-springing tears in her eyes: "But you mustn't be sorry for having done what you had to do; you have nothing to reproach yourself for."

"Oh, but I have!" she said; and so they parted.

XXIII

When the Receiver Guilfords, great and small, set
their official guillotines at work lopping off department
heads, they commonly ignore a consequence overlooked
by many; namely, the possible effect of such wholesale
changes in leadership upon the rank and file.

The American railroad in its unconsolidated stage is
a modern feudalism. Its suzerains are the president
and board of directors; its clan chiefs are the men who
have built it and fought for its footing in the sharply
contested field of competition. To these leaders the
rank and file is loyal, as loyalty is accorded to the men
who build and do, rather than to their successors who
inherit and tear down. Add to this the supplanting of
competent executive officers by a staff of political trench-
ermen, ignorant alike of the science of railroading, and
the equally important sub-science of industrial manhandling, and you have the kindling for the fire of in-
surrection which had been slowly smoldering in the

(283)

Trans-Western service since the day when Major Guilford had issued his general order Number One.

At first the fire had burned fitfully, eating its way into the small economies; as when the section hands pelt stray dogs with new spikes from the stock keg, and careless freight crews seed down the right of way with cast-off links and pins; when engineers pour oil where it should be dropped, and firemen feed the stack instead of the steam-dome.

But later, when the incompetence of the new officials became the mocking gibe of the service, and the cut-rate avalanche of traffic had doubled all men's tasks, the flames rose higher, and out of the smoke of them loomed the shape of the dread demon of demoralization.

First it was Hank Brodrick, who misread his orders and piled two freights in a mountain of wreckage in the deep cut between Long Pine and Argenta. Next it was an overworked night man who lost his head and cranked a switch over in front of the west-bound Flyer, laying the 1020 on her side in the ditch, with the postal and the baggage-car neatly telescoped on top to hold her down.

Two days later it was Patsy Callahan; and though he escaped with his life and his job, it was a close call. He was chasing a time freight with the fast mail, and the freight was taking the siding at Delhi to let him pass. One of the red tail-lights of the freight had gone out, and Callahan mistook the other for the target lamp of the second switch. He had time to yell at his fireman, to fling himself upon the throttle-bar and to set the air-brake before he began to turn Irish handsprings down the embankment; but the wrecking crew camped two whole days at Delhi gathering up the debris.

It was well on in the summer, when the two divisions, east and west, were strewn with wreckage and the pit tracks in the shops and shop yard were filled to over-flowing with crippled engines, that the insurrectionaries began to gather in their respective labor groups to dis-cuss the growing hazards of railroading on the Trans-Western.

The outcome was a protest from the Brotherhood of Locomotive Engineers, addressed to the receiver in the name of the organization, setting forth in plain terms the grievance of the members, and charging it bluntly to bad management. This was followed immediately by similar complaints from the trainmen, the telegraphers, and the firemen; all praying for relief from the incubus of incompetent leadership. Not to be behind these, came the Amalgamated Machinists, demanding an increase of pay for night work and overtime; and last, but not least, an intimation went forth from the Federative Council of all these labor unions hinting at possible political consequences and the alienation of the labor vote if the abuses were not corrected.

"What d'ye calc'late the major will do about it?" said Brodrick, in the roundhouse conclave held daily by the trainmen who were hung up or off duty. "Will he listen to reason and give us a sure-enough railroad man or two at the top?"

"Not in *ein* t'ousand year," quoth "Dutch" Tischer, Callahan's alternate on the fast mail. "Haf you not de *Arkoos* been reading? It is bolotics from der beginning to der ent; mit der governor *vorwärts.*"

"Then I am tellin' you-all right now there's goin' to be a heap o' trouble," drawled "Pike County" Griggs, the oldest engineer on the line. "The shopmen are b'ilin'; and if the major puts on that blanket cut in wages he's talkin' about—"

" 'If'," broke in Callahan, with fine scorn. " 'Tis slaping on yer injuries ye are, Misther Griggs. The notice is out; 'twas posted in the shops this day."

"Then that settles it," said Griggs, gloomily. "When does it take hold?"

"The first day av the month to come. An' they're telling me it catches everybody, down to the missinger b'ys in the of'ces."

Griggs got upon his feet, yawning and stretching before he dropped back into his corner of the wooden settle.

"You lissen at me: if that's the fact, I'm tellin' you-all that every wheel on this blame', hoodooed railroad is goin' to stop turnin' at twelve o'clock on the night before that notice takes hold."

An oil-begrimed wiper crawled from under the 1031, spat at the dope-bucket and flung his bunch of waste therein.

"Gur-r-r! Let 'em stop," he rasped. "The dope's bad, and the waste's bad; and the old man has cut out the 'lectrics and put us back on *them*," kicking a small jacket lamp to the bottom of an empty stall. "Give 's a chaw o' yer smokin' plug, Mr. Callahan," and he held out his hand.

Callahan emptied the hot ashes from his black pipe into the open palm.

" 'Tis what ye get f'r yer impidunce, an' f'r layin' tongue to ould man Durgan, ye scut. 'Tis none av his doin's—the dhirty oil an' the chape waste an' the jacket lamps. It's ay-conomy, me son; an' the other name f'r that is a rayceiver."

"Is Durgan with us?" asked Brodrick.

"He's wit' himself, as a master-mechanic shu'd be," said Callahan. "So's M'Tosh. But nayther wan n'r t'other av thim'll take a thrain out whin the strike's on. They're both Loring min."

At the mention of Loring's name Griggs looked up from the stick he was whittling.

"No prospects o' the Boston folks getting the **road back** again, I reckon," he remarked tentatively.

"You should read dose *Arkoos* newsbapers: den you should know somet'ings alretty, ain'd it?" said Tischer.

Brodrick laughed.

"If you see it in the papers, it's so," he quoted. "What the *Argus* doesn't say would make a 'nough sight bigger book than what it does. But I've been kind o' watchin' that man Kent. He's been hot after the major, right from the jump. You rec'lect what he said in them Civic League talks o' his: said these politicians had stole the road, hide, hair an' horns."

"I'm onto him," said Callahan. "'Tis a bird he is. Oleson was telling me. The Scandehoovian was thryin' to get him down to Gaston the day they ray-ceivered us. Jarl says he wint a mile a minut', an' the little man never turned a hair."

"Is he here yet; or did he go back to God's country?" asked Engineer Scott, leaning from the cab window of the 1031.

"He's here; and so is Mr. Loring. They're stopping at the Clarendon," said Brodrick.

"Then they haven't quit," drawled Griggs; adding: "I wonder if they have a ghost of a show against the politicals?"

"Has annybody been to see 'em?" asked Callahan.

"There's a notion for you, Scott," said Brodrick. Scott was the presiding officer in the B. of L. E. local.

"Get up a committee from the Federative to go and ask Mr. Loring if there's any use in our tryin' to hold on."

The wiper was killing time at a window which commanded a view of the upper yards, with the Union Passenger Station at the end of the three-mile vista. Being a late comer in the field, the Trans-Western had scanty track rights in the upper yard; its local headquarters were in the shops suburb, where the two division main lines proper began and ended, diverging, the one to the eastward and the other to the west.

"Holy smut!" said the wiper. "See Dicky Dixon comin' out with the Flyer! How's that for ten miles an hour in the city limits?"

It was a foot-note commentary on the way the service was going to pieces. Halkett, the "political" general superintendent, had called Dixon on the carpet for not making time with his train. "If you're afraid to run, say so, and we'll get a man that isn't," Halkett had said; and here was Dixon coming down a borrowed track in a busy yard at the speed which presupposes a ninety-pound rail and nothing in the way.

The conclave had gathered at the wiper's window.

"The dum fool!" said Brodrick. "If anything gets in front of him—"

There was a suburb street-crossing three hundred yards townward from the "yard limits" telegraph office,

which stood in the angle formed by the diverging
tracks of the two divisions. Beyond the yard the
street became a country road, well traveled as the principal southern inlet to the city. When Dixon was within two train-lengths of the crossing, a farm wagon appeared, driven between the cut freight trains on the
sidings directly in the path of the Flyer. The men at
the roundhouse window heard the crash of the splinter-
ing wagon above the roar of the train; and the wiper
on the window seat yelped like a kicked dog and went
sickly green under his mask of grime.

"There it is again," said Scott, when Dixon had
brought his train to a stand two hundred yards beyond
the "limits" office where he should have stopped for
orders. "We're all hoodooed, the last one of us. I'll
get that committee together this afternoon and go and
buzz Mr. Loring."

Now it fell out that these things happened on a day
when the tide of retrieval was at its lowest ebb; the
day, namely, in which Kent had told Loring that he
was undecided as to his moral right to use the evidence
against Bucks as a lever to pry the Trans-Western out
of the grip of the junto. It befell, also, that it was the
day chosen by two other men, not members of the labor
unions, in which to call upon the ex-manager; and
Loring found M'Tosh, the train-master, and Durgan,
the master-mechanic, waiting for him in the hotel cor-

ridor when he came in from a late luncheon at the Camelot Club.

"Can you give us a few minutes, Mr. Loring?" asked M'Tosh, when Loring had shaken hands with them, not as subordinates.

"Surely. My time is not very valuable, just at present. Come in, and I'll see if Mr. Kent has left me any cigars."

"Humph!" said Durgan, when the ex-manager had gone into Kent's room to rummage for the smoke offering. "And they give us the major in the place of such a man as that!" with a jerk of his thumb toward the door of the bedroom.

"Come off!" warned M'Tosh; "he'll hear you." And when Loring came back with the cigars there was dry humor in his eye.

"You mustn't let your loyalty to the old guard get you into trouble with the receiver," he cautioned; and they both smiled.

"The trouble hasn't waited for our bringing," said M'Tosh. "That is why we are here. Durgan has soured on his job, and I'm more than sick of mine. It's hell, Mr. Loring. I have been at it twenty years, and I never saw such crazy railroading in any one of them."

"Bad management, you mean?"

"Bad management at the top, and rotten demoralization at the bottom as a natural consequence. We can't

be sure of getting a train out of the yards without
accident. Dixon is as careful a man as ever stepped on
an engine, and he smashed a farmer's wagon and killed
the farmer this morning within two train-lengths of
the shop junction."

"Drunk?" inquired the ex-manager.

"Never a drop; Dixon's a Prohibitionist, dyed in the
wool. But just before he took his train, Halkett had
him in the sweat-box, jacking him up for not making
his time. He came out red in the face, jumped on his
engine, and yanked the Flyer down the yards forty
miles an hour."

"And what is your trouble, Durgan?" asked Loring.

"Another side of the same thing. I wrote Major Guilford yesterday, telling him that six pit gangs, all the
roundhouse 'emergencies' and two outdoor repair squads
couldn't begin to keep the cripples moving; and within
a week every one of the labor unions has kicked through
its grievance committee. His reply is an order announc-
ing a blanket cut in wages, to go into effect the first of
the month. That means a strike and a general tie-up."

Loring shook his head regretfully.

"It hurts me," he admitted. "We had the best-hand-
led piece of railroad in the West, and I give the credit
to the men that did the handling. And to have it
wrecked by a gang of incompetent salary-grabbers—"

The two left-overs nodded.

"That's just it, Mr. Loring," said M'Tosh. "And we're here to ask you if it's worth while for us to stick to the wreck any longer. Are you folks doing anything?"

"We have been trying all legal means to break the grip of the combination—yes."

"And what are the prospects?" It was the master-mechanic who wanted to know.

"They are not very bright at present, I must confess. We have the entire political ring to fight, and the odds are overwhelming."

"You say you've been trying 'legal means'," M'Tosh put in. "Can't we down them some other way? I believe you could safely count on the help of every man in the service, barring the politicals."

Loring smiled.

"I don't say we should scruple to use force if there were any way to apply it. But the way doesn't offer."

"I didn't know," said the train-master, rising to close the interview. "But if the time ever comes, all you or Mr. Kent will have to do will be to pass the word. Maybe you can think of some way to use the strike. It hasn't been declared yet, but you can bet on it to a dead moral certainty."

It was late in the afternoon of the same day that the Federative Council sent its committee, chairmaned by Engineer Scott, to interview the ex-general manager

at his rooms in the Clarendon. Scott acted as spokesman, stating the case with admirable brevity and con-
ciseness, and asking the same question as that pro-
pounded by the train-master, to wit, if there were any
prospect of a return of the road to its former management.

Loring spoke more hopefully to the committee than
he had to Durgan and M'Tosh. There had been a little
more time for reflection, and there was the heartening
which comes upon the heels of unsolicited help-tender-
ings, however futile. So he told the men that the stock-
holders were moving heaven and earth in the effort to
recover their property; that until the road should be
actually sold under an order from the court, there was
always room for hope. The committee might rest assured that no stone would be left unturned; also that
the good will of the rank and file would not be forgotten
in the day of restitution, if that day should ever dawn.

When Loring was through, Engineer Scott did a thing
no union man had ever done before: he asked an ex-
general manager's advice touching the advisability of a
strike.

"I can't say as to that," was the prompt reply. "You
know your own business best—what it will cost, and
what it may accomplish. But I've been on the other
side often enough to be able to tell you why most strikes
fail, if you care to know."

A broad grin ran the gamut of the committee.

"Tell us what to do, and we'll do it, Mr. Loring," said Scott, briefly.

"First, then, have a definite object and one that will stand the test of public opinion; in this case we'll say it is the maintenance of the present wage-scale and the removal of incompetent officers and men. Secondly, make your protest absolutely unanimous to a man. Thirdly, don't give the major time to fortify: keep your own counsels, and don't send in your ultimatum until the final moment. And, lastly, shun violence as you would a temptation of the devil."

"Yon's a man," said Angus Duncan, the member from the Amalgamated Machinists, when the committee was filing out through the hotel corridor.

"Now you're shouting!" said Engineer Scott. "And you might say a man and a brother."

XXIV

INTO THE PRIMITIVE

Tested upon purely diplomatic principles, Miss Van Brock's temper was little less than angelic, exhibiting itself under provocation only in guarded pin-pricks of sarcasm, or in small sharp-clawed kitten-buffetings of repartee. But she was at no pains to conceal her scornful disappointment when David Kent made known his doubts concerning his moral right to use the weapon he had so skilfully forged.

He delayed the inevitable confession to Portia until he had told Loring; and in making it he did not tell Miss Van Brock to whom he owed the sudden change in the point of view. But Portia would have greatly discredited her gift of insight if she had not instantly reduced the problem to its lowest terms.

"You have been asking Miss Brentwood to lend you her conscience, and she has done it," was the form in which she stated the fact. And when Kent did not deny it: "You lack at least one quality of greatness, David; you sway too easily."

"No, I don't!" he protested. "I am as obstinate as a mule. Ask Ormsby, or Loring. But the logic of the thing is blankly unanswerable. I can either get down to the dirty level of these highbinders—fight the devil with a brand taken out of his own fire; or—"

"Or what?" she asked.

"Or think up some other scheme; some plan which doesn't involve a surrender on my part of common decency and self-respect."

"Yes?" she retorted. "I suppose you have the other plan all wrought out and ready to drop into place?"

"No, I haven't," he admitted reluctantly.

"But at least you have some notion of what it is going to be?"

"No."

She was pacing back and forth in front of his chair in a way that was almost man-like; but her contemptuous impatience made her dangerously beautiful. Suddenly she stopped and turned upon him, and there were sharp claws in the kitten-buffetings.

"Do you know you are spoiling a future that most men would hesitate to throw away?" she asked. "While you have been a man of one idea in this railroad affair, we haven't been idle—your newspaper and political friends, and Ormsby and I. You are ambitious; you want to succeed; and we have been laying the foundations for you. The next election would give you anything in the gift of the State that a man of your years could aspire to. Have you known this?"

"I have guessed it," he said quite humbly.

"Of course you have. But it has all been contingent upon one thing: you were to crush the grafters in this railroad struggle—show them up—and climb to distinction yourself on the ladder from which you had shaken them. It might have been done; it was in a fair way to be done. And now you turn back and leave the plow in the furrow!"

There was more of a like quality—a good bit more; some of it regretful; all of it pungent and logical from Miss Van Brock's point of view; and Kent was no rock not to be moved by the small tempest of disappointed vicarious ambition. Wherefore he escaped when he could, though only to begin the ethical battle all over again; to fight and to wander among the tombs in the valley of indecision for a week and a day, eight miserable twirlings of the earth in space, during which interval he was invisible to his friends and innocuous to his enemies.

On the morning of the ninth day Editor Hildreth telephoned Miss Van Brock to ask if she knew where Kent could be found. The answer was a rather anxious negative; though the query could have been answered affirmatively by the conductor and motorman of an early morning electric car which ran to the farthest outskirts of the eastern suburb of the city. Following a boyish habit he had never fully outgrown, Kent had once more taken his problem to the open, and the hour after luncheon time found him plodding wearily back to the end of the car line, jaded, dusty and stiff from much tramping of the brown plain, but with the long duel finally fought out to some despairing conclusion.

The City Hall clock was upon the stroke of three when the inbound trolley-car landed him in front of the Clarendon. It was a measure of his purposeful abstraction that he went on around the corner to the Security Bank, dusty and unpresentable as he was, and transferred the packet of incriminating affidavits from the safety deposit box to his pocket before going to his rooms in the hotel.

This paper weapon was the centering point of the struggle which had now lasted for nearly a fortnight. So long as the weapon was his to use or to cast away, the outcome of the moral conflict hung in the balance. But now he was emerging from the night wanderings among the tombs of the undecided.

"I can't give it up; there is too much at stake," he muttered, as he trudged heavily back to the hotel. And before he went above stairs he asked the young woman at the house telephone exchange to ascertain if Governor Bucks were in his office at the capitol, and if so, if he were likely to remain there for an hour.

When he reached his rooms he flung the packet of papers on the writing-table and went to freshen himself with a bath. That which lay before him called for fitness, mental and physical, and cool sanity. In other times of stress, as just before a critical hour in court, the tub and the cold plunge had been his fillip where other men resorted to the bottle.

He was struggling into clean linen, and the packet was still lying where he had tossed it on entering, when a bell-boy came up with a card. Kent read the name with a ghost of a smile relaxing the care-drawn lines about his mouth. There are times when a man's fate rushes to meet him, and he had fallen upon one of them.

"Show him up," was the brief direction; and when the door of the elevator cage clacked again, Kent was waiting.

His visitor was a man of heroic proportions; a large man a little breathed, as it seemed, by the swift upward rush of the elevator. Kent admitted him with a nod; and the governor planted himself heavily in a chair and begged a light for his cigar. In the match-passing he gathered his spent breath and declared his errand.

"I think we have a little score to settle between us as man to man, Kent," he began, when Kent had clipped the end from his own cigar and lighted it in stolid silence.

"Possibly: that is for you to say," was the unencouraging reply.

Bucks rose deliberately, walked to the bath-room door, and looked beyond it into the bedroom.

"We are quite alone, if that is what you want to make sure of," said Kent, in the same indifferent tone; and the governor came back and resumed his chair.

"I came up to see what you want—what you will take to quit," he announced, crossing his legs and locking the huge ham-like hands over his knee. "That is putting it rather abruptly, but business is business, and we can dispense with the preliminaries, I take it."

"I told your attorney-general some time ago what I wanted, and he did not see fit to grant it," Kent responded. "I am not sure that I want anything now—anything you can have to offer." This was not at all what he had intended to say; but the presence of the adversary was breeding a stubborn antagonism that was more potent on the moral side than all the prickings of conscience.

The yellow-lidded eyes of the governor began to close down, and the look came into them which had been there when he had denied a pardon to a widow pleading for the life of her convicted son.

"I had hoped you were in the market," he demurred. "It would be better for all concerned if you had something to sell, with a price attached. I know what you have been doing, and what you think you have got hold of. It's a tissue of mistakes and falsehoods and back-bitings from beginning to end, but it may serve your purpose with the newspapers. I want to buy that package of stuff you've got stowed away in the Security vaults."

The governor's chair was on one side of the writing-table, and Kent's was on the other. In plain sight between the two men lay the packet Bucks was willing to bargain for. It was inclosed in a box envelope, bearing the imprint of the Security Bank. Kent was looking steadily away from the table when he said:

"What if I say it isn't for sale?"

"Don't you think it had better be?"

"I don't know. I hadn't thought much about the advisable phase of it."

"Well, the time has come when you've got it to do," was the low-toned threat.

"But not as a matter of compulsion," said Kent, coolly enough. "What is your bid?"

Bucks made it promptly.

"Ten thousand dollars: and you promise to leave the State and stay away for one year from the first Tuesday in November next."

"That is, until after the next State election." Kent blew a whiff of smoke to the ceiling and shook his head slowly. "It is not enough."

The governor uncrossed his legs, crossed them the other way, and said:

"I'll make it twenty thousand and two years."

"Or thirty thousand and three years," Kent suggested amiably. "Or suppose we come at once to the end of that string and say one hundred thousand and ten years. That would still leave you a fair price for your block of suburban property in Guilford and Hawk's addition to the city of Gaston, wouldn't it?"

The governor set his massive jaw with a sharp little click of the teeth.

"You are joking on the edge of your grave, my young friend. I taught you in Gaston that you were not big enough to fight me: do you think you are big enough now?"

"I don't think; I know," said Kent, incisively. "And since you have referred to the Gaston days: let me ask if I ever gave you any reason to believe that I could be scared out?"

"Keep to the point," retorted Bucks, harshly. "This State isn't broad enough to hold you and me on opposite sides of the fence. I could make it too hot to hold you without mixing up in it myself, but I choose to fight my own battles. Will you take twenty thousand dollars spot cash, and MacFarlane's job as circuit judge when I'm through with him? Yes or no."

"No."

"Then what will you take?"

"Without committing myself in any sense, I might say that you are getting off too cheaply on your most liberal proposition. You and your friends have looted a seventy-million-dollar railroad, and—"

"You might have stood in on that if you had taken Guilford's offer," was the brusk rejoinder. "There was more than a corporation lawyer's salary in sight, if you'd had sense enough to see it."

"Possibly. But I stayed out—and I am still out."

"Do you want to get in? Is that your price?"

"I intend to get in—though not, perhaps, in the way you have in mind. Are you ready to recall Judge Mac-Farlane with instructions to give us our hearing on the merits?"

The governor's face was wooden when he said:

"Is that all you want? I understand MacFarlane is returning, and you will doubtless have your hearing in due season."

"Not unless you authorize it," Kent objected.

"And if I do? If I say that I have already done so, will you come in and lay down your arms?"

"No."

"Then I'm through. Give me your key and write me an order on the Security Bank for those papers you are holding."

"No," said Kent, again.

"I say *yes!*" came the explosive reassertion; and Kent found himself looking down the bright barrel of a pistol thrust into his face across the table.

For a man who had been oftenest an onlooker on the football half of life, Kent was measurably quick and resourceful. In one motion he clamped the weapon and turned it aside; in another he jammed the fire end of his cigar among the fingers of the grasping hand. The governor jerked free with an oath, pain-extorted; and Kent dropped the captured weapon into the table drawer. It was all done in two breaths, and when it was over, Kent flung away the broken cigar and lighted a fresh one.

"That was a very primitive expedient, your Excellency, to say the best of it," he remarked. "Have you nothing better to offer?"

The reply was a wild-beast growl, and taking it for a negative, Kent went on.

"Then perhaps you will listen to my proposal. The papers you are so anxious about are here,"—tapping the envelope on the table. "No, don't try to snatch them; you wouldn't get out of here alive with them, lacking my leave. Such of them as relate to your complicity in the Universal Oil deal are yours—on one condition; that your health fails and you get yourself ordered out of the State for the remainder of your term."

"No!" thundered the governor.

"Very well; you may stay and take a course of home treatment, if you prefer. It's optional."

"By God! I don't know what keeps me from throttling you with my hands!" Bucks got upon his feet, and Kent rose, also, slipping the box envelope into his pocket and laying a precautionary hand on the drawer-pull.

The governor turned away and walked to the window, nursing his burned fingers. When he faced about it was to return to the charge.

"Kent, what is it you want? Say it in two words."

"Candidly, I didn't know, until a few minutes ago, Governor. It began with a determination to break your grip on my railroad, I believe."

"You can have your railroad, if you can get it—and be damned to it, and to you, too!"

"I said it began that way. My sole idea in gathering up this evidence against you and your accomplices was to whittle out a club that would make you let go of the Trans-Western. For two weeks I have been debating with myself as to whether I should buy you or break you; and half an hour before you came, I went to the bank and took these papers out, meaning to go and hunt you up."

"Well?" said the governor, and the word bared his teeth because his lips were dry.

"I thought I knew, in the old Gaston days, how many

different kinds of a scoundrel you could be, but you've succeeded in showing me some new variations in the last few minutes. It's a thousand pities that the people of a great State should be at the mercy of such a gang of pirates as you and Hendricks and Meigs and MacFarlane, and—"

"Break it off!" said Bucks.

"I'm through. I was merely going to add that I have concluded not to buy you."

"Then it's to be war to the knife, is it?"

"That is about the size of it," said Kent; and the governor found his hat.

"I'll trouble you to return my property," he growled, pointing to the table drawer.

"Certainly." Kent broke the revolver over the blotting pad, swept the ejected cartridges into the open drawer, and passed the empty weapon to its owner.

When the door closed behind the outgoing visitor the victor in the small passage at arms began to walk the floor; but at four o'clock, which was Hildreth's hour for coming down-town, he put on his hat and went to climb the three flights of stairs to the editor's den in the *Argus* building.

XXV

DEAD WATER AND QUICK

The cubby-hole in which Hildreth earned his bread by the sweat of his brain was dark even at midday; and during working hours the editor sat under a funnel-shaped reflector in a conic shower-bath of electric light which flooded man and desk and left the corners of the room in a penumbra of grateful twilight.

Kent sat just outside of the cone of radiance, watching Hildreth's face as the editor read stolidly through the contents of the box envelope. It was an instructive study in thought dynamics. There was a gleam of battle satisfaction in the editorial eye when Hildreth faced the last sheet down upon the accumulation of evidence, saying:

"You didn't overstate the fact in your brag about the political graves. Only this isn't a spade; it's a steam shovel. Do I understand you are giving me this stuff to use as I please?"

"Just that," said Kent.

"And you have made it serve your turn, too?"

(308)

"No." Kent's voice was sharp and crisp.

"Isn't that what you got it for?"

"Yes."

"Then why don't you use it?"

"That was what Bucks wanted to know a little while ago when he came to my rooms to try to buy me off. I don't think I succeeded in making him understand why I couldn't traffic with it; and possibly you wouldn't understand."

"I guess I do. It's public property, and you couldn't divert it into private channels. Is that the way it struck you?"

"It is the way it struck a friend of mine whose sense of ultimate right and wrong hasn't lost its fine edge in the world-mill. I did not want to do it."

"Naturally," said the editor. "Giving it up means the loss of all you have been working for in the railroad game. I wish I could use it, just as it stands."

"Can't you?"

"I am afraid not—effectively. It would make an issue in a campaign; or, sprung on the eve of an election, it might down the ring conclusively. I think it would. But this is the off year, and the people won't rise to a political issue—couldn't make themselves felt if they should."

"I don't agree with you. You have your case all

made out, with the evidence in sound legal form. What
is to prevent your trying it?"

"The one thing that you ought to be lawyer enough
to see at a glance. There is no court to try it in. With
the Assembly in session we might do something: as it
is, we can only yap at the heels of the ringsters, and
our yapping won't help you in the railroad fight. What
do you hear from Boston?"

"Nothing new. The stock is still flat on the market,
with the stock-holders' pool holding a bare majority,
and the Plantagould brokers buying in driblets wherever they can find a small holder who is willing to let
go. It is only a question of time; and a very short
time at that."

The editor wagged his head in sympathy.

"I wish I could help you, David. You've done a big
thing for me—for the *Argus;* and all I have to hand
you in return is a death sentence. MacFarlane is back."

"Here? In town?"

"Yes. And that isn't the worst of it. The governor
sent for him."

"Have you any idea what is in the wind?" asked
Kent, dry-lipped.

"I am afraid I have. My young men have been nos-
ing around in the Trans-Western affair, and several
things have developed. Matters are approaching a crisis. The cut-rate boom is about to collapse, and there

is trouble brewing in the labor organizations. If Bucks
doesn't get his henchmen out of it pretty soon, they will
be involved in the smash—which will be bad for them
and for him, politically."

"I developed most of that a good while ago," Kent
cut in.

"Yes; I know. But there is more to follow. The
stock-smashing plan was all right, but it is proving too
slow. Now they are going to do something else."

"Can you give it a name?" asked Kent, nerving himself.

"I can. But first tell me one thing: as matters stand,
could Guilford dispose of the road—sell it or lease it?"

"No; he would first have to be made permanent receiver and be given authority by the court."

"Ah! that explains Judge MacFarlane's return. Now
what I am going to tell you is the deadest of secrets.
It came to me from one of the Overland officials, and
I'm not supposed to gossip. Did you know the Overland Short Line had passed under Plantagould domi-
nation?"

"I know they elected a Plantagould directory at the
annual meeting."

"Exactly. Well, Guilford is going to lease the Trans-
Western to its competitor for a term of ninety-nine
years. That's your death sentence."

Kent sprang to his feet, and what he said is unrecordable. He was not a profane man, but the sanguine temperament would assert itself explosively in moments of sudden stress.

"When is this thing to be done?" he demanded, when the temperamental gods were appeased a little.

Hildreth shrugged.

"I have told you all I could, and rather more than I had any right to. Open the door behind you, won't you? The air is positively sulphurous."

Kent opened the door, entirely missing the point of the sarcasm in his heat.

"But you must have some idea," he insisted.

"I haven't; any more than the general one that they won't let the grass grow under their feet."

"No. God blast the whole—I wish I could swear in Sanscrit. The mother-tongue doesn't begin to do justice to it. Now I know what Bucks meant when he told me to take my railroad, *if I could get it*. He had the whole thing coopered up in a barrel at that minute."

"I take it you have no alternative to this," said the editor, tapping the pile of affidavits.

"Not a cursed shred of an idea! And, Hildreth—" he broke off short because once again the subject suddenly grew too large for coherent speech.

Hildreth disentangled himself from the legs of his chair and stood up to put his hands on Kent's shoulders.

"You are up against it hard, David," he said; and

he repeated: "I'd give all my old shoes to be able to help you out."

"I know it," said Kent; and then he turned abruptly and went away.

Between nine and ten o'clock the same evening Kent was walking the floor of his room, trying vainly to persuade himself that virtue was its own reward, and wondering if a small dose of chloral hydrate would be defensible under the cruel necessity for sleep. He had about decided in favor of the drug when a tap at the door announced the coming of a bell-boy with a note. It was a message from Portia.

"If you have thrown away your chance definitely, and are willing to take a still more desperate one, come to see me," she wrote; and he went mechanically, as a drowning man catches at a straw, knowing it will not save him.

The house in Alameda Square was dark when he went up the walk; and while he was feeling for the bell-push his summoner called to him out of the electric stencilings of leaf shadows under the broad veranda.

"It is too fine a night to stay indoors," she said. "Come and sit in the hammock while I scold you as you deserve." And when he had taken the hammock: "Now give an account of yourself. Where have you been for the past age or two?"

"Wallowing around in the lower depths of the place that Dante visited," he admitted.

"Don't you think you deserve a manhandling?"

"I suppose so; and if you have it in mind, I shall probably get it. But I may say I'm not especially anxious for a tongue-lashing to-night."

"Poor boy!" she murmured, in mock sympathy. "Does it hurt to be truly good?"

"Try it some time when you have a little leisure, and see for yourself," he retorted.

She laughed.

"No; I'll leave that for the Miss Brentwoods. By the way, did you go to tell the household good-by? Penelope was wondering audibly what had become of you."

"I didn't know they were gone. I have been nowhere since the night you drove me out with contumely and opprobrium."

She laughed again.

"You must have dived deep. They went a week ago Tuesday, and you lost your ghostly adviser and your political stage manager at one fell swoop. But it isn't wonderful that you haven't missed Mr. Ormsby. Having elected Miss Brentwood your conscience-keeper-in-chief, you have no further use for the P. S. M."

"And you have no further use for me, apparently,"

he complained. "Did you send for me so that you might abuse me in the second edition?"

"No; I wanted to give you a bit of news, and to repeat an old question of mine. Do you know what they are going to do next with your railroad?"

"Yes; Hildreth told me this afternoon."

"Well, what are *you* going to do?"

"Nothing. There is nothing to be done. They have held to the form of legal procedure thus far, but they won't do it any more. They will take MacFarlane off in a corner somewhere, have him make Guilford permanent receiver, and the lease to the Overland will be consummated on the spot. I sha'n't be in it."

"Probably not; certainly not if you don't try to get in it. And that brings me back to the old question. Are you big enough, David?"

"If you think I haven't been big enough to live up to my opportunities thus far, I'm afraid I may disappoint you again," he said doubtfully.

"You have disappointed me," she admitted. "That is why I am asking: I'd like to be reasonably sure your Jonathan Edwardsy notions are not going to trip us again."

"Portia, if I thought you really meant that. . . A conscienceless man is bad enough, God knows; but a conscienceless woman—"

Her laugh was a decorous little shriek.

"David, you are *not* big; you are narrow, narrow, *narrow!* Is there then no other code of morals in the round world save that which the accident of birth has interleaved with your New England Bible? What is conscience? Is it an absolute standard of right and wrong? Or is it merely your ideal or mine, or Shafiz Ullah Khan's?"

"You may call it all the hard names you can lay tongue to," he allowed. "I'm not getting much comfort out of it, and I rather enjoy hearing it abused. But you are thrusting at a shadow in the present instance. Do you know what I did this afternoon?"

"How should I know?"

"I don't know why you shouldn't: you know everything that happens. But I'll tell you. I had been fighting the thing over from start to finish and back again ever since you blessed me out a week ago last Monday, and at the wind-up this afternoon I took the papers out of the bank vault, having it in mind to go and give his Excellency a bad quarter of an hour."

"But you didn't do it?"

"No, he saved me the trouble. While I was getting ready to go and hunt him, his card came up. We had it out in my rooms."

"I'm listening," she said; and he rehearsed the facts for her, concealing nothing.

"What a curious thing human nature is!" she commented, when he had made an end. "My better judgment says you were all kinds of a somebody for not clinching the nail when you had it so well driven home. And yet I can't help admiring your exalted fanaticism. I do love consistency, and the courage of it. But tell me, if you can, how far these fair-fighting scruples of yours go. You have made it perfectly plain that if a thief should steal your pocketbook, you would suffer loss before you'd compromise with him to get it back. But suppose you should catch him at it: would you feel compelled to call a policeman—or would you—"

He anticipated her.

"You are doing me an injustice on the other side, now. I'll fight as furiously as you like. All I ask is to be given a weapon that won't bloody my hands."

"Good!" she said approvingly. "I think I have found the weapon, but it's desperate, desperate! And O David! you've got to have a cool head and a steady hand when you use it. If you haven't, it will kill everybody within the swing of it—everybody but the man you are trying to reach."

"Draw it and let me feel its edge," he said shortly.

Her chair was close beside the low-swung hammock. She bent to his ear and whispered a single sentence. For a minute or two he sat motionless, weighing and balancing the chance of success against the swiftly multiplying difficulties and hazards.

"You call it desperate," he said at length; "if there is a bigger word in the language, you ought to find it and use it. The risk is that of a forlorn hope; not so much for me, perhaps, as for the innocent—or at least ignorant—accomplices I'll have to enlist."

She nodded.

"That is true. But how much is your railroad worth?"

"It is bonded for fifty millions first, and twenty millions second mortgage."

"Well, seventy millions are worth fighting for: worth a very considerable risk, I should say."

"Yes." And after another thoughtful interval: "How did you come to think of it?"

"It grew out of a bit of talk with the man who will have to put the apex on our pyramid after we have done our part."

"Will he stand by us? If he doesn't, we shall all be no better than dead men the morning after the fact."

She clasped her hands tightly over her knee, and said:

"That is one of the chances we must take, David; one of the many. But it is the last of the bridges to be crossed, and there are lots of them in between. Are the details possible? That was the part I couldn't go into by myself."

He took other minutes for reflection.

"I can't tell," he said doubtfully. "If I could only know how much time we have."

Her eyes grew luminous.

"David, what would you do without me?" she asked. "To-morrow night, in Stephen Hawk's office in Gaston, you will lose your railroad. MacFarlane is there, or if he isn't, he'll be there in the morning. Bucks, Guilford and Hawk will go down from here to-morrow evening; and the Overland people are to come up from Midland City to meet them."

There was awe undisguised in the look he gave her, and it had crept into his voice when he said:

"Portia, are you really a flesh-and-blood woman?"

She smiled.

"Meaning that your ancestors would have burned me for a witch? Perhaps they would: I think quite likely they burned women who made better martyrs. But I didn't have to call in Flibbertigibbet. The programme is a carefully guarded secret, to be sure; but it is known—it had to be known—to a number of people outside of our friends the enemy. You've heard the story of the inventor and his secret, haven't you?"

"No."

"Well, the man had invented something, and he told the secret of it to his son. After a little the son wanted to tell it to a friend. The old man said, 'Hold on; I know it—that's one'—holding up one finger—'you know it—that's eleven'—holding up another finger beside the first; 'and now if you tell this other fellow, that'll be one hundred and eleven'—holding up three fingers. That is the case with this programme. One of the one hundred and eleven—he is a person high up in the management of the Overland Short Line—dropped a few words in my hearing and I picked them up. That's all."

"It is fearfully short—the time, I mean," he said after another pause. "We can't count on any help from any one in authority. Guilford's broom has swept the high-salaried official corners clean. But the wage-people are mutinous and ripe for anything. I'll go and find out where we stand." And he groped on the floor of the veranda for his hat.

"No, wait a minute," she interposed. "We are not quite ready to adjourn yet. There remains a little matter of compensation—your compensation—to be considered. You are still on the company's pay-rolls?"

"In a way, yes; as its legal representative on the ground."

"That won't do. If you carry this thing through

successfully it must be on your own account, and not
as the company's paid servant. You must resign and
make terms with Boston beforehand; and that, too,
without telling Boston what you propose to do."

He haggled a little at that.

"The company is entitled to my services," he asserted.

"It is entitled to what it pays for—your legal services.
But this is entirely different. You will be acting upon
your own initiative, and you'll have to spend money
like water at your own risk. You must be free to deal
with Boston as an outsider."

"But I have no money to spend," he objected.

Again the brown eyes grew luminous; and again she
said:

"What would you do without me? Happily, my information came early enough to enable me to get a letter to Mr. Ormsby. He answered promptly by wire this
morning. Here is his telegram."

She had been winding a tightly folded slip of paper
around her fingers, and she smoothed it out and gave
it to him. He held it in a patch of the electric light
between the dancing leaf shadows and read:

"Plot Number Two approved. Have wired one hundred thousand to Kent's order Security Bank. Have
him draw as he needs."

"So now you see," she went on, "you have the sinews of war. But you must regard it as an advance and name your fee to the Boston folk so you can pay it back."

He protested again, rather weakly.

"It looks like extortion; like another graft," he said; and now she lost patience with him.

"Of all the Puritan fanatics!" she cried. "If it were a simple commercial transaction by which you would save your clients a round seventy million dollars, which would otherwise be lost, would you scruple to take a proportionate fee?"

"No; certainly not."

"Well, then; you go and tell Mr. Loring to wire his Advisory Board, and to do it to-night."

"But I'll have to name a figure," said Kent.

"Of course," she replied.

Kent thought about it for a long minute. Then he said: "I wonder if ten thousand dollars, and expenses, would paralyze them?"

Miss Van Brock's comment was a little shriek of derision.

"I knew you'd make difficulties when it came to the paying part of it, and since I didn't know, myself, I wired Mr. Ormsby again. Here is what he says," and she untwisted a second telegram and read it to him. "'Fee should not be less than five per cent. of bonded indebtedness; four-fifths in stock at par; one-fifth cash; no cure, no pay.' "

"Three million five hundred thousand dollars!" gasped Kent.

"It's only nominally that much," she laughed. "The stock part of it is merely your guaranty of good faith: it is worth next to nothing now, and it will be many a long day before it goes to par, even if you are successful in saving its life. So your magnificent fee shrinks to seven hundred thousand dollars, less your expenses."

"But heavens and earth! that's awful!" said Kent.

"Not when you consider it as a surgeon's risk. You happen to be the one man who has the idea, and if it isn't carried out, the patient is going to die to-morrow night, permanently. You are the specialist in this case, and specialists come high. Now you may go and attend to the preliminary details, if you like."

He found his hat and stood up. She stood with him; but when he took her hand she made him sit down again.

"You have at least three degrees of fever!" she exclaimed; "or is it only the three-million-five-hundred-thousand-dollar shock? What have you been doing to yourself?"

"Nothing, I assure you. I haven't been sleeping very well for a few nights. But that is only natural."

"And I said you must have a cool head! Will you do exactly as I tell you to?"

"If you don't make it too hard."

"Take the car down-town—don't walk—and after you have made Mr. Loring send his message to Boston, you go straight to Doctor Biddle. Tell him what is the matter with you, and that you need to sleep the clock around."

"But the time!" he protested. "I shall need every hour between now and to-morrow night!"

"One clear-headed hour is worth a dozen muddled ones. You do as I say."

"I hate drugs," he said, rising again.

"So do I; but there is a time for everything under the sun. It is a crying necessity that you go into this fight perfectly fit and with all your wits about you. If you don't, somebody—several somebodies—will land in the penitentiary. Will you mind me?"

"Yes," he promised; and this time he got away.

XXVI

ON THE HIGH PLAINS

Much to Elinor's relief, and quite as much, perhaps, to Penelope's, Mrs. Brentwood tired of Breezeland Inn in less than a fortnight and began to talk of returning to the apartment house in the capital.

Pressed to give a reason for her dissatisfaction, the younger sister might have been at a loss to account for it in words; but Elinor's desire to cut the outing short was based upon pride and militant shame. After many trap-settings she had succeeded in making her mother confess that the stay at Breezeland was at Ormsby's expense; and not all of Mrs. Brentwood's petulant justifyings could remove the sting of the nettle of obligation.

"There is no reason in the world why you should make so much of it: I am your mother, and I ought to know," was Mrs. Brentwood's dictum. "You wouldn't have any scruples if we were his guests on the *Amphitrite* or in his country house on Long Island."

(325)

"That would be different," Elinor contended. "We are not his guests here; we are his pensioners."

"Nonsense!" frowned the mother. "Isn't it beginning to occur to you that beggars shouldn't be choosers? And, besides, so far as you are concerned, you are only anticipating a little."

It was an exceedingly injudicious, not to say brutal way of putting it; and the blue-gray eyes flashed fire.

"Can't you see that you are daily making a marriage between us more and more impossible?" was the bitter rejoinder. Elinor's *métier* was cool composure under fire, but she was not always able to compass it.

Mrs. Brentwood fanned herself vigorously. She had been aching to have it out with this self-willed young woman who was playing fast and loose with attainable millions, and the hour had struck.

"What made you break it off with Brookes Ormsby?" she snapped; adding: "I don't wonder you were ashamed to tell me about it."

"I did not break it off; and I was not ashamed." Elinor had regained her self-control, and the angry light in the far-seeing eyes was giving place to the cool gray blankness which she cultivated.

"That is what Brookes told me, but I didn't believe him," said the mother. "It's all wrong, anyway, and I more than half believe David Kent is at the bottom of it."

Elinor left her chair and went to the window, which looked down on the sanatorium, the ornate parterre, and the crescent driveway. These family bickerings were very trying to her, and the longing to escape them was sometimes strong enough to override cool reason and her innate sense of the fitness of things.

In her moments of deepest depression she told herself that the prolonged struggle was making her hard and cynical; that she was growing more and more on the Grimkie side and shrinking on the Brentwood. With the unbending uprightness of the Grimkie forebears there went a prosaic and unmalleable strain destructive alike of sentiment and the artistic ideals. This strain was in her blood, and from childhood she had fought it, hopefully at times, and at other times, as now, despairingly. There were tears in her eyes when she turned to the window; and if they were merely tears of self-pity, they were better than none. Once, in the halcyon summer, David Kent had said that the most hardened criminal in the dock was less dangerous to humanity than the woman who had forgotten how to cry.

But into the turmoil of thoughts half indignant, half self-compassionate, came reproach and a great wave of tenderness filial. She saw, as with a sudden gift of retrospection, her mother's long battle with inadequacy, and how it had aged her; saw, too, that the battle had been fought unselfishly, since she knew her mother's declaration that she could contentedly "go back to noth-ing" was no mere petulant boast. It was for her daugh-ters that she had grown thin and haggard and irritable under the persistent reverses of fortune; it was for them that she was sinking the Grimkie independence in the match-making mother.

The tears in Elinor's eyes were not altogether of self-pity when she put her back to the window. Ormsby was coming up the curved driveway in his automobile, and she had seen him but dimly through the rising mist of emotion.

"Have you set your heart upon this thing, mother?—but I know you have. And I—I have tried as I could to be just and reasonable; to you and Penelope, and to Brookes Ormsby. He is nobleness itself: it is a shame to give him the shadow when he so richly de-serves the substance."

She spoke rapidly, almost incoherently; and the mother-love in the woman who was careful and troubled about the things that perish put the match-maker to the wall. It was almost terrifying to see Elinor, the strong-hearted, the self-contained, breaking down like other mothers' daughters. So it was the mother who held out her arms, and the daughter ran to go down on her knees at the chair-side, burying her face in the lap of com-forting.

"There, there, Ellie, child; don't cry. It's terrible

to hear you sob like that," she protested, her own voice shaking in sympathy. "I have been thinking only of you and your future, and fearing weakly that you couldn't bear the hard things. But we'll bear them together—we three; and I'll never say another word about Brookes Ormsby and what might have been."

"O mother! you are making it harder than ever, now," was the tearful rejoinder. "I—there is no reason why I should be so obstinate. I haven't even the one poor excuse you are making for me down deep in your heart."

"David Kent?" said the mother.

The bowed head nodded a wordless assent.

"I sha'n't say that I haven't suspected him all along, dear. I am afraid I have. I have nothing against him. But he is a poor man, Elinor; and we are poor, too. You'd be miserably unhappy."

"If he stays poor, it is I who am to blame,"—this most contritely. "He had a future before him: the open door was his winning in the railroad fight, and I closed it against him."

"You?" said the mother, astonished.

"Yes. I told him he couldn't go on in the way he meant to. I made it a matter of conscience; and he— he has turned back when he might have fought it out and made a name for himself, and saved us all. And it was such a hair-splitting thing! All the world would have applauded him if he had gone on; and there was only one woman in all the world to pry into the secret places of his soul and stir up the sleeping doubt!"

Now, if all the thrifty, gear-getting "faculty" of the dead and gone Grimkies had become thin and diluted and inefficient in this Mrs. Hepzibah, last of the name, the strong wine and iron of the blood of uprightness had come down to her unstrained.

"Tell me all about it, daughter," she adjured; and when the tale was told, she patted the bowed head tenderly and spoke the words of healing.

"You did altogether right, Ellie, dear; I—I am proud of you, daughter. And if, as you say, you were the only one to do it, that doesn't matter; it was all the more necessary. Are you sure he gave it up?"

Elinor rose and stood with clasped hands beside her mother's chair; a very pitiful and stricken half-sister of the self-reliant, dependable young woman who had boasted herself the head of the household.

"I have no means of knowing what he has done," she said slowly. "But I know the man. He has turned back."

There was a tap at the door and a servant was come to say that Mr. Brookes Ormsby was waiting with his auto-car. Was Miss Brentwood nearly ready?

Elinor said, "In a minute," and when the door closed,

she made a confidante of her mother for the first time since her childhood days.

"I know what you have suspected ever since that summer in New Hampshire, and it is true," she confessed. "I do love him—as much as I dare to without knowing whether he cares for me. Must I—may I—say yes to Brookes Ormsby without telling him the whole truth?"

"Oh, my dear! You couldn't do that!" was the quick reply.

"You mean that I am not strong enough? But I am; and Mr. Ormsby is manly enough and generous enough to meet me half-way. Is there any other honest thing to do, mother?"

Mrs. Hepzibah shook her head deliberately and determinedly, though she knew she was shaking the Ormsby millions into the abyss of the unattainable.

"No; it is his just due. But I can't help being sorry for him, Ellie. What will you do if he says it doesn't make any difference?"

The blue-gray eyes were downcast.

"I don't know. Having asked so much, and accepted so much from him—it shall be as he says, mother."

The afternoon had been all that a summer afternoon on the brown highlands can be, and the powerful touring car had swept them from mile to mile over the dun hills like an earth-skimming dragon whose wing-beat was the muffled, explosive thud of the motor.

Through most of the miles Elinor had given herself up to silent enjoyment of the rapture of swift motion, and Ormsby had respected her mood, as he always did. But when they were on the high hills beyond the mining-camp of Megilp, and he had thrown the engines out of gear to brake the car gently down the long inclines, there was room for speech.

"This is our last spin together on the high plains, I suppose," he said. "Your mother has fixed upon to-morrow for our return to town, hasn't she?"

Elinor confirmed it half-absently. She had been keyed up to face the inevitable in this drive with Ormsby, and she was afraid now that he was going to break her resolution by a dip into the commonplaces.

"Are you glad or sorry?" he asked.

Her reply was evasive.

"I have enjoyed the thin, clean air and the freedom of the wide horizons. Who could help it?"

"But you have not been entirely happy?"

It was on her lips to say some conventional thing about the constant jarring note in all human happiness, but she changed it to a simple "No."

"May I try if I can give the reason?"

She made a reluctant little gesture of assent; some

such signal of acquiescence as Marie Antoinette may have given the waiting headsman.

"You have been afraid every day lest I should begin a second time to press you for an answer, haven't you?"

She could not thrust and parry with him. They were past all that.

"Yes," she admitted briefly.

"You break my heart, Elinor," he said, after a long pause. "But"—with a sudden tightening of the lips—"I'm not going to break yours."

She understood him, and her eyes filled quickly with the swift shock of gratitude.

"If you had made a study of womankind through ten lifetimes instead of a part of one, you could not know when and how to strike truer and deeper," she said; and then, softly: "Why can't you make me love you, Brookes?"

He took his foot from the brake-pedal, and for ten seconds the released car shot down the slope unhindered. Then he checked the speed and answered her.

"A little while ago I should have said I didn't know; but now I do know. It is because you love David Kent: you loved him before I had my chance."

She did not deny the principal fact, but she gave him his opportunity to set it aside if he could—and would.

"Call it foolish, romantic sentiment, if you like. Is there no way to shame me out of it?"

He shook his head slowly.

"You don't mean that."

"But if I say that I do; if I insist that I am willing to be shamed out of it."

His smile was that of a brother who remembers tardily to be loving-kind.

"I shall leave that task for some one who cares less for you and for your true happiness than I do, or ever shall. And it will be a mighty thankless service that that 'some one' will render you."

"But I ought to be whipped and sent to bed," she protested, almost tearfully. "Do you know what I have done?—how I have—"

She could not quite put it in words, even for him, and he helped her generously, as before.

"I know what Kent hasn't done; which is more to the point. But he will do it fast enough if you will give him half a chance."

"No," she said definitively.

"I say yes. One thing, and one thing only, has kept him from telling you any time since last autumn: that is a sort of finical loyalty to me. I saw how matters stood when he came aboard of our train at Gaston— I'm asking you to believe that I didn't know it before—

and I saw then that my only hope was to make a hand-fast friend of him. And I did it."

"I believe you can do anything you try to do," she said warmly.

This time his smile was a mere grimace.

"You will have to make one exception, after this; and so shall I. And since it is the first of any consequence in all my mounting years, it grinds. I can't throw another man out of the window and take his place."

"If you were anything but what you are, you would have thrown him out of the window another way," she rejoined.

"That would have been a dago's trick; not a white man's," he asserted. "I suppose I might have got in his way and played the dog in the manger generally, and you would have stuck to your word and married me, but I am not looking for that kind of a winning. I don't mind confessing that I played my last card when I released you from your engagement. I said to myself: If that doesn't break down the barriers, nothing will."

She looked up quickly.

"You will never know how near it came to doing it, Brookes."

"But it didn't quite?"

"No, it didn't quite."

The brother-smile came again.

"Let's paste that leaf down and turn the other; the one that has David Kent's name written at the top. He is going to succeed all around, Elinor; and I am going to help him—for his sake, as well as yours."

"No," she dissented. "He is going to fail; and I am to blame for it."

He looked at her sidewise.

"So you were at the bottom of that, were you? I thought as much, and tried to make him admit it, but he wouldn't. What was your reason?"

"I gave it to him: I can't give it to you."

"I guess not," he laughed. "I wasn't born on the right side of the Berkshire Hills to appreciate it. But really, you mustn't interfere. As I say, we are going to make something of David; and a little conscience—of the right old Pilgrim Fathers' brand—goes a long way in politics."

"But you promised me you were not going to spoil him—only it doesn't matter; you can't."

Ormsby chuckled openly, and when she questioned "What?" he said:

"I was just wondering what you would say if you knew what he is into now; if you could guess, for instance, that his backers have put up a cool hundred thousand to be used as he sees fit?"

"Oh!" she exclaimed; and there was dismay and sharp disappointment in her voice. "You don't mean that he is going to bribe these men?"

"No," he said, relenting. "As a matter of fact, I don't know precisely what he is doing with the money, but I guess it is finding its way into legitimate channels. I'll make him give me an itemized expense account for your benefit when it's all over, if you like."

"It would be kinder to tell me more about it now," she pleaded.

"No; I'll let him have that pleasure, after the fact— if we can get him pardoned out before you go back East."

She was silent so long that he stole another sidewise look between his snubbings of the brake-pedal. Her face was white and still, like the face of one suddenly frost-smitten, and he was instantly self-reproachful.

"Don't look that way," he begged. "It hurts me; makes me feel how heavy my hand is when I'm doing my best to make it light. He is trying a rather desperate experiment, to be sure, but he is in no immediate personal danger. I believe it or I shouldn't be here; I should be with him."

She asked no more questions, being unwilling to tempt him to break confidence with Kent. But she was thinking of all the desperate things a determined man with temperamental unbalancings might do when the touring car rolled noiselessly down the final hill into the single street of Megilp.

There was but one vehicle in the street at the moment; a freighter's ore-wagon drawn by a team of mules, meekest and most shambling-prosaic of their tribe. The motor-car was running on the spent velocity of the descent, and Ormsby thought to edge past without stopping. But at the critical instant the mules gave way to terror, snatched the heavy wagon into the opposite plank walk, and tried to climb a near-by telephone pole. Ormsby put his foot on the brake and something snapped under the car.

"What was that?" Elinor asked; and Ormsby got down to investigate.

"It is our brake connection," he announced, after a brief inspection. "And we are five good miles from Hudgins and his repair kit."

A ring of town idlers was beginning to form about them. An automobile was still enough of a rarity in the mining-camp to draw a crowd.

"Busted?" inquired one of the onlookers.

Ormsby nodded, and asked if there were a machinist in the camp.

"Yep," said the spokesman; "up at the Blue Jay mine."

"Somebody go after him," suggested Ormsby, flipping a coin; and a boy started on a run.

The waiting was a little awkward. The ringing idlers were good-natured but curious. Ormsby stood by and answered questions multiform, diverting curiosity from the lady to the machine. Presently the spokesman said:

"Is this here the steam-buggy that helped a crowd of you fellers to get away from Jud Byers and his posse one day a spell back?"

"No," said Ormsby. Then he remembered the evening of small surprises—the racing tally-ho with the Inn auto-car to help; and, more pointedly now, the singular mirage effect in the lengthening perspective as the east-bound train shot away from Agua Caliente.

"What was the trouble that day?" he asked, putting in a question on his side.

"A little ruction up at the Twin Sisters. There was a furss, an' a gun went off, accidintally on purpose killin' Jim Harkins," was the reply.

The machinist was come from the Blue Jay, and Ormsby helped Elinor out of her seat while the repairs were making. The town office of the Blue Jay was just across the street, and he took her there and begged house-room and a chair for her, making an excuse that he must go and see to the brake-mending.

But once outside he promptly stultified himself, letting the repairs take care of themselves while he went in search of one Jud Byers. The deputy sheriff was not hard to find. Normally and in private life he was the weigher for the Blue Jay; and Ormsby was directed to the scale shanty which served as the weigher's office.

The interview was brief and conclusive; was little more than a rapid fire of question and answer; and for the greater part the sheriff's affirmatives were heartily eager. Yes, certainly; if the thing could be brought to pass, he, Byers, would surely do his part. All he asked was an hour or two in which to prepare.

"You shall have all the time there is," was the reply. "Have you a Western Union wire here?"

"No; nothing but the railroad office."

"That won't do; they'd stop the message. How about the Inn?"

"Breezeland has a Western Union all right; wire your notice there, and I'll fix to have it 'phoned over. I don't believe it can be worked, though," added the deputy, doubtfully.

"We can't tell till we try," said Ormsby; and he hurried back to his car to egg on the machinist with golden promises contingent upon haste.

Miss Brentwood found her companion singularly silent on the five-mile race to Breezeland; but the lightning speed at which he drove the car put conversation out of the question. At the hotel he saw her into the lift with decent deliberation; but the moment she was off his hands he fairly ran to the telegrapher's alcove in the main hall.

"Have you a Western Union wire to the capital direct?" he inquired.

The young man snapped his key and said he had.

"It has no connection with the Trans-Western railroad offices?"

"None whatever."

Ormsby dashed off a brief message to Kent, giving three or four addresses at which he might be found.

"Send that, and have them try the Union Station train platform first. Don't let them spare expense at the other end, and if you can bring proof of delivery to Room 261 within half an hour, it means a month's pay to you, individually. Can you do it?"

But the operator was already claiming the wire, writing "deth," "deth," "deth," as rapidly as his fingers could shake off the dots and dashes.

XXVII

Between the hours of eight-thirty and ten P. M. the Union Passenger Station at the capital presents a moving and spirited spectacle. Within the hour and a half, four through and three local trains are due to leave, and the space within the iron grille that fences off the track platforms from the public part of the station is filled with hurrying throngs of train-takers.

Down at the outer end of the train-shed the stuttering pop-valves of the locomotives, the thunderous trundling of the heavy baggage trucks, and the shrill, monotonous chant of the express messengers checking in their cargoes, lift a din harmonious to the seasoned traveler; a medley softened and distance-diminished for those that crowd upon the gate-keepers at the iron grille.

It was the evening of the last day in the month; the day when the Federative Council of Railway Workers had sent its ultimatum to Receiver Guilford. The reduction in wages was to go into effect at midnight; if,

(342)

by midnight, the order had not been rescinded, and the
way opened for a joint conference touching the removal
of certain obnoxious officials, a general strike and tie-up
would be ordered. Trains in transit carrying passengers or United States mail would be run to their respective destinations; trains carrying perishable freight
would be run to division stations: with these exceptions
all labor would cease promptly on the stroke of twelve.

Such was the text of the ultimatum, a certified copy
of which Engineer Scott had delivered in person into
the hands of the receiver at noon.

It was now eight forty-five P. M. The east-bound
night express was ready for the run to A. & T. Junction; the fast mail, one hour and thirty-five minutes
late from the east, was backing in on track nine to take
on the city mail. On track eight, pulled down so that
the smoke from the engine should not foul the air of
the train-shed, the receiver's private car, with the 1010
for motive power and "Red" Callahan in the cab, had
been waiting since seven o'clock for the order to run
special to Gaston. And as yet the headquarters office
had made no sign; sent no word of reply to the strike
notice.

Griggs was on for the night run eastward with the
express; and "Dutch" Tischer had found himself slated
to take the fast mail west. The change of engines on
the mail had been effected at the shops; and when

Tischer backed his train in on track nine his berth was beside the 1010. Callahan swung down from his cab and climbed quickly to that of the mail engine.

"Annything new at the shops, Dutchy?" he inquired.

"I was not somet'ings gehearing, *nein*. You was dot *Arkoos* newsbaper dis evening *sehen?* He says nodings too, alretty, about dot strike."

"Divil a worrd. Ye might think Scotty'd handed the major a bit av blank paper f'r all the notice he's taking. More thin that, he's lavin' town, wid me to pull him. The Naught-seven's to run special to Gaston—bad cess to ut!"

"Vell, I can'd hellup id," said the phlegmatic Bavarian. "I haf the mail and egspress got, and I go mit dem t'rough to Pighorn. You haf der brivate car got, and you go mit dem t'rough to Gaston. Den ve qvits, ain'd it?"

Callahan nodded and dropped to the platform. But before he could mount to the foot-board of the 1010, M'Tosh collared him.

"Patsy, I have your orders, at last. Your passengers will be down in a few minutes, and you are to pull out ahead of the express."

"Is it to Gaston I'm goin', Misther M'Tosh?"

The fireman was standing by with the oil can and torch, ready to Callahan's hand, and the train-master drew the engineer aside.

"Shovel needn't hear," he said in explanation. And then: "Are you willing to stand with us, Patsy? You've had time enough to think it over."

Callahan stood with his arms folded and his cap drawn down over his eyes.

" 'Tis not f'r meself I'm thinkin', Misther M'Tosh, as ye well know. But I'm a widdy man; an' there's the bit colleen in the convint."

"She'll be well cared for, whatever happens to you," was the quick reply.

"Thin I'm yer man," said Callahan; and when the train-master was gone, he ordered Shovel to oil around while he did two or three things which, to an initiated onlooker, might have seemed fairly inexplicable. First he disconnected the air-hose between the car and the engine, tying the ends up with a stout cord so that the connection would not seem to be broken. Next he crawled under the Naught-seven and deliberately bled the air-tank, setting the cock open a mere hair's-breadth so that it would leak slowly but surely until the pressure was entirely gone.

Then he got a hammer and sledge out of the engine tool-box, and after hooking up the safety-chain couplings between the private car and the 1010, he crippled the points of the hooks with the hammer so that they could not be disengaged without the use of force and the proper tools.

"There ye are, ye ould divil's band-wagon," he said, apostrophizing the private car when his work was done. "Ye'll ride this night where Patsy Callahan dhrives, an' be dommed to ye."

Meanwhile the train-master had reached the iron grille at the other end of the long track platform. At a small wicket used by the station employees and trainmen, Kent was waiting for him.

"Is it all right, M'Tosh? Will he do it?" he asked anxiously.

"Yes, Patsy's game for it; I knew he would be. He'd put his neck in a rope to spite the major. But it's a crazy thing, Mr. Kent."

"I know it; but if it will give me twenty-four hours—"

"It won't. They can't get home on our line because we'll be tied up. But they can get the Naught-seven put on the Overland's Limited at A. & T. Junction, and that will put them back here before you've had time to turn around twice. Have they come down yet?"

"No," said Kent; and just then he saw Loring coming in from the street entrance and went to meet him.

"I have the final word from Boston," said the ex-manager, when he had walked Kent out of earshot of the train-takers. "Your terms are accepted—with all sorts of safeguards thrown about the 'no cure, no pay' proviso; also with a distinct repudiation of you and

your scheme if there is anything unlawful afoot. Do
you still think it best to keep me in the dark as to what
you are doing?"

"Yes; there are enough of us involved, as it stands.
You couldn't help; and you might hinder. Besides,
if the mine should happen to explode in our direction
it'll be a comfort to have a foot-loose friend or two on
the outside to pick up the pieces of us."

Loring was polishing his eye-glasses with uncommon
vigor.

"I wish you'd drop it, David, if it isn't too late. I
can't help feeling as if I had prodded you into it, whatever it is."

Kent linked arms with him and led him back to the
street entrance.

"Go away, Grantham, and don't come back again,"
he commanded. "Then you can swear truthfully that
you didn't know anything about it. It is too late to
interfere, and you are not responsible for me. Go up
to see Portia; she'll keep you interested while you wait."

When Loring was gone, Kent went back to the wicket
in the grille; but M'Tosh, who was always a busy man
at train-time, had disappeared again.

It was a standing mystery to the train-master, and to
the rank and file, why Receiver Guilford had elected to
ignore the fact that he was within three hours of a
strike which promised to include at least **four-fifths of**

his operatives; had taken no steps for defense, and had not confided, as it appeared, in the members of his own official staff.

But Kent was at no loss to account for the official silence. If the secret could be kept for a few hours longer, the junto would unload the Trans-Western, strike, tie-up and general demoralization, upon an unsuspecting Overland management.

None the less, there were other things unexplainable even to Kent; for one, this night flitting to Gaston to put the finishing touch on an edifice of fraud which had been builded shamelessly in the light of day.

Kent had not the key to unlock this door of mystery; but here the master spirit of the junto was doing, not what he would, but what he could. The negotiations for the lease had consumed much time at a crisis when time was precious. Judge MacFarlane had to be recalled and once more bullied into subjection; and Falkland, acting for the Plantagould interest, had insisted upon some formal compliance with the letter of the law.

Bucks had striven masterfully to drive and not be driven; but the delays were inexorable, and the impending strike threatened to turn the orderly charge into a rout. The governor had postponed the *coup* from day to day, waiting upon the leisurely movements of Falkland; and at the end of the ends there remained but three hours of the final day of grace when the telegram came from Falkland with the welcome news that the Overland officials were on their way from Midland City to keep the appointment in Gaston.

Of all this Kent knew nothing, and was anxious in just proportion as the minutes elapsed and the time for the departure of the east-bound express drew near. For the success of the desperate venture turned upon this: that the receiver's special must leave ahead of the passenger train. With the express blocking the way the difficulties became insurmountable.

Kent was still standing at the trainmen's wicket when Callahan sent the private car gently up to the trackhead of track eight. M'Tosh had been telephoning again, and the receiver and his party were on the way to the station.

"I was afraid you'd have to let the express go first," said Kent, when the train-master came his way again. "How much time have we?"

"Five minutes more; and they are on the way down—there they come."

Kent looked and saw a group of six men making for the nearest exit in the grille. Then he smote his fist into his palm.

"Damn!" he muttered; "they've got the vice-president of the Overland with them! That's bad."

"It's bad for Mr. Callafield," growled M'Tosh. "We're in too deep now to back down on his account."

Kent moved nearer and stood in the shadow of the gate-keeper's box, leaving M'Tosh, who was on the track platform, free to show himself. From his new point of espial Kent checked off the members of the party. When Major Guilford left it to come back for a word with M'Tosh, there were five others: the governor, his private secretary, Hawk, Halkett, the general superintendent, and the Overland's vice-president.

"All ready, M'Tosh?" said the receiver.

"Ready and waiting, Major," was the bland reply.

"Who is our engineer?"

"Patrick Callahan."

"That wild Irishman? The governor says he'd as soon ride behind the devil."

"Callahan will get you there," said the train-master, with deliberate emphasis. Then he asked a question of his own. "Is Mr. Callafield going with you?"

"No. He came down to see us off. How is the fast mail to-night?"

"She's just in—an hour and thirty-five minutes late."

The major swore pathetically. He was of the generation of railway officials, happily fast passing, which cursed and swore itself into authority.

"That's another five hundred dollars' forfeit to the Post-office Department! Who's taking it west?"

"Tischer."

"Give him orders to cut out all the stops. If he is

more than fifty-five minutes late at Bighorn, he can come in and get his time."

Tischer had just got the word to go, and was pulling out on the yard main line.

"I'll catch him with the wire at yard limits," said M'Tosh. Then: "Would you mind hurrying your people a little, Major? The express is due to leave."

Guilford was a heavy man for his weight, and he waddled back to the others, waving his arms as a signal for them to board the car.

Kent saw the vice-president of the Overland Short Line shake hands with Bucks and take his leave, and was so intent upon watching the tableau of departure that he failed to notice the small boy in Western Union blue who was trying to thrust a telegram, damp from the copying rolls, into his hand.

"It's a rush, sir," said the boy, panting from his quick dash across the track platforms.

It was Ormsby's message from Breezeland; and while Kent was trying to grasp the tremendous import of it, M'Tosh was giving Callahan the signal to go. Kent sprang past the gate-keeper and gave the square of damp paper to the train-master.

"My God! read that!" he gasped, with a dry sob of excitement. "It was our chance—one chance in a million—and we've lost it!"

M'Tosh was a man for a crisis. The red tail-lights of

the private-car special were yet within a sprinter's dash
of the trackhead, but the train-master lost no time
chasing a ten-wheel flyer with "Red" Callahan at the
throttle.

"Up to my office!" he shouted; and ten seconds later
Kent was leaning breathless over the desk in the despatcher's room while M'Tosh called Durgan over the
yard limits telephone.

"Is that you, Durgan?" he asked, when the reply
came. Then: "Drop the board on the mail, quick! and
send somebody to tell Tischer to side-track, leaving the
main line Western Division clear. Got that?"

The answer was evidently prompt and satisfactory,
since he began again almost in the same breath.

"Now go out yourself and flag Callahan before he
reaches the limits. Tell him the time-card's changed
and he is to run *west* with the special to Megilp as first
section of the mail—no stops, or Tischer will run him
down. Leg it! He's half-way down the yard, now!"

The train-master dropped the ear-piece of the telephone and crossed quickly to the despatcher's table.

"Orders for the Western Division, Donohue," he said
curtly, "and don't let the grass grow. 'Receiver's car,
Callahan, engineer, runs to Megilp as first section of
fast mail. Fast mail, Hunt, conductor; Tischer, engineer; runs to the end of the division without stop, mak-

ing up all time possible.' Add to that last, 'By order of the receiver.' "

The orders were sent as swiftly as the despatcher could rattle them off on his key; and then followed an interval of waiting more terrible than a battle. Kent tried to speak, but his lips were parched and his tongue was like a dry stick between his teeth. What was doing in the lower yard? Would Durgan fail at the pinch and mismanage it so as to give the alarm? The minutes dragged leaden-winged, and even the sounders on the despatcher's table were silent.

Suddenly the clicking began again. The operator at "yard limits" was sending the O. K. to the two train orders. So far, so good. Now if Callahan could get safely out on the Western Division. . .

But there was a hitch in the lower yard. Durgan had obeyed his orders promptly and precisely, and had succeeded in stopping Callahan at the street-crossing where Engineer Dixon had killed the farmer. Durgan climbed to the cab of the 1010, and the changed plan was explained in a dozen words. But now came the crux.

"If I stand here till you'd be bringin' me my orders, I'll have the whole kit av thim buzzin' round to know fwhat's the matthēr," said Callahan; but there was no other thing to do, and Durgan hurried back to the telegraph office to play the messenger.

He was too long about it. Before he got back, Halkett was under the cab window of the 1010, demanding to know—with many objurgations—why Callahan had stopped in the middle of the yards.

"Get a move on you!" he shouted. "The express is right behind us, and it'll run us down, you damned bog-trotter!"

Callahan's gauntleted hand shot up to the throttle-bar.

"I'm l'avin', Misther Halkett," he said mildly. "Will yez go back to the car, or ride wit' me?"

The general superintendent took no chance of catching the Naught-seven's hand-rails in the darkness, and he whipped up into the cab at the first sharp cough of the exhaust.

"I'll go back when you stop for your orders," he said; but a shadowy figure had leaped upon the engine-step a scant half-second behind him, and Callahan was stuffing the crumpled copy of the order into the sweat-band of his cap. The next instant the big 1010 leaped forward like a blooded horse under an unmerited cut of the whip, slid past the yard limits telegraph office and shot out upon the main line of the Western Division.

"Sit down, Misther Halkett, an' make yerself aisy!" yelled Callahan across the cab. " 'Tis small use Jimmy Shovel 'll have for his box this night."

"Shut off, you Irish madman!" was the shouted command. "Don't you see you're on the wrong division?"

Callahan gave the throttle-bar another outward hitch, tipped his seat and took a hammer from the tool-box.

"I know where I'm goin', an' that's more thin you know, ye blandhanderin' divil! Up on that box wit' you, an' kape out av Jimmy Shovel's road, or I'll be the death av yez! Climb, now!"

It was at this moment that the tense strain of suspense was broken in the despatcher's room on the second floor of the Union Station. The telephone skirled joyously, and the train-master snatched up the ear-piece.

"What does he say?" asked Kent.

"It's all right. He says Callahan is out on the Western Division, with Tischer chasing him according to programme. Halkett's in the cab of the 1010 with Patsy, and—hold on— By George! he says one of them jumped the car as it was passing the limits station!"

"Which one was it?" asked Kent; and he had to wait till the reply came from Durgan.

"It was Hawk, the right-of-way man. He broke and ran for the nearest electric-car line the minute he hit the ground, Durgan says. Does he count?"

"No," said Kent; but it is always a mistake to underrate an enemy's caliber—even that of his small arms.

XXVIII

THE NIGHT OF ALARMS

If Editor Hildreth had said nothing in his evening edition about the impending strike on the Trans-Western, it was not because public interest was waning. For a fortnight the newspapers in the territory tributary to the road had been full of strike talk, and Hildreth had said his say, deprecating the threatened appeal to force as fearlessly as he condemned the mismanagement which was provoking it.

But it was Kent who was responsible for the dearth of news on the eve of the event. Early in the morning of the last day of the month he had sought out the editor and begged him to close the columns of the *Evening Argus* to strike news, no matter what should come in during the course of the day.

"I can't go into the reasons as deeply now as I hope to a little later," he had said, his secretive habit holding good to the final fathom of the slipping hawser of events. "But you must bear with me once more, and

(356)

whatever you hear between now and the time you go to press, don't comment on it. I have one more chance to win out, and it hangs in a balance that a feather's weight might tip the wrong way. I'll be with you between ten and twelve to-night, and you can safely save two columns of the morning paper for the sensation I'm going to give you."

It was in fulfilment of this promise that Kent bestirred himself after he had sent a wire to Ormsby, and M'Tosh had settled down to the task of smoothing Callahan's way westward over a division already twitching in the preliminary rigor of the strike convulsion.

"I am going to set the fuse for the newspaper explosion," he said to his ally. "Barring accidents, there is no reason why we shouldn't begin to figure definitely upon the result, is there?"

M'Tosh was leaning over Despatcher Donohue's shoulder. He had slipped Donohue's fingers aside from the key to cut in with a peremptory "G. S." order suspending, in favor of the fast mail, the rule which requires a station operator to drop his board on a following section that is less than ten minutes behind its file-leader.

"The fun is beginning," said the train-master. "Tischer has his tip from Durgan to keep Callahan's tail-lights in sight. With the mail treading on their heels the gentlemen in the Naught-seven will be chary about pulling Patsy down too suddenly in mid career. They have just passed Morning Dew, and the operator reports Tischer for disregarding his slow signal."

"Can't you fix that?" asked Kent.

"Oh, yes; that is one of the things I can fix. But there are going to be plenty of others."

"Still we must take something for granted, Mr. M'Tosh. What I have to do up-town won't wait until Callahan has finished his run. I thought the main difficulty was safely overcome."

"Umph!" said the train-master; "the troubles are barely getting themselves born. You must remember that we swapped horses at the last minute. We were ready for the race to the east. Everybody on the Prairie Division had been notified that a special was to go through to-night without stop from Lesterville to A. & T. Junction."

"Well?"

"Now we have it all to straighten out by wire on another division; meeting points to make, slow trains to side-track, fool operators to hold down; all on the dizzy edge of a strike that is making every man on the line lose his balance. But you go ahead with your newspaper business. I'll do what a man can here. And if you come across that right-of-way agent, I wish you'd make it a case of assault and battery and get him locked up. I'm leery about him."

Kent went his way dubiously reflective. In the moment of triumph, when Durgan had announced the success of the bold change in the programme, he had made light of Hawk's escape. But now he saw possibilities. True, the junto was leaderless for the moment, and Bucks had no very able lieutenants. But Hawk would give the alarm; and there was the rank and file of the machine to reckon with. And for weapons, the ring controlled the police power of the State and of the city. Let the word be passed that the employees of the Trans-Western were kidnapping their receiver and the governor, and many things might happen before "Red" Callahan should finish his long race to the westward.

Thinking of these things, David Kent walked uptown when he might have taken a car. When the toxin of panic is in the air there is no antidote like vigorous action.

Passing the Western Union central office, he stopped to send Ormsby a second telegram, reporting progress and asking him to be present in person at the dénouement to put the facts on the wire at the earliest possible instant of time. "Everything depends upon this," he added, when he had made the message otherwise emphatic. "If we miss the morning papers, we are done."

While he was pocketing his change at the receiving clerk's pigeon-hole, a cab rattled up with a horse at a gallop, and Stephen Hawk sprang out. Kent saw him through the plate-glass front and turned quickly to the public writing-desk, hoping to be overlooked. He was. For once in a way the ex-district attorney was too nearly rattled to be fully alert to his surroundings. There were others at the standing desk; and Hawk wrote his message, after two or three false starts, almost at Kent's elbow.

Kent heard the chink of coin and the low-spoken urgings for haste at the receiving clerk's window; but he forbore to move until the cab had rattled away. Then he gathered up the spoiled blanks left behind by Hawk and smoothed them out. Two of them bore nothing but the date line, made illegible, it would seem, by the writer's haste and nervousness. But at the third attempt Hawk had got as far as the address: "To All Trans-Western agents on Western Division."

Kent stepped quickly to the receiver's window. The only expedient he could think of was open to reproach, but it was no time to be over-scrupulous.

"Pardon me," he began, "but didn't the gentleman who was just here forget to sign his message?"

The little hook caught its minnow. The receiving clerk was folding Hawk's message to place it in the leather carrier of the pneumatic tube, but he opened and examined it.

"No," he said; "it's signed all right: 'J. B. Halkett, G. S.'"

"Ah!" said Kent. "That's a little odd. Mr. Halkett is out of town, and this gentleman, Mr. Hawk, is not in his department. I believe I should investigate a little before sending that, if I were you."

Having thus sown the small seed of suspicion, which, by the by, fell on barren soil, Kent lost no time in calling up M'Tosh over the nearest telephone.

"Do our agents on the Western Division handle Western Union business?" he asked.

The reply came promptly.

"Yes; locally. The W-U. has an independent line to Breezeland Inn and points beyond."

"Well, our right-of-way man has just sent a telegram to all agents, signing Halkett's name. I don't know what he said in it, but you can figure that out for yourself."

"You bet I can!" was the emphatic rejoinder. And then: "Where are you now?"

"I'm at the Clarendon public 'phone, but I am going over to the *Argus* office. I'll let you know when I leave there. Good-by."

When Kent reached the night editor's den on the third floor of the *Argus* building he found Hildreth immersed chin-deep in a sea of work. But he quickly extricated himself and cleared a chair for his visitor.

"Praise be!" he ejaculated. "I was beginning to get anxious. Large things are happening, and you didn't turn up. I've had Manville wiring all over town for you."

"What are some of the large things?" asked Kent, lighting his first cigar since dinner.

"Well, for one: do you know that your people are on the verge of the much-talked-of strike?"

"Yes; I knew it this morning. That was what I wanted you to suppress in the evening edition."

"I suppressed it all right; I didn't know it—day and date, I mean. They kept it beautifully quiet. But that isn't all. Something is happening at the capitol. I was over at the club a little while ago, and Hendricks was there. Somebody sent in a note, and he positively ran to get out. When I came back, I sent Rogers over to Cassatti's to see if he could find you. There was a junto dinner confab on; Meigs, Senator Crowley, three or four of the ring aldermen and half a dozen wa-ward politicians. Rogers has a nose for news, and when he had 'phoned me you weren't there, he hung around on the edges."

"Good men you have, Hildreth. What did the unimpeachable Rogers see?"

"He saw on a large scale just what I had seen on a small one: somebody pup-passed a note in, and when it had gone the round of the dinner-table those fellows tumbled over each other trying to get away."

"Is that all?" Kent inquired.

"No. Apart from his nose, Rogers is gifted with horse sense. When the dinner crowd boarded an up-town car, our man paid fare to the same conductor. He wired me from the Hotel Brunswick a few minutes ago. There is some sort of a caucus going on in Hendricks' office in the capitol, and mum-messengers are flying in all directions."

"And you wanted me to come and tell you all the whys and wherefores?" Kent suggested.

"I told the chief I'd bet a bub-blind horse to a broken-down mule you could do it if anybody could."

"All right; listen: something worse than an hour ago the governor, his private secretary, Guilford, Hawk and Halkett started out on a special train to go to Gaston."

"What for?" interrupted the editor.

"To meet Judge MacFarlane, Mr. Semple Falkland, and the Overland officials. You can guess what was to be done?"

"Sure. Your railroad was to be sold out, lock, stock and barrel; or leased to the Overland for ninety-nine years—which amounts to the same thing."

"Precisely. Well, by some unaccountable mishap the receiver's special was switched over to the Western Division at yard limits, and the engineer seems to think he has orders to proceed westward. At all events, that is what he is doing. And the funny part of it is that he can't stop to find out his blunder. The fast mail is right behind him, with the receiver's order to smash anything that gets in its way; so you see—"

"That will do," said the night editor. "We don't print fairy stories in the *Argus.*"

"None the less, you are going to print this one to-morrow morning, just as I'm telling it to you," Kent asserted confidently. "And when you get the epilogue you will say that it makes my little preface wearisome by contrast."

The light was slowly dawning in the editorial mind.

"My heaven!" he exclaimed. "Kent, you're good for twenty years, at the very lul-least!"

"Am I? It occurs to me that the prosecuting attorney in the case will have a hard time proving anything. Doesn't it look that way to you? At the worst, it is only an unhappy misunderstanding of orders. And if the end should happen to justify the means—"

Hildreth shook his head gravely.

"You don't understand, David. If you could be sure of a fair-minded judge and an unbiased jury—you and those who are implicated with you: but you'll get neither in this machine-ridden State."

"We are going to have both, after you have filled your two columns—by the way, you are still saving those two columns for me, aren't you?—in to-morrow morning's *Argus.* Or rather, I'm hoping there will be no need for either judge or jury."

The night editor shook his head again, and once more
he said, "My heaven!" adding: "What could you possibly hope to accomplish? You'll get the receiver and
his big boss out of the State for a few minutes, or possibly for a few hours, if your strike makes them hunt
up another railroad to return on. But what will it
amount to? Getting rid of the receiver doesn't annul
the decree of the court."

Kent fell back on his secretive habit yet once again.

"I don't care to anticipate the climax, Hildreth. By
one o'clock one of two things will have happened:
you'll get a wire that will make your back hair sit up,
or I'll get one that will make me wish I'd never been
born. Let it rest at that for the present; you have work
enough on hand to fill up the interval, and if you
haven't, you can distribute those affidavits I gave you
among the compositors and get them into type. I want
to see them in the paper to-morrow morning, along with
the other news."

"Oh, we can't do that, David! The time isn't ripe.
You know what I told you about—"

"If the time doesn't ripen to-night, Hildreth, it never
will. Do as I tell you, and get that stuff into type. Do
more; write the hottest editorial you can think of, demanding to know if it isn't time for the people to rise
and clean out this stable once for all."

"By Jove! David, I've half a mum-mind to do it.

If you'd only unbutton yourself a little, and let me see what my backing is going to be—"

"All in good season," laughed Kent. "Your business for the present moment is to write; I'm going down to the Union Station."

"What for?" demanded the editor.

"To see if our crazy engineer is still mistaking his orders properly."

"Hold on a minute. How did the enemy get wind of your plot so quickly? You can tell me that, can't you?"

"Oh, yes; I told you Hawk was one of the party in the private car. He fell off at the yard limits station and came back to town."

The night editor stood up and confronted his visitor.

"David, you are either the coolest plunger that ever drew breath—or the bub-biggest fool. I wouldn't be standing in your shoes to-night for two such railroads as the T-W."

Kent laughed again and opened the door.

"I suppose not. But you know there is no accounting for the difference in tastes. I feel as if I had never really lived before this night; the only thing that troubles me is the fear that somebody or something will get in the way of my demented engineer."

He went out into the hall, but as Hildreth was closing the door he turned back.

"There is one other thing that I meant to say: when

you get your two columns of sensation, you've got to be decent and share with the Associated Press."

"I'm dud-dashed if I do!" said Hildreth, fiercely.

"Oh, yes, you will; just the bare facts, you know. You'll have all the exciting details for an 'exclusive,' to say nothing of the batch of affidavits in the oil scandal. And it is of the last importance to me that the facts shall be known to-morrow morning wherever the Associated has a wire."

"Go away!" said the editor, "and dud-don't come back here till you can uncork yourself like a man and a Cuc-Christian! Go off, I say!"

It wanted but a few minutes of eleven when Kent mounted the stair to the despatcher's room in the Union Station. He found M'Tosh sitting at Donohue's elbow, and the sounders on the glass-topped table were crackling like overladen wires in an electric storm.

"Strike talk," said the train-master. "Every man on both divisions wants to know what's doing. Got your newspaper string tied up all right?"

Kent made a sign of assent.

"We are waiting for Mr. Patrick Callahan. Any news from him?"

"Plenty of it. Patsy would have a story to tell, all right, if he could stop to put it on the wires. Durgan ought to have caught that blamed right-of-way man and chloroformed him."

"I found him messing, as I 'phoned you. Anything come of it?"

"Nothing fatal, I guess, since Patsy is still humping along. But Hawk's next biff was more to the purpose. He came down here with Halkett's chief clerk, whom he had hauled out of bed, and two policemen. The plan was to fire Donohue and me, and put Bicknell in charge. It might have worked if Bicknell'd had the sand. But he weakened at the last minute; admitted that he wasn't big enough to handle the despatcher's trick. The way Hawk cursed him out was a caution to sinners."

"When was this?" Kent asked.

"Just a few minutes ago. Hawk went off ripping; swore he would find somebody who wasn't afraid to take the wires. And, between us three, I'm scared stiff for fear he will."

"Can it be done?"

"Dead easy, if he knows how to go about it—and Bicknell will tell him. The Overland people don't love us any too well, and if they did, the lease deal would make them side with Guilford and the governor. If Hawk asks them to lend him a train despatcher for a few minutes, they'll do it."

"But the union?" Kent objected.

"They have three or four non-union men."

"Still, Hawk has no right to discharge you."

"Bicknell has. He is Halkett's representative, and—"

The door opened suddenly and Hawk danced in, followed by a man bareheaded and in his shirt-sleeves, the superintendent's chief clerk, and the two officers.

"Now, then, we'll trouble you and your man to get out of here, Mr. M'Tosh," said the captain of the junto forces, vindictively.

But the train-master was of those who die hard. He protested vigorously, ·addressing himself to Bicknell and ignoring the ex-district attorney as if he were not. He, McTosh, was willing to surrender the office on an official order in writing over the chief clerk's signature. But did Bicknell fully understand what it might mean in loss of life and property to put a new man on the wires at a moment's notice?

Bicknell would have weakened again, but Hawk was not to be frustrated a second time.

"Don't you see he is only sparring to gain time?" he snapped at Bicknell. Then to M'Tosh: "Get out of here, and do it quick! And you can go, too," wheeling suddenly upon Kent.

Donohue had taken no part in the conflict of authority. But now he threw down his pen and clicked his key to cut in with the "G. S.," which claims the wire instantly. Then distinctly, and a word at a time so that the slowest operator on the line could get it, he spelled out the message: "All Agents: Stop and hold all trains except first and second fast mail, west-bound. M'Tosh fired, and office in hands of police—"

"Stop him!" cried the shirt-sleeved man. "He's giving it away on the wire!"

But Donohue had signed his name and was putting on his coat.

"You're welcome to what you can find," he said, scowling at the interloper. "If you kill anybody now, it'll be your own fault."

"Arrest that man!" said Hawk to his policemen; but Kent interposed.

"If you do, the force will be two men shy to-morrow. The Civic League isn't dead yet." And he took down the numbers of the two officers.

There were no arrests made, and when the ousted three were clear of the room and the building, Kent asked an anxious question.

"How near can they come to smashing us, M'Tosh?"

"That depends on Callahan's nerve. The night operators at Donerail, Schofield and Agua Caliente are all Guilford appointees, and when the new man explains the situation to them, they'll do what they are told to do. But I'm thinking Patsy won't pull up for anything milder than a spiked switch."

"Well, they might throw a switch on him. I wonder somebody hasn't done it before this."

The train-master shook his head.

"If Tischer is keeping close up behind, that would jeopardize more lives than Callahan's. But there is another thing that doesn't depend on nerve—Patsy's or anybody's."

"What is that?"

"Water. The run is one hundred and eighty miles. The 1010's tank is good for one hundred with a train, or a possible hundred and sixty, light. There is about one chance in a thousand that Callahan's crown-sheet won't get red-hot and crumple up on him in the last twenty miles. Let's take a car and go down to yard limits. We can sit in the office and hear what goes over the wires, even if we can't get a finger in to help Patsy out of his troubles."

They boarded a Twentieth Avenue car accordingly, but when they reached the end of the line, which was just across the tracks from the junction in the lower yards, they found the yard limits office and the shops surrounded by a cordon of militia.

"By George!" said M'Tosh. "They got quick action, didn't they? I suppose it's on the ground of the strike and possible violence."

Kent spun on his heel, heading for the electric car they had just left.

"Back to town," he said; "unless you two want to jump the midnight Overland as it goes out and get away while you can. If Callahan fails—"

XXIX

THE RELENTLESS WHEELS

But Engineer Callahan had no notion of failing. When he had drawn the hammer on his superior officer, advising discretion and a seat on Jimmy Shovel's box, the 1010 was racking out over the switches in the Western Division yards. Three minutes later the electric beam of Tischer's following headlight sought and found the first section on the long tangent leading up to the high plains, and the race was in full swing.

At Morning Dew, the first night telegraph station out of the capital, the two sections were no more than a scant quarter of a mile apart; and the operator tried to flag the second section down, as reported. This did not happen again until several stations had been passed, and Callahan set his jaw and gave the 1010 more throttle. But at Lossing, a town of some size, the board was down and a man ran out at the crossing, swinging a red light.

Callahan looked well to the switches, with the steam shut off and his hand dropping instinctively to the air;

(372)

and the superintendent shrank into his corner and gripped the window ledge when the special roared past the warning signals and on through the town beyond. He had maintained a dazed silence since the episode of the flourished hammer, but now he was moved to yell across the cab.

"I suppose you know what you're in for, if you live to get out of this! It's twenty years, in this State, to pass a danger signal!" This is not all that the superintendent said: there were forewords and interjections, emphatic but unprintable.

Callahan's reply was another flourish of the hammer, and a sudden outpulling of the throttle-bar; and the superintendent subsided again.

But enforced silence and the grindstone of conscious helplessness will sharpen the dullest wit. The swerving lurch of the 1010 around the next curve set Halkett clutching for hand-holds, and the injector lever fell within his grasp. What he did not know about the working parts of a modern locomotive was very considerable; but he did know that an injector, half opened, will waste water as fast as an inch pipe will discharge it. And without water the Irishman would have to stop.

Callahan heard the chuckling of the wasting boiler feed before he had gone a mile beyond the curve. It was a discovery to excuse bad language, but his protest was lamb-like.

"No more av that, if ye plaze, Misther Halkett, or me an' Jimmy Shovel'll have to—Ah! would yez, now?"

Before his promotion to the superintendency Halkett had been a ward boss in the metropolis of the State. Thinking he saw his chance, he took it, and the blow knocked Callahan silly for the moment. Afterward there was a small free-for-all buffeting match in the narrow cab in which the fireman took a hand, and during which the racing 1010 was suffered to find her way alone. When it was over, Callahan spat out a broken tooth and gave his orders concisely.

"Up wid him over the coal, an' we'll put him back in the car where he belongs. Now, thin!"

Halkett had to go, and he went, not altogether unwillingly. And when it came to jumping across from the rear of the tender to the forward vestibule of the Naught-seven, or being chucked across, he jumped.

Now it so chanced that the governor and his first lieutenant in the great railway steal had weighty matters to discuss, and they had not missed the superintendent or the lawyer, supposing them to be still out on the rear platform enjoying the scenery. Wherefore Halkett's sudden appearance, mauled, begrimed and breathless from his late tussle with the two enginemen, was the first intimation of wrong-going that had penetrated to the inner sanctum of the private car.

"What's that you say, Mr. Halkett?—on the Western Division? Whereabouts?" demanded the governor.

"Between Lossing and Skipjack siding—if we haven't passed the siding in the last two or three minutes. I've been too busy to notice," was the reply.

"And you say you were on the engine? Why the devil didn't you call your man down?"

"I knocked him down," gritted the superintendent, savagely, "and I'd have beat his face in for him if there hadn't been two of them. It's a plot of some kind, and Callahan knows what he is about. He had me held up with a hammer till just a few minutes ago, and he's running past stop-signals and over red lights like a madman!"

Bucks and Guilford exchanged convictions by the road of the eye, and the governor said:

"This is pretty serious, Major. Have you anything to suggest?" And without waiting for a reply he turned upon Halkett: "Where is Mr. Hawk?"

"I don't know. I supposed he was in here with you. Or maybe he's out on the rear platform."

The three of them went to the rear, passing the private secretary comfortably asleep in his wicker chair. When they stepped out upon the recessed observation platform they found it empty.

"He must have suspected something and dropped off

in the yard or at the shops," said Halkett. And at the saying of it he shrank back involuntarily and added: "Ah! Look at that, will you?"

The car had just thundered past another station, and Callahan had underrun one more stop-signal at full speed. At the same instant Tischer's headlight swung into view, half blinding them with its glare.

"What is that following us?" asked Bucks.

"It's the fast mail," said Halkett.

Guilford turned livid and caught at the hand-rail.

"S-s-say—are you sure of that?" he gasped.

"Of course: it was an hour and thirty-five minutes late, and we are on its time."

"Then we can't stop unless somebody throws us on a siding!" quavered the receiver, who had a small spirit in a large body. "I told M'Tosh to give the mail orders to make up her lost time or I'd fire the engineer—told him to cut out all the stops this side of Agua Caliente!"

"That's what you get for your infernal meddling!" snapped Halkett. In catastrophic moments many barriers go down; deference to superior officers among the earliest.

But the master spirit of the junto was still cool and collected.

"This is no time to quarrel," he said. "The thing to

be done is to stop this train without getting ourselves ripped open by that fellow behind the headlight yonder. The stop-signals prove that Hawk and the others are doing their best, but we must do ours. What do you say, Halkett?"

"There is only one thing," replied the superintendent; "we've got to make the Irishman run ahead fast enough and far enough to give us room to stop or take a siding."

The governor planned it in a few curt sentences. Was there a weapon to be had? Danforth, the private secretary, roused from his nap in the wicker chair, was able to produce a serviceable revolver. Two minutes later, the sleep still tingling in his nerves to augment another tingling less pleasurable, the secretary had spanned the terrible gap separating the car from the engine and was making his way over the coal, fluttering his handkerchief in token of his peaceful intentions.

He was charged with a message to Callahan, mandatory in its first form, and bribe-promising in its second; and he was covered from the forward vestibule of the private car by the revolver in the hands of a resolute and determined state executive.

"One of them's comin' ahead over the coal," warned James Shovel; and Callahan found his hammer.

"Run ahead an' take a siding, is ut?" he shouted, glaring down on the messenger. "I have me ordhers fr'm betther men than thim that sint you. Go back an' tell thim so."

"You'll be paid if you do, and you'll be shot if you don't," yelled the secretary, persuasively.

"Tell the boss he can't shoot two av us to wanst; an' the wan that's left 'll slap on the air," was Callahan's answer; and he slacked off a little to bring the following train within easy striking distance.

Danforth went painfully and carefully back with this defiance, and while he was bridging the nerve-trying gap, another station with the stop-board down and red lights frantically swinging was passed with a roar and a whistle shriek.

"Fwhat are they doing now?" called Callahan to his fireman.

"They've gone inside again," was the reply.

"Go back an' thry the tank," was the command; and Jimmy Shovel climbed over the coal and let himself down feet foremost into the manhole. When he slid back to the footplate his legs were wet to the mid shin.

"It's only up to there," he reported, measuring with his hand.

Callahan looked at his watch. There was yet a full hour's run ahead of him, and there was no more than a scant foot of water in the tank with which to make it.

Thereafter he forgot the Naught-seven, and whatever

menace it held for him, and was concerned chiefly with
the thing mechanical. Would the water last him
through? He had once made one hundred and seventy
miles on a special run with the 1010 without refilling
his tank; but that was with the light engine alone.
Now he had the private car behind him, and it seemed
at times to pull with all the drag of a heavy train.

But one expedient remained, and that carried with it
the risk of his life. An engine, not overburdened, uses
less water proportionately to miles run as the speed is
increased. He could outpace the safe-guarding mail,
save water—and take the chance of being shot in the
back from the forward vestibule of the Naught-seven
when he had gained lead enough to make a main-line
stop safe for the men behind him.

Callahan thought once of the child mothered by the
Sisters of Loretto in the convent at the capital, shut his
eyes to that and to all things extraneous, and sent the
1010 about her business. At the first reversed curve he
hung out of his window for a backward look. Tischer's
headlight had disappeared and his protection was gone.

On the rear platform of the private car four men
watched the threatening second section fade into the
night.

"Our man has thought better of it," said the governor, marking the increased speed and the disappear-
ance of the menacing headlight.

Guilford's sigh of relief was almost a groan.

"My God!" he said; "it makes me cold to think what might happen if he should pull us over into the other State!"

But Halkett was still smarting from the indignities put upon him, and his comment was a vindictive threat.

"I'll send that damned Irishman over the road for this, if it is the last thing I ever do!" he declared; and he confirmed it with an oath.

But Callahan was getting his punishment as he went along. He had scarcely settled the 1010 into her gait for the final run against the failing water supply when another station came in sight. It was a small cattle town, and in addition to the swinging red lights and a huge bonfire to illuminate the yards, the obstruction-ists had torn down the loading corral and were piling the lumber on the track.

Once again Callahan's nerve flickered, and he shut off the steam. But before it was too late he reflected that the barrier was meant only to scare him into stop-ping. One minute later the air was full of flying splint-ers, and that danger was passed. But one of the broken planks came through the cab window, missing the en-gineer by no more than a hand's-breadth. And the shower of splinters, sucked in by the whirl of the train, broke glass in the private car and sprinkled the quar-tet on the platform with split kindling and wreckage.

"What was that?" gasped the receiver.

Halkett pointed to the bonfire, receding like a fading star in the rearward distance.

"Our friends are beginning to throw stones, since clods won't stop him." he said.

Bucks shook his head.

"If that is the case, we'll have to be doing something on our own account. The next obstruction may derail us."

Halkett stepped into the car and pulled the cord of the automatic air.

"No good," he muttered. "The Irishman bled our tank before he started. Help me set the hand brakes, a couple of you."

Danforth and the governor took hold of the brake wheel with him, and for a minute or two the terrible speed slackened a little. Then some part of the disused hand-gear gave way under the three-man strain and that hope was gone.

"There's one thing left," said the superintendent, indomitable to the last. "We'll uncouple and let him drop us behind."

The space in the forward vestibule was narrow and cramped, and with the strain of the dragging car to make the pin stick, it took two of them lying flat, waiting for the back-surging moment and wiggling it for slack, to pull it. The coupling dropped out of the hook and the engine shot ahead to the length of the safety-chains; thus far, but no farther.

Halkett stood up.

"It's up to you, Danforth," he said, raising his voice to be heard above the pounding roar of the wheels. "You're the youngest and lightest: get down on the 1010's brake-beam and unhook those chains."

The secretary looked once into the trap with the dodging jaws and the backward-flying bottom and declined the honor.

"I can't get down there," he cried. "And I shouldn't know what to do if I could."

Once more the superintendent exhibited his nerve. He had nothing at stake save a desire to defeat Callahan; but he had the persistent courage of the bull-terrier. With Bucks and the secretary to steady him he lowered himself in the gap till he could stand upon the brake-beam of the 1010's tender and grope with one free hand for the hook of the nearest safety-chain. Death nipped at him every time the engine gave or took up the slack of the loose coupling, but he dodged and hung on until he had satisfied himself.

"It's no good," he announced, when they had dragged him by main strength back to a footing in the narrow vestibule. "The hooks are bent into the links. We're due to go wherever that damned Irishman is taking us."

Shovel was firing, and the trailing smoke and cinders quickly made the forward vestibule untenable. When they were driven in, Bucks and the receiver went through to the rear platform, where they were presently joined by Halkett and Danforth.

"I've been trying the air again," said the superintendent, "but it's no go. What's next?"

The governor gave the word.

"Wait," he said; and the four of them clung to the hand-rails, swaying and bending to the bounding lurches of the flying car.

Mile after mile reels from beneath the relentless wheels, and still the speed increases. Station Donerail is passed, and now the pace is so furious that the watchers on the railed platform can not make out the signals in the volleying wake of dust. Station Schofield is passed, and again the signals, if any there be, are swiftly drowned in the gray dust-smother. From Schofield to Agua Caliente is but a scant ten miles; and as the flying train rushes on toward the State boundary, two faces in the quartet of watchers show tense and drawn under the yellow light of the Pintsch platform lamp.

The governor swings himself unsteadily to the right-hand railing and the long look ahead brings the twinkling arc-star of the tower light on Breezeland Inn into view. He turns to Guilford, who has fallen limp into one of the platform chairs.

"In five minutes more we shall pass Agua Caliente," he says. "Will you kill the Irishman, or shall I?" Guilford's lips move, but there is no audible reply; and Bucks takes Danforth's weapon and passes quickly and alone to the forward vestibule.

The station of Agua Caliente swings into the field of 1010's electric headlight. Callahan's tank has been bone dry for twenty minutes, and he is watching the glass water-gage where the water shows now only when the engine lurches heavily to the left. He knows that the crown-sheet of the fire-box is bare, and that any moment it may give down and the end will come. Yet his gauntleted hand never falls from the throttle-bar to the air-cock, and his eyes never leave the bubble appearing and disappearing at longer intervals in the heel of the water-glass.

Shovel has stopped firing, and is hanging out of his window for the straining look ahead. Suddenly he drops to the footplate to grip Callahan's arm.

"See!" he says. "They have set the switch to throw us in on the siding!" In one motion the flutter of the exhaust ceases, and the huge ten-wheeler buckles to the sudden setting of the brakes. The man standing in the forward vestibule of the Naught-seven lowers

his weapon. Apparently it is not going to be necessary to kill the engineer, after all.

But Callahan's nerve has failed him only for the moment. There is one chance in ten thousand that the
circumambulating side track is empty; one and one
only, and no way to make sure of it. Beyond the station,
as Callahan well knows, the siding comes again into
the main line, and the switch is a straight-rail "safety."
Once again the thought of his motherless child flickers
into the engineer's brain; then he releases the air and
throws his weight backward upon the throttle-bar. Two
gasps and a heart-beat decide it; and before the man
in the vestibule can level his weapon and fire, the one-
car train has shot around the station, heaving and
lurching over the uneven rails of the siding, and grind-
ing shrilly over the points of the safety switch to race
on the down grade to Megilp.

At the mining-camp the station is in darkness save
for the goggle eyes of an automobile drawn up beside
the platform, and deep silence reigns but for the muffled,
irregular thud of the auto-car's motor. But the beam of
the 1010's headlight shows the small station building
massed by men, a score of them poising for a spring to
the platforms of the private car when the slackening
speed shall permit. A bullet tears into the woodwork at
Callahan's elbow, and another breaks the glass of the

window beside him, but he makes the stop as steadily as if death were not snapping at him from behind and roaring in his ears from the belly of the burned engine.

"Be doomping yeɽ fire lively, now, Jimmy, b'y," he says, dropping from his box to help. And while they wrestle with the dumping-bar, these two, the poising figures have swarmed upon the Naught-seven, and a voice is lifted above the Babel of others in sharp protest.

"Put away that rope, boys! There's law here, and by God, we're going to maintain it!"

At this a man pushes his way out of the thick of the crowd and climbs to a seat beside the chauffeur in the waiting automobile.

"They've got him," he says shortly. "To the hotel for all you're worth, Hudgins; our part is to get this on the wires before one o'clock. Full speed; and never mind the ruts."

XXX

SUBHI SADIK

The dawn of a new day was graying over the capital city, and the newsboys were crying lustily in the streets, when David Kent felt his way up the dark staircases of the Kittleton Building to knock at the door of Judge Oliver Marston's rooms on the top floor. He was the bearer of tidings, and he made no more than a formal excuse for .the unseemly hour when the door was opened by the lieutenant-governor.

"I am sorry to disturb you, Judge Marston," he began, when he had the closed door at his back and was facing the tall thin figure in flannel dressing gown and slippers, "but I imagine I'm only a few minutes ahead of the crowd. Have you heard the news of the night?"

The judge pressed the button of the drop-light and waved his visitor to a chair.

"I have heard nothing, Mr. Kent. Have a cigar?"— passing the box of unutterable stogies.

(387)

"Thank you; not before breakfast," was the hasty reply. Then, without another word of preface: "Judge Marston, for the time being you are the governor of the State, and I have come to—"

"One moment," interrupted his listener. "There are some stories that read better for a foreword, however brief. What has happened?"

"This: last night it was the purpose of Governor Bucks and Receiver Guilford to go to Gaston by special train. In some manner, which has not yet been fully explained, there was a confusion of orders. Instead of proceeding eastward, the special was switched to the tracks of the Western Division; was made the first section of the fast mail, which had orders to run through without stop. You can imagine the result."

Marston got upon his feet slowly and began pacing the length of the long room. Kent waited, and the shrill cries of the newsboys floated up and in through the open windows. When the judge finally came back to his chair the saturnine face was gray and haggard.

"I hope it was an accident that can be clearly proved," he said; and a moment later: "You spoke of Bucks and Guilford; were there others in the private car?"

"Two others; Halkett, and the governor's private secretary."

"And were they all killed?"

A great light broke in upon Kent when he saw how Marston had misapprehended. Also, he saw how much it would simplify matters if he should be happy enough to catch the ball in the reactionary rebound.

"They are all alive and uninjured, to the best of my knowledge and belief; though I understand that one of them narrowly escaped lynching at the hands of an excited mob."

The long lean figure erected itself in the chair, and the weight of years seemed to slip from its shoulders.

"But I understood you to say that the duties of the executive had devolved upon me, Mr. Kent. You also said I could imagine the result of this singular mistaking of train-orders, and I fancied I could. What was the result?"

"A conclusion not quite as sanguinary as that you had in mind, though it is likely to prove serious enough for one member of the party in the private car. The special train was chased all the way across the State by the fast mail. It finally outran the pursuing section and was stopped at Megilp. A sheriff's posse was in waiting, and an arrest was made."

"Go on," said the lieutenant-governor.

"I must first go back a little. Some weeks ago there was a shooting affray in the mining-camp, arising out of a dispute over a 'salted' mine, and a man was killed.

The murderer escaped across the State line. Since the authorities of the State in which the crime was committed had every reason to believe that a governor's requisition for this particular criminal would not be honored, two courses were open to them: to publish the facts and let the moral sentiment of the neighboring commonwealth punish the criminal as it could, or would; or, suppressing the facts, to bide their chance of catching their man beyond the boundaries of the State which gave him an asylum. They chose the latter."

A second time Marston left his chair and began to pace the floor. After a little he paused to say:

"This murderer is James Guilford, I take it; and the governor—"

"No," said Kent, gravely. "The murderer is—Jasper G. Bucks." He handed the judge a copy of the *Argus*. "You will find it all in the press despatches; all I have told you, and a great deal more."

The lieutenant-governor read the newspaper story as he walked, lighting the electric chandelier to enable him to do so. When it was finished he sat down again.

"What a hideous cesspool it is!" was his comment. "But we shall clean it, Mr. Kent; we shall clean it if it shall leave the People's Party without a vote in the State. Now what can I do for you? You didn't come here at this hour in the morning merely to bring me the news."

"No, I didn't, Judge Marston. I want my railroad."

"You shall have it," was the prompt response. "What have you done since our last discussion of the subject?"

"I tried to 'obliterate' Judge MacFarlane, as you suggested. But I failed in the first step. Bucks and Meigs refused to approve the *quo warranto*."

The judge knitted his brows thoughtfully.

"That way is open to you now; but it is long and devious, and delays are always dangerous. You spoke of the receivership as being part of a plan by which your road was to be turned over to an eastern monopoly. How nearly has that plan succeeded?"

Kent hesitated, not because he was afraid to trust the man Oliver Marston, but because there were some things which the governor of the State might feel called upon to investigate if the knowledge of them were thrust upon him. But in the end he took counsel of utter frankness.

"So nearly that if Bucks and the receiver had reached Gaston last night, our road would now be in the hands of the Plantagoulds under a ninety-nine-year lease."

The merest ghost of a smile flitted over the lieutenant-governor's face when he said, with his nearest approach to sarcasm:

"How extremely opportune the confusion of train-orders becomes as we go along! But answer one more question if you please—it will not involve these singularly heedless railway employees of yours: is Judge Mac-Farlane in Gaston now?"

"He is. He was to have met the others on the arrival of the special train."

There were footsteps on the stair and in the corridor, and Marston rose.

"Our privacy is about to be invaded, Mr. Kent. This is a miserable business; miserable for everybody, but most of all for the deceived and hoodwinked people of an unhappy State. God knows, I did not seek this office; but since it has fallen on me, I shall do my duty as I see it, and my hand shall be heaviest upon that man who makes a mockery of the justice he is sworn to administer. Come to the capitol a little later in the day, prepared to go at once to Gaston. I think I can promise you your hearing on the merits without further delay."

"Thank you," said Kent, simply, grasping the hand of leave-taking. Then he tried to find other and larger words. "I wish I could do something to show my appreciation of your—"

But the lieutenant-governor was pushing him toward the door.

"You have done something, Mr. Kent, and you can

do more. Head those people off at the door and say that for the present I refuse positively to be seen or interviewed. They will find me at the capitol during office hours."

It was seven o'clock in the evening of the fiercest working day Kent had ever fought through when the special train—his own private special, sent to Gaston and brought back again over the strike-paralyzed road by the express permission and command of the strikers themselves—set him down in the Union Station at the capital.

Looking back to the gray of the morning when he had shaken hands with Governor Marston at the door of the room on the top floor of the Kittleton Building, the crowding events made the interval seem more like a week; and now the events themselves were beginning to take on dream-like incongruities in the haze of utter weariness.

"*Evening Argus!* all about the p'liminary trial of Governor Bucks. *Argus,* sir?" piped a small boy at the station exit; but Kent shook his head, found a cab and had himself conveyed quickly through streets still rife with excitement to the Clarendon Hotel.

In the lobby was the same bee-buzzing crowd with which he had been contending all day, and he edged his way through it to the elevator, praying that he might go unrecognized—as he did. Once safe in his rooms he sent for Loring, stretching himself on the bed in a very ecstasy of relaxation until the ex-manager came up. Then he emptied his mind as an overladen ass spills its panniers.

"I'm done, Grantham," he said; "and that is more different kinds of truth than you have heard in a week. Go and reorganize your management, and M'Tosh is the man to put in Halkett's place. The strike will be declared off at the mere mention of your name and his. That's all. Now go away and let me sleep."

"Oh, hold on!" was the good-natured protest; "I'm not more curious than I have to be, but I'd like to know how it was done."

"I don't know, myself; and that's the plain fact. But I suspect Marston fell upon Judge McFarlane: gave him a wire hint of what was due to arrive if he didn't give us a clean bill of health. I had my preliminary interview with the governor at daybreak this morning; and I was with him again between nine and ten. He went over the original papers with me, and about all he said was, 'Be in Gaston by two o'clock this afternoon, and MacFarlane will give you the hearing in chambers.' I went on my knees to the Federative Council to get a train."

"You shouldn't have had any trouble there."

"I didn't have, after the men understood what was in the wind. Jarl Oleson took me down and brought me back. The council did it handsomely, dipping into its treasury and paying the mileage on a Pullman car."

"And MacFarlane reversed his own order?"

"Without a question. It was the merest formality. Jennison, Hawk's former law partner, stood for the other side; but he made no argument."

"Good!" said Loring. "That will do for the day's work. But now I'd like to know how last night's job was managed."

"I'm afraid you want to know more than is good for you. What do the papers say? I haven't looked at one all day."

"They say there was a misunderstanding of orders. That will answer for the public, perhaps, but it won't do for me."

"I guess it will have to do for you, too, Grantham," said Kent, yawning shamelessly. "Five men, besides myself—six of us in all—know the true inwardness of last night's round-up. There will never be a seventh."

Loring's eye-glasses fell from his nose, and he was smiling shrewdly when he replaced them.

"There is one small consequence that doesn't please you, I'm sure. You'll have to bury the hatchet with MacFarlane."

"Shall I?" flashed Kent, sitting up as if he had been struck with a whip. "Let me tell you: Marston is going to call an extra session of the Assembly. There is a death vacancy in this district, and I shall be a candidate in the special election. If there is no other way to get at MacFarlane, he shall be impeached!"

"H'm: so you're going into politics?"

"You've said it," said Kent, subsiding among the pillows. "Now will you go?"

It took the general manager a wakeful twenty-four hours to untangle the industrial snarl which was the receiver's legacy to his successor; and David Kent slept through the major part of that interval, rising only in time to dress for dinner on the day following the retrieval of the Trans-Western.

In the grill-room of the Camelot he came face to face with Ormsby, and learned, something to his astonishment, that the Breezeland party had returned to the capital on the first train in from the west.

"I thought you were going to stay a month or more," he said, with his eyes cast down.

"So did I," said Ormsby. "But Mrs. Brentwood cut it short. She's a town person, and so is Penelope." And it was not until the soup plates had been removed that he added a question. "Are you going out to see them this evening, David? You have my royal permission."

"No"—bluntly.

"Isn't it up to you to go and give them a chance to

jolly you a little? I think they are all aching to do it.
Mrs. Hepzibah has seen the rising stock quotations,
and she thinks you are It."

"No; I can't go there any more," said Kent, and
his voice was gruffer than he meant it to be.

"Why not?"

"There were good reasons before: there are better
ones now."

"A seven-hundred-thousand-dollar difference?" suggested Ormsby, who had had speech with Loring.

Kent flushed a dull red.

"I sha'n't strike you, Ormsby, no matter what you
say," he said doggedly.

"Humph! There is one difference between you and
Rabbi Balaam's burro, David: it could talk sense, and
you can't," was the offensive rejoinder.

Kent changed the subject abruptly.

"Say, Ormsby; I'm going into a political office-hunt.
There is a death vacancy in the House, and I mean
to have the nomination and election. I don't need
money now, but I do need a friend. Are you with me?"

"Oh, sure. Miss Van Brock will answer for that."

"But I don't want you to do it on her account; I
want you to do it for me."

"It's all one," said the club-man.

Kent looked up quickly.

"You are right; that is the truest word you've said

to-night," and he went away, leaving the dessert untouched.

The evening was still young when Kent reached the house in Alameda Square. Within the week the weather had changed, and the first chill of the approaching autumn was in the air. The great square house was lighted and warmed, and the homelikeness of the place appealed to him as it never had before. To her other gifts, which were many and diverse, Miss Van Brock added that of home-making; and the aftermath of battle is apt to be an acute longing for peace and quiet, for domesticity and creature comforts.

He had not seen Portia since the night when she had armed him for the final struggle with the enemy; he told himself that he should not see her again until the battle was fought and won. But in no part of the struggle had he been suffered to lose sight of his obligation to her. He had seen the chain lengthen link by link, and now the time was come for the welding of it into a shackle to bind. He did not try to deceive himself, nor did he allow the glamour of false sentiment to blind him. With an undying love for Elinor Brentwood in his heart, he knew well what was before him. None the less, Portia should have her just due.

She was waiting for him when he entered the comfortable library.

"I knew you would come to-night," she said cheerfully. "I gave you a day to drive the nail—and, O David! you have driven it well!—another day to clinch it, and a third to recover from the effects. Have you fully recovered?"

"I hope so. I took the day for it, at all events," he laughed. "I am just out of bed, as you might say."

"I can imagine how it took it out of you," she assented. "Not so much the work, but the anxiety. Night before last, after Mr. Loring went away, I sat it out with the telephone, nagging poor Mr. Hildreth for news until I know he wanted to murder me."

"How much did you get of it?" he asked.

"He told me all he dared—or perhaps it was all he knew—and it made me feel miserably helpless. The little I could get from the *Argus* office was enough to prove that all your plans had been changed at the last moment."

"They were," he admitted; and he began at the beginning and filled in the details for her.

She heard him through without comment other than a kindling of the brown eyes at the climaxes of daring; but at the end she gave him praise unstinted.

"You have played the man, David, as I knew you would if you could be once fully aroused. I've had faith in you from the very first."

"It has been more than faith, Portia," he asserted soberly. "You have taken me up and carried me when

I could neither run nor walk. Do you suppose I am so besotted as not to realize that you have been the head, while I have been only the hand?"

"Nonsense!" she said lightly. "You are in the dumps of the reaction now. You mustn't say things that you will be sorry for, later on."

"I am going to say one thing, nevertheless; and will remain for you to make it a thing hard to be remembered, or the other kind. Will you take what there is of me and make what you can of it?"

She laughed in his face.

"No, my dear David; no, no, no." And after a little pause: "How deliciously transparent you are, to be sure!"

He would have been less than a man if his self-love had not been touched in its most sensitive part.

"I am glad if it amuses you," he frowned. "Only I meant it in all seriousness."

"No, you didn't; you only thought you did," she contradicted, and the brown eyes were still laughing at him. "Let me tell you what you did mean. You are pleased to think that I have helped you—that an obligation has been incurred; and you meant to pay your debt like a man and a gentleman in the only coin a woman is supposed to recognize."

"But if I should say that you are misinterpreting the motive?" he suggested.

"It would make your nice little speech a perjury instead of a simple untruth, and I should say no, again, on other, and perhaps better, grounds."

"Name them," he said shortly.

"I will, David, though I am neither a stick nor a stone to do it without wincing. You love another woman with all your heart and soul, and you know it."

"Well? You see I am neither admitting nor denying."

"As if you needed to!" she scoffed. "But don't interrupt me, please. You said I might take what there is of you and make what I can of it: I might make you anything and everything in the world, David, except that which a woman craves most in a husband—a lover."

His eyes grew dark.

"I wish I knew how much that word means to you, Portia."

"It means just as much to me as it does to every woman who has ever drawn the breath of life in a passionate world, David. But that isn't all. Leaving Miss Brentwood entirely out of the question, you'd be miserably unhappy."

"Why should I?"

"Because I shouldn't be able to realize a single one of your ideals. I know what they are—what you will expect in a wife. I could make you a rich man, a successful man, as the world measures success, and perhaps

I could even give you love: after the first flush of youth
is past, the heavenly-affinity sentiment loses its hold
and a woman comes to know that if she cares to try hard
enough she can love any man who will be thoughtful
and gentle, and whose habits of life are not hopelessly at
war with her own. But that kind of love doesn't breed
love. Your vanity would pique itself for a little while,
and then you would know the curse of unsought love
and murder me in your heart a thousand times a day.
No, David, I have read you to little purpose if these are
the things you will ask of the woman who takes your
name and becomes the mother of your children." She
had risen and was standing beside his chair, with her
hand lightly touching his shoulder. "Will you go now?
There are others coming, and—"

He made his adieux gravely and went away half
dazed and a prey to many emotions, but strangely light-
hearted withal: and as once before, he walked when he
might have ridden. But the mixed-emotion mood was
not immortal. At the Clarendon he found a committee
of Civic Leaguers waiting to ask him if he would stand
as a "Good Government" candidate in the special election to fill the House vacancy in the capital district;
and in the discussion of ways and means, and the setting of political pins which followed there was little
food for sentiment.

It was three weeks and more after Governor Marston's call summoning the Assembly for an investigative session. Kent had fought his way triumphantly through the special election to a seat in the House, aided and abetted manfully by Ormsby, Hildreth, and the entire Trans-Western influence and vote. And now men were beginning to say that without the tireless blows of the keen-witted, sharp-tongued young corporation lawyer, the junto might still have reasserted itself.

But the House committee, of which Kent was the youngest member and the chairman, had proved incorruptible, and the day of the Gaston wolf-pack was over. Hendricks resigned, to escape a worse thing; Meigs came over to the majority with a show of heartiness that made Kent doubly watchful of him; heads fell to the right and left, until at the last there was left only one member of the original cabal to reckon with; the judicial tool of the capitol ring.

Kent had hesitated when MacFarlane's name came up; and the judge never knew that he owed his escape from the inquisitorial House committee, and his permission to resign on the plea of broken health, to a young woman whom he had never seen.

It was Elinor Brentwood who was his intercessor; and the occasion was the last day of the third week of the extra session—a Saturday afternoon and a legislative recess when Kent had borrowed Ormsby's auto-car, and had driven Elinor and Penelope out to Pentland Place to look at a house he was thinking of buying. For with means to indulge it, Kent's Gaston-bred mania for plunging in real estate had returned upon him with all the acuteness of a half-satisfied passion.

They had gone all over the house and grounds with the caretaker, and when there was nothing more to see, Penelope had prevailed on the woman to open the venetians in the music-room. There was a grand piano in the place of honor, presided over by a mechanical piano-player; and Penelope went into ecstasies of mockery.

"Wait till I can find the music scrolls, and I'll hypnotize you," she said gleefully; and Kent and Elinor beat a hasty retreat to the wide entrance hall.

"I don't quite understand it," was Elinor's comment, when they had put distance between themselves and Penelope's joyous grinding-out of a Wagner scroll. "It looks as if the owners had just walked out at a moment's notice."

"They did," said Kent. "They went to Europe, I believe. And by the way; I think I have a souvenir here somewhere. Will you go up to the first landing of the stair and point your finger at that window?"

She did it, wondering; and when he had the line of direction he knelt in the cushioned window-seat and began to probe with the blade of his pen-knife in a small round hole in the woodwork.

"What is it?" she asked, coming down to stand beside him.

"This." He had cut out a flattened bullet and was holding it up for her to see. "It was meant for me, and I've always had an idea that I heard it strike the woodwork."

"For you? Were you ever here when the house was occupied?"

"Yes, once; it is the Senator Duvall place. This is the window where I broke in."

She nodded intelligence.

"I know now why you are going to buy it. The senator is another of those whom you haven't forgiven."

His laugh was a ready denial.

"I have nothing against Duvall. He was one of Bucks' dupes, and he is paying the price. The property is to be sold at a forced sale, and it is a good investment."

"Is that all it means to you? It is too fine to be hawked about as a thing to make money with. It's a splendidly ideal home—leaving out that thing that Penelope is quarreling with." And she made a feint of stopping her ears.

He laughed again.

"Ormsby says I ought to buy it, and marry and settle down."

She took him seriously.

"You don't need it. Miss Van Brock has a very lovely home of her own," she said soberly.

It was at his tongue's end to tell the woman he loved how the woman he did not love had refused him, but he saved himself on the brink and said:

"Why Miss Van Brock?"

"Because she is vindictive, too, and—"

"But I am not vindictive."

"Yes, you are. Do you know anything about Judge MacFarlane's family affairs?"

"A little. He has three daughters; one of them rather unhappily married, I believe."

"Have you considered the cost to these three women if you make their father's name a byword in the city where they were born?"

"He should have considered it," was the unmoved reply.

"David!" she said; and he looked up quickly.

"You want me to let him resign? It would be compounding a felony. He is a judge, and he was bribed."

She sat down beside him in the cushioned window seat and began to plead with him.

"You must let him go," she insisted. "It is entirely

in your hands as chairman of the House committee;
the governor, himself, told me so. I know all you say
about him is true; but he is old and wretched, with only
a little while to live, at best."

There was a curious little smile curling his lip when
he answered her.

"He has chosen a good advocate. It is quite like a
man of his stamp to try to reach me through you."

"David!" she said again. Then: "I really shouldn't
know him if I were to see him."

"Then why—" he began; but there was a love-light
in the blue-gray eyes to set his heart afire. "You are
doing this for me?" he said, trembling on the verge
of things unutterable.

"Yes. You don't know how it hurts me to see you
growing hard and merciless as you climb higher and
higher in the path you have marked out for yourself."

"The path you have marked out for me," he corrected. "Do you remember our little talk over the embers of the fire in your sitting-room at home? I knew
then that I had lost the love I might have won; but the
desire to be the kind of leader you were describing
was born in me at that moment. I haven't always been
true to the ideal. I couldn't be, lacking the right to
wear your colors on my heart—"

"Don't!" she said. "I haven't been true to my
ideals. I—I sold them, David!"

She was in his arms when she said it, and the bachelor maid was quite lost in the woman.

"I'll never believe that," he said loyally. "But if you did, we'll buy them back—together."

Penelope was good to them. It was a full half-hour before she professed herself satisfied with the mechanical piano-toy; and when she was through, she helped the woman caretaker to shut the venetians with clangings that would have warned the most oblivious pair of lovers.

And afterward, when they were free of the house, she ran ahead to the waiting auto-car, leaving Kent and Elinor to follow at a snail's pace down the leaf-covered walk to the gate. There was a cedar hedge to mark the sidewalk boundary, and while it still screened them Kent bent quickly to the upturned face of happiness.

"One more," he pleaded; and when he had it: "Do you know now, dearest, why I brought you here to-day?"

She nodded joyously.

"It is the sweetest old place. And, David, dear; we'll bring our ideals—all of them; and it shall be your haven when the storms beat."

Americans in Fiction

*A series of reprints of 19th century American novels important
to the study of American folklore, culture and literary history*

THOMAS BAILEY ALDRICH
The Stillwater Tragedy

JAMES LANE ALLEN
A Kentucky Cardinal

GERTRUDE ATHERTON
Los Cerritos: A Romance of Modern Times
The Californians
Senator North
Aristocrats
The Splendid Idle Forties

ARLO BATES
The Puritans

OLIVER THOMAS BEARD
Bristling With Thorns

ALICE BROWN
Tiverton Tales
The County Road

FRANCIS H. BURNETT
Through One Administration

WILLIAM A. CARUTHERS
Kentuckian in New York, or the Adventures of Three Southerns
The Cavaliers of Virginia

CHARLES WADDELL CHESNUTT
The Conjure Woman
The Wife of His Youth; and Other Stories of the Colour Line
The House Behind the Cedars

KATE CHOPIN
Bayou Folk

JOHN ESTEN COOKE
The Virginia Comedians
Surry of Eagle's Nest
Mohun: or the Last Days of Lee and His Paladins
My Lady Pokahontas

ROSE TERRY COOKE
Rootbound and Other Sketches

MARGARET DELAND
John Ward, Preacher

THOMAS DIXON
The Leopard's Spots
The Clansman

EDWARD EGGLESTON
Roxy
The Faith Doctor

MARY HALLOCK FOOTE
The Led-Horse Claim

PAUL LEICESTER FORD
The Honorable Peter Stirling

HAROLD FREDERIC
Seth's Brother's Wife

MARY E. WILKINS FREEMAN
A New England Nun; and Other Stories
The Portion of Labor

HENRY B. FULLER
The Cliff Dwellers